RISING

LISA SWALLOW

Cover designed by Najla Qamber Designs

Cover Image by Lindee Robinson

Editing by Hot Tree Editing

About Rising

An intense and emotionally charged story of love, redemption, and finding a second chance in life.

Jem Jones, the self-destructive Blue Phoenix lead guitarist, meets the fierce and volatile Ruby, lead singer of Ruby Riot, in this standalone book in the Blue Phoenix rock star romance series.

Three attempts at staying clean after rehab and Jem Jones, Blue Phoenix guitarist, is determined this time he'll succeed. Haunted by his recent past, Jem throws himself into the one addiction he still has left: music. With Blue Phoenix on a break, he looks elsewhere for a place to channel his creativity and discovers up-and-coming band Ruby Riot.

For lead singer, Ruby, breaking into the music scene could break the cycle of abuse that's controlled her life since she was a child. Finding release through music, the growing success of the band has set Ruby on the path to regaining her identity and self-esteem.

Ruby Riot brings Jem and Ruby together, but Ruby's tangled personal life pushes her closer to a reluctant Jem. Living and touring together, Jem and Ruby discover they have more in common than their passion for music. Can this understanding break down the carefully constructed barriers they're trapped behind? Or is loving somebody too big a risk to take?

For all the Blue Phoenix groupies.
Thanks for making 2014 a year to remember!

Rising ~ Blue Phoenix

the heat has a way of changing you
as it beats down upon your skin
and just when you think you're losing again
you find a new way to win

I heard that a storm is coming
and it's really gonna take its toll
through a rebirth of the person i am
and a transformation of my soul

chorus:

I was burned alive but now I'm rising
now everyone finds it quite surprising
that I made it without compromising
I was burned alive and now I'm rising

when you travel through the flames
and they scorch you to the core
your old ways are incinerated
by a change you cannot ignore

PROLOGUE

Fifteen Years Ago

Jem

The front door slams. Twelve-sixteen a.m. He's late. When he's late, everything is worse.

The shouting starts and the TV volume rises, too, but this never drowns the argument. The neighbours in our row of terraced houses must hear but nobody ever speaks. No one gets involved.

The shouting is okay. I can deal with that. The quiet afterwards is what turns my stomach and leaves me torn between creeping downstairs to see her, and hiding in my bedroom.

I'm a coward. She's my mum. I should be there to help.

I tried once, last month, and Alan belted me for interfering. The next morning, Mum screamed at me, blamed me for making things worse. *I made things worse*. Mum worried because the bruises were on the side of my face; she can hide her bruises under her clothes. I've seen them; she doesn't think I have. Questions were asked at school but Alan was careful to make sure those and the bruises in the following weeks weren't visible, so I could hide them. Mum said they'd take me away if somebody knew, and I don't want to lose her completely.

Tonight, I grab my headphones and turn up the sound, drowning the fear and anger with the sound of Metallica. I lie back and stare at the ceiling, allowing the guitar and screaming vocals to take over, to numb myself, and stop the need to run downstairs and help. I'll get the crap kicked out of me if I do. Instead, I close my eyes and watch the red and black colours of the music dancing through my mind, obliterating thoughts.

One day I won't be a kid. One day I can look after her. If I can look after my mum, she wouldn't leave me alone. She'd need me instead of the men who come into our life, who tear our world apart and leave again. I'll be a teenager in two years, almost a man. I can do their job. If I'm not enough, and Mum doesn't want me, I'll be big enough to take care of myself when she leaves me again.

Now I'm older, when she goes away, I can already look after myself. I'm not scared any more like I was a few years ago, when I'd sleep with a cricket bat by my bed in case somebody came into the house. Now I'm bigger, I'm not such a baby about these things; it's just my life. Mum always comes back, even if she doesn't tell me when she's going away or why. Sometimes she's gone for a couple of days. That's okay. If the time stretches into weeks, I worry in case she's hurt or lost.

I never tell anybody.

The thoughts edge through the music:

If I was older and I could look after Mum, she'd be safer.

I wouldn't be alone, if I was a good enough son for her.

What is it I do wrong that makes her go away?

What if one day my mum goes away and never comes back?

1

Jem

Every cliché, rock, love song crashes into my head as if they were all written for this girl. Long legs in black, skinny jeans, tattoos emerging from the tight tank top stretching across her tits and crimson hair spilling across her shoulders. She leans against the bar, one elbow propped behind her. This girl stepped from my fantasies and landed in the new version of reality I live in these days.

When she turns her head, it's as if she takes a sawn-off shotgun, holds it to my temples, and pulls the fucking trigger. My head explodes because in her eyes I can see she exists in the same place I do: a lost place at the edge of the world.

Did time stand still? The world fade away? Souls meet across the stars? I should give this to Dylan for one of his pathetic love songs. That shit doesn't happen.

The chick looks away, snapping me back to the real world. Another club, another band. Not the best place for a recovering addict to hang out, but Blue Phoenix manager, Steve reckons I make a good scout for a new support act. Blue Phoenix don't tour again until next year and I worry he's trying to replace us. Steve claims he's looking for a decent support he can whip into shape ready for the tour. Hedging his bets, more like.

The world waits for Jem Jones to fall back into his drug addicted self, poised to hold me up as a fucked up loser again. If I'm in public, I'm less likely to slip than if I'm hidden at home amongst the spectre of my old life. This time I make it count.

The kids in the club are young; some are too young to be here. Sure, eighteen is a great age in this country because it's legal to drink in clubs but what a mess. Why come and watch a band if you're too drunk to stand up? At least I could hold my drink by the time I hit the legal age, but I started early and had plenty of practice.

I'm half-hidden in the shadows at the edge of the bar waiting for Ruby Riot. Everything's set up on stage but no band. I check my phone - eight p.m. They're late. If they don't appear soon, I'm leaving. I don't have time for a band who can't get their shit together. This was a last minute anyway; normally I research before I waste my time, but I needed to get out of the house and away from my thoughts. I rocked up at the nearest pub with a band playing tonight, and here I am.

The white glow from the lights above the bar illuminates the girl, highlighting the scarlet red of her hair. Do I speak to her? Why am I hesitating? Since when is Jem Jones nervous of talking to a chick? She must know who I am or she wouldn't have her eyes glued to me again. Problem is, if I step out of the shadows, the kids around will spot me. As I debate this like a nervous teen, she drains her beer and places the empty bottle on the bar.

Fuck it.

"You want another?" I ask, approaching the girl.

"No. Thanks."

I wait for the parted lip, moment of realisation at who I am but it doesn't come. Instead, she scans the room, ignoring me. Do I have to bloody introduce myself?

She smells of flowers, roses maybe, which is odd because she doesn't look like a flowery girl. In her boots and with those legs, she's almost to my eye height and her face is close enough to see the 'back off me' purse of her lips. Now I'm closer, I'm struck she could be younger than she looks under all the make-up and my neck prickles as an image of Liv trips into my head.

"What's the band like?" I ask.

She turns her black-painted eyes toward me. "Yeah, they're okay. Do you know much about Ruby Riot?"

"No, I heard good things so came to check them out."

"Why ask? You'll see them soon, make your own mind up."

"I want to know people's opinions."

Does she *really* not recognise me? There isn't a glimmer of anything apart from a disinterested girl being hit on by some guy in a bar.

A new track filters from the speakers and through the room. I smirk when I hear Blue Phoenix; this should prompt her memory. I watch and wait but her expression remains detached, no flicker of recognition. *For fuck's sake.*

"Hmm. Okay, I gotta go." The girl pulls herself away from the bar.

"Leaving? The band are due onstage soon."

She fixes me with a curious look. "I have somewhere I need to be."

This I'm not used to. I almost utter the cliché 'don't you know who I am' but she'll laugh at me. Nah, she must have a boyfriend. That's who she's looking for. Damn shame.

"I hope you like the band, Jem Jones," she says and stalks away.

Okay. That was unexpected. I stretch out my neck and consider my next move. Drunk Jem would've ignored the rejection by picking up some chick who'd love to get her hands on me. Sober Jem can't be bothered. I shuffle back into the shadows before someone spots me, but the crowd is jammed tight and not looking at anyone but each other.

When I was younger and went to clubs, we smoked. Now it's banned. At most places in my Blue Phoenix life, this makes no difference. I do it anyway, but here it's a no go. Shaking my head, I disappear out of the bar to indulge the one vice I've not weaned myself off yet. So? I can't stop every drug in the space of three months.

I head to the back of the club, staying to the shadows and edging around the sweaty crowd. Security knows who I am; they were pre-warned in case I attracted attention. No hassle from anyone so far and the niggling feeling I'm a 'has-been' edges around. I'm paranoid - I don't go from top of the world to nothing. The location I'm in is the reason I look like just another grungy dude in the corner. Suits me.

I duck out through the room filled with empty crates and fresh kegs, then out of the propped open fire door. The warmth of the summer evening surprises me but you can never tell with English summers. It's pissing it down one minute, bright, sunny days the next. I pull the pack of cigs from my pocket and light one, gratefully inhaling the nicotine. Good thing I can't do this by the bar; reckon I'd have ordered a beer by now. Filling my lungs with the harsh smoke, I close my eyes and rest my head against the cool bricks. The nicotine buzzes into my system. Yeah, I'll give up. Eventually.

A scuffling sound and a woman's voice alerts me. The alleyway is narrow, brick walls overhanging the space between. The sound carries from around the corner.

"I fucking saw you, you stupid bitch!" The man's voice alerts me. I have zero tolerance of this shit thrown at women. Peeling myself from the wall, I approach the corner.

A woman's voice, low and placating, travels toward me; I quietly step out of where I am.

And see red.

Literally, because against the wall, partially illuminated by the car park streetlight, is a girl with red hair. What makes me see red in the other sense - of wanting to rip the fucker's head off - is a man with his hands around the girl's throat, pressing her into the wall. The worst part is she's not fighting back.

The man slams the girl's head against the bricks and trips a primal anger in my brain. Striding toward him, I yank him by the back of his jacket, and he loosens his grip in surprise. The guy draws himself to his full height, but he's still a few inches shorter than me. He has close-cropped hair, and the muscles barely covered by his t-shirt suggest he works out. A lot.

"What the fuck?" he growls.

"Was gonna ask you the same thing," I say in a low voice.

"I'm fine; it's okay." The girl's panicked voice confuses me, as if my interference is unwarranted.

I stare back at the girl from the bar, but she rubs her head, keeps her gaze to the floor, and doesn't meet mine. "A guy has his hands around your throat and you say it's fine?"

"None of your fucking business, mate." The man curls his hand around the girl's arm and she winces.

Assault charge. Do not get an assault charge. I close my eyes and fight the urge to smash my fist into his face. My history with chicks isn't the best, but I sure as hell never beat a woman.

"Please leave us alone," says the girl quietly.

I open my eyes and meet hers, the lost soul behind them pleading with me not to make things worse.

"Hands off her and I'll go," I growl at the guy.

He snorts and pulls his hand away so she stumbles, and then he raises them in a gesture of surrender. The red-haired girl steps back and disappears through the nearby fire exit before I can ask if she's okay.

The dickhead and me stand off against each other for a moment. He's drunk, his eyes not focused on me properly. Man, he'd be so easy to fight. I open and close my fist, fighting down the Jem who'd solve things without words. Then I turn away, taking a drag from my cigarette. If the dickhead hits me first, I'll have an excuse.

Unfortunately, or maybe fortunately, he doesn't. When I resume the position against the wall to finish my smoke, I glance over and he's gone.

Not my problem.

I leave the empty alley and return to the busy club, the contrast in sound pushing away thoughts about my weird encounter. The lighting in the space between the bathrooms and the door is brighter and girls queue outside. At least one of them recognises me. I hear my name whispered. Beneath the heavy make-up and long, black hair, she's young. Too young for me. Wow, I'm maturing. I laugh to myself, no, just getting too old for screwing girls in darkened corners. Not my style these days. Any more than a glance toward a chick, and I'm asking for attention so I adopt my 'don't fucking talk to me' stance and stalk back to the bar.

I order a Coke, again questioning my wisdom in surrounding myself with one of the drugs that fucked my life up. Why? Because in these bars I'm at the beginning, before I became Jem Jones, lead guitarist of the stratospheric Blue Phoenix. Where else can I immerse myself in the raw music that reminds me of the early days before I got lost?

Suddenly, the band launches into their set, no introduction, just a jarring guitar pitching into a frenzied song.

Powerful. Arresting.

I turn from the bar toward the stage, encouraged I might be hearing something decent after weeks listening to wannabes who need to rehearse a lot more before they play in public. Bodies fill the sticky, wooden floor between me and the band; strobe lights pick out the band members.

Front of stage, mic in hand is the red-haired girl.

What the hell? Her voice cuts into the sound, an energy and depth to compliment the overpowering music. She has the crowd transfixed. I'm transfixed and that never happens. She's fucking amazing. Beautiful. Intoxicating.

How can someone with the strength and presence holding the crowd by the balls, be weakened by the dickhead who was holding her throat outside?

The rest of the band members are guys and I smirk with recognition as I watch the lead guitarist. He's good, not as good as me, but makes up for it in his presence. He shakes his blond hair from his face and picks out a girl in the crowd before turning on the kind of smile I used myself. *Tag, you're it*. Yeah, there's a fair few chicks fixated on this wiry, muscular guy with the looks to match his swagger.

The drummer is half-hidden but pretty damn good too, and the bassist is lost at the opposite end of the stage, intently focused on his performance. You get that, some people have no idea how to perform to a crowd. Blue Phoenix bass player, Liam, isn't big into performing but he gets to hide behind his long hair; this guy's short spiky black hair hides nothing, including the piercings covering his face.

The more I stay, and the more I hear, I know Ruby Riot is beyond special. The acoustics in the place are shit, some of their gear is crap, but with decent equipment and sound engineers, this band would rock the fucking world. The world needs to hear Ruby Riot and at that moment, I decide to make it my job to see that they do.

I close my eyes to see what colour their music is – I see music as colour, always have and I was pretty damn happy when I discovered I share this condition with Jimi Hendrix. I suspect the drugs are responsible for the synaesthesia becoming stronger over time, more damage to my brain, but in this case, I'm happy about it. This song is purple; red and blue melded into a vibrancy to match her voice.

I don't let the girl see me. I don't need to; she knows I'm here. Other nights, when bands knew Jem Jones was scouting them, it reflected in their performance. I scared them into mistakes and if that's going to happen, they're not ready to step outside their pubs and club circuits. This chick, no. If anything, I suspect she's performing better.

I guess I'll have to find her afterwards.

Toward the end of the set, I disappear outside for another nicotine fix and when I get back, Ruby Riot has left the stage. I head to the Green Room, hoping to hell Mr Muscles isn't the band spokesperson. The flaking blue painted door is ajar so I walk in.

"I said I'm sorry," says the red-haired girl as she turns. "Oh. You."

Her face glows from the performance and she drags her hair above her head, twisting the damp tendrils into a ponytail. The movement is impossibly sexy, her flushed face and wide-eyes adding to the almost innocent attraction. Her plain black tank top is soaked at the front, perspiration slicking her skin. This chick is hot. I blink. And too young.

"You never told me it was your band," I say.

"Thought you might leave if I did." She reaches for a bottle of water behind her and when she wraps her painted red lips around it, I immediately picture them around my dick. Yeah, I guess some things will never change.

"Why would I leave?"

"Can't see Jem Jones scouting out a band with a girl as lead singer."

"Why not?"

She wipes sweat from her brow with the back of her hand. "Dunno. Just never seen Blue Phoenix with a female support band."

"You're not all chicks."

She pulls a sour face. "That's okay then, only one of the band members is the weaker sex."

"You're twisting my words."

"What do you want, Jem Jones?"

"You."

Her eyebrows rise along with her tone. "And you think I'll fuck you because you're the famous Jem Jones? We're good. I don't need to sleep with anyone to get Ruby Riot on the map. We'll get there."

I laugh at her, at her presumption and the hovering meaning behind. She thinks either I'm a complete asshole or she's considering me in a fuckable light. Funny. Closing the door, I lean against it and cross my legs at the ankles.

The girl stiffens.

"I meant the band," I say in a low voice. "Not your delightful self."

"Oh. Shit." Despite her bravado, the girl's hands shake. She roots around in a large bag and pulls out a small bottle of whiskey.

This time when she drinks straight from the bottle, I lick my lips imagining my mouth around the bottle instead.

"What's your name?" I ask.

"Ruby."

"Ruby from Ruby Riot. Cute." I flick my fingers at her. "You dyed your hair to match your name?"

"Kind of."

"Kind of?"

"It's not my real name."

"What's your real name?"

"What does it matter?"

Our staccato conversation is accompanied by much more beneath the words. Ruby's pale blue eyes get me. Completely freak me out. Why is she so lost?

"You guys are good," I tell her.

"Thanks, I know."

"Wow, you're hard to talk to." I pull out one of Steve's business cards and wave it at Ruby. "This is my manager. I'm helping him find a support act for the next Blue Phoenix tour, send him a demo."

Ruby looks at the card as if I'm handing her a bomb. "Blue Phoenix split."

I huff. "No, we're taking time out. We're touring again early next year." I step forward, still holding out the card. "Gonna take it?"

I'm close enough to inhale Ruby - her scent, her warmth, her loneliness - and close enough to see the fading bruise beneath the make-up on her cheek. For a split second, I want to reach out and touch Ruby's face, stroke away the mark. One hand goes to her cheek, eyes warning me not to speak.

Ruby snatches the card. "I'll ask the guys. Jax - the guitarist - makes the big decisions."

Somehow, I can't see anyone telling this chick what to do. "Sure."

Turning away, Ruby sits on the table and places her feet on the chair. Damn those boots are sexy, half way up those amazing legs. "And you can leave now."

"You can't be found alone in a room with Jem Jones, huh?"

"Yeah, exactly. Mind you, I always preferred Dylan. I might not have said no to him given the chance," she shoots back.

Burned. "It's always Dylan."

Ruby parts her lips, as if she had an afterthought, but she doesn't speak.

I head to the door and open it, the buzz of voices and music from the bar enter the quiet space.

No. Wait. I turn back. "Don't waste the opportunity. You guys are good. Really, bloody good."

Ruby nods slowly, the curious look still on her face. "I was lying by the way."

"About the guitarist making the decisions for the band?"

"No, about preferring Dylan."

When our gazes lock again, I'm dragged back to the place we belong; the one I saw behind her eyes earlier.

But I'm not going there again, not for anybody. I can't fix people. I only kill them, don't I?

"Sure," I say and close the door on my way out.

2

Ruby

I'm late.

I run from the bus stop toward my small terraced house, heart heaving, short of breath. Not because I'm unfit, but because I'm shit scared. He warned me. I've been late three times this week and it's not my fault. Ben, who runs the cafe, asks me to stay and clean up later and later each night, attempting to persuade me to go out with him somewhere. I know why. He wants to talk to me about the bruises from last week.

Dan's slipping, leaving visible marks on my skin where before they were hidden. I'm slipping too, away from what's left of myself.

When the lights are off in the house, my breath rushes from my lungs in relief. Dan's not home yet. He doesn't realise I'm late. I unhook my black messenger bag from over my shoulders and dump it on the floor, pulling my phone from my pocket with shaking hands. What if Dan's texted me, telling me to be somewhere else? The only message is from Nate, asking if I can make rehearsals this weekend. I don't know if I can yet.

I walk toward the lounge room and when Dan steps out of the kitchen as I pass, I stifle a scream and drop my phone. The hallway is dark, Dan's face shadowed and his bulky frame between the lounge and me.

"You scared me!" I pick up my phone.

"Why are you late?"

"Same as yesterday. Ben is being a dick and keeping me back late."

"Back late?" he steps closer. "Why?"

The smell of Dan, the fresh scent of detergent and the powerful deodorant he uses, fills the space between us; it's a nauseating reminder of last night, one that twinges the pain in my bruised shoulder. "I don't know."

Dan catches my chin and yanks my face to look at him. "You told him about me?"

This question has many answers. The fact I have a boyfriend? Or that he occasionally smacks me around when the psychological abuse fails? That I live with the man who helped me years ago, but who I now need help getting away from?

"He knows I have a boyfriend, yeah." I pull my scarlet hair over my shoulder and he catches my hand as I do, squeezing the delicate bones of my wrist. I wince. "Don't. You'll bruise me."

Dan runs his tongue along his teeth, sweeping a gaze up and down my thin figure. My blue jeans and tight, faded-to-grey Blue Phoenix t-shirt take an extra few pounds off me. He ignores my loaded comment about visible injuries. "I'm not worried about that, nobody else would be interested in you. What have you got to offer? Nothing."

"Have you eaten?" I ask him before the rant starts.

"No, waiting for you. There's nothing in to eat; did you go shopping?"

Shit. I knew there was something I forgot. "No," I say in a small voice.

"What the fuck, Ruby? Why not?"

"You could've picked some things up from the shop near the gym," I reply, immediately regretting my words.

Dan straightens. "I don't do the fucking shopping! That's your job! I gave you the money. Where is it?"

I pull bank notes from my back pocket. He snatches them from me and folds the notes, counting. "You get paid today?"

"Yes."

Dan holds his large palm out again.

I dig around for the money Ben gave me. "I need to keep some, Dan, for..."

"I'll give you some when you've done the shopping." He thrusts some twenty-pound notes at me. "Make sure you get everything on the list I gave you."

"Now? I wanted to get something to eat."

"We don't have anything to eat!"

"Just some toast."

Dan straightens and leans closer. "You don't have time."

Tonight I have to ask him about Friday, whether I can go to the gig. If Dan can't come with me, I won't be allowed to. I need to keep Dan calm, be who he wants me to be, and hopefully, he'll say yes.

"Okay, is there anything special you want?" I ask.

"Yeah, but I'm stuck with you."

The way Dan looks at me, as if I'm an annoying insect he wants to squash, hurts. He's not stuck with me; he could let me go. I could move on. I *would* move on if I could seize back the control Dan's taken.

Three years ago, when he helped me out of the abuse I'd stuck with too long, I let him take over. Dan told me if he looked after everything – money, housing, me – I'd be safe because nobody could take them away and threaten my future. That Dan was a different man, one who saved me from the gathering nightmares. I soon learned that I'd moved from one bad dream to a new one. Dan wanted someone he could control. Own. Before I realised, that person was me.

Now I have new plans of my own, once I find the courage and means to see them through. My last attempt at leaving a couple of months ago failed; when his screaming abuse and attempt to shut me in the lounge room failed, Dan sat against the front door so I couldn't escape. I don't have a key to our tiny backyard or the windows.

I was trapped. I'm still trapped.

3

Jem

I dreamt about Liv.

I fucking dreamt about her again.

The dreams had stopped. The images looping around my head like a continuous horror movie retreated a month ago, the spectre of her death finally beaten. Last night I was there again. In the hotel. Drugged to the eyeballs trying to wake up my dead girlfriend. My broken girl who looked the calmest she had the whole time I'd known her.

Calm? No, dead because of my drugs.

What really sucks is because my subconscious has such a tight grip on the memories, the fact I was high at the time is no defence against the torture my mind believes I deserve. So much of my life back then is a hazy blur, but that day is seared on my mind forever.

Liv follows me everywhere the day after I have the dreams. Glimpses of her tucked into the armchair in the corner of the lounge, strung out, or reading, catch my eye but she's never there. Screaming arguments encroach my memories, followed by images of holding and wanting to save her. Liv was twenty-one, a woman, but still a little girl in so many ways, stunted by her past.

Days like these, the oblivion of the bottle seems the lesser of two evils - alcohol or drugs. Neither is in the house but both are in easy reach. Alone, unable to distract myself away from the coiling nightmare tightening around my chest, I get closer to walking out and getting something to numb the pain.

Padding the room in circles in my bare feet, I scroll through the contacts on my phone. If I walk out of the door now, I'll be back with something to obliterate the world.

Therapist? Too tired for that shit.

Bryn. The Blue Phoenix drummer is in the country, or he was last week, and he's always ready to listen. I dial and wait, willing him to answer quickly.

"Jem?"

"Hey, Bryn."

"You okay, man?" asks my new go-to guy now Dylan's on his endless holiday with the love of his life.

In the past lead singer Dylan would be the first person I'd call. Not anymore. My relationship with Dylan is rocky at the best of times, we've only recently started talking again after my attempt to ruin his relationship with Sky.

"You back from overseas?" I ask.

"Yeah. What do you need?"

A shitload of drugs. "Fancy another trip to London? I'm scouting bands for Steve. Wanna help?"

Bryn makes a soft sound. "Steve has you looking for bands? In clubs?"

"Yeah, I can handle it, Bryn. When we go back on tour, I need to be confident I can stay clean around this stuff."

"Hmm. Isn't this a bit soon?"

I settle onto the sofa and rest my head on the back, staring at the ceiling. Maybe. A month since I came back from Thailand, from my discreet rehab centre. Like the world didn't know where I was. Back in my house in Notting Hill, I focus on writing new tracks but without the rest of the band to work with, I'm disconnected. The way Ruby Riot's music vibrated beneath my skin last night is the most excited I've been about music for a long time. They remind me of the raw Blue Phoenix, a perfect blend of talent and synchronicity between the musicians. Hell, if I can focus on helping them make it, it could keep my mind off my other addictions

"So, come babysit me."

"Seriously, Jem, think about this. Third stint in rehab, make this one count."

"So you don't want to come over? I've found a good one. Check them out online: Ruby Riot."

"You're complimenting a band? This is worth seeing. Okay, I'll come over this evening for a couple of days." He pauses. "You obviously need me to."

Trust Bryn to spot my real reason for calling.

Bryn's decision to come and stay lifts some of the darkness and compulsion to blot out the world. That and the fact he'll be here in a few hours means I can't exactly greet him when I'm stoned, can I?

4

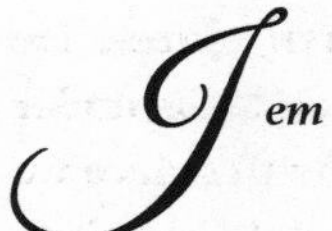*em*

Two Blue Phoenix guys are harder to hide than one. The Camden venue is bigger than the last place I saw Ruby Riot, and jammed with students. Most pretend not to notice us, if anyone thinks Blue Phoenix are old school, it's these guys. This both suits and amuses me. On my way through, I check out some of the chicks and none of them responds. I'm long overdue getting laid and judging by their indifference, this could be fun. A challenge could be the thing to take my mind off obsessing about sex with scarlet-haired rock chicks.

The venue owner gives Bryn and me one of the back rooms to hang out in. The chipped wall is decorated with band posters dating back years and it doesn't take long to locate a tatty Blue Phoenix one near the top. I remember playing here. And I'm pretty sure I remember getting an awesome blowjob in this very room.

"What you thinking about?" asks Bryn.

"Old times." I indicate the poster with my bottle of water.

"Reckon this band could be the next Phoenix?" he asks.

I choke a laugh. "Come on, nobody can be the next Phoenix. It's like saying, 'can Phoenix be the next Stones'. Close but not close enough."

Bryn shakes his head with a small smile. "Such humility, Jem."

"Have you listened to them? Ruby Riot?"

Now he fixes me with a half-disparaging look, lips pouting slightly. "I not only heard but saw them, too, on YouTube. I can see one of the attractions for you."

"The chick? I wouldn't rate a band based on how hot the singer is!"

Bryn gives me a disparaging look. "If only I could believe that."

"But you heard them? You can see this is beyond my dick's opinion?"

"I'm winding you up. Yeah. Be interesting to see them live."

Five minutes into their set and I can see Bryn agrees. He doesn't have to say anything for me to know the sound gets under his skin too. Again, Ruby's voice travels to my soul, to the place we share that I don't want to be. The crowd, a sweaty sea of black, is as spellbound as the last time I saw them play, and again I hover near the bar. Wearing a tank top and short skirt with knee high striped socks and kick-ass boots, she's sexy as hell. I have a thing for huge ass boots wrapping half of a girl's leg. I really, really shouldn't picture them wrapped around me. *Too late.* I shift against my hardening reaction to her; one I bet a few other guys are having.

I doubt Ruby can see me from here, but I want her to look at me. Instead, she spends a lot of tonight singing to the floor or the ceiling, hair flying around her as she moves around the stage. Oblivious. Despite the synchronicity of the band, she's on the edge in her own space. It's as if Ruby's something rare the guys have captured and she won't allow herself to be part of them. Not completely.

A girl with long, dark hair sits on a stool nearby, facing the band. She's petite, dressed in a short black dress that barely covers her ass and tits, and red and black striped leggings. Is this a thing? Chicks with stripy legs? She side glances me and her mouth makes an 'o' of recognition, so I nod.

She smiles. I smile back.

Awesome.

Bryn's halfway into the crowd, partly blended in although his height sets him head and shoulders above the others. Nobody notices. A lot of the guys are fixated on the vision of sexual fantasies incarnated in the girl who'd eat them alive. I can't equate this girl with the ballsy voice and the meek girl held against the wall by her dickhead boyfriend or whatever he is. I can only hope she uses some of that strength to kick his backside, and soon.

"You're Jem Jones, aren't you?" calls the girl over the music, as I approach her.

"I guess I don't need a lame chat-up line for you then."

"Try one if you like."

"No, sweetheart, I don't need to."

She licks her bottom lip slowly, and trains her eyes on me. "I came here tonight because I heard you'd be here."

Aha. I move closer and lean against the wooden bar next to her. "Oh? And why would that be?"

"I have fantasies about sex with rock stars."

"You don't mess around do you?" I say with a laugh.

"Why play games? I bet you don't."

"Oh, I do, interesting games..."

The music fades as the band pauses, set finished and the encore cheered for.

The girl sips from her glass. Seriously, did this chick come here tonight to fuck Jem Jones? Girls as forward as this set off my 'media alarm'. Will our night be a double-page spread in the daily newspaper? Night? Huh. She'll be lucky. I consider all this as I weigh up whether I'll indulge her fantasies.

Groupies come in several categories, some less pleasant than others, but this kind I enjoy. Wide-eyed and breathless, she introduces herself as Sara and tells me stories of her relationship with Blue Phoenix - you know, first heard us, first gig, blah, blah, and apparently tried to get backstage a few times, but never succeeded. I apologise and slide my hand underneath her dress. This kind of girl is my favourite type, pretends to be brazen, but melts into star-struck the moment I touch them.

"I see you made a friend, Jem." *Nice timing, Bryn.*

"Sara." I gesture between the pair by way of introduction.

Her star-struck look grows. "Hey, Bryn."

Bryn picks up my coke from the bar and drinks. I bristle. "It's fucking coke!"

"Yeah, okay." He sets the glass back down.

"Don't big brother me!"

Before our exchange cools any further, I'm alerted by a familiar sound. The opening bars of "Rising", Blue Phoenix's first hit. I look over to the stage and Ruby is staring straight at me, one hand gripping the mic, the other on the stand. I count the beats before the lyrics start and every single one pushes another person around us out of my awareness.

Usually when I hear a cover version of "Rising," I cringe at how badly the lead guitarist fails to reach my expectation. This time I've no idea whether this guitarist does or not, because I'm waiting. Waiting to hear Ruby's vocals, how she interprets the song I wrote with Dylan about getting through the fire and coming out the other side burnt but alive. Nobody ever sang the words with the same understanding Dylan has.

Ruby? She's almost there but she should stick to her own songs. Harsh? Yeah, but these tracks are my babies. This is a song you need to sing like you mean it and not pretend you do. This isn't a song you can perform to the crowd and hope they get sucked in.

Realisation rips through me. Ruby-who-isn't-really-Ruby is playing a role and her whole self isn't in the performance. She's still in the fire and until she pushes through the other side, she won't sing this convincingly.

Bryn nudges me and gives the thumbs up. Seems the cover is good enough for him, but the band killed the mood for me the moment they covered one of my songs. Ruby Riot is phenomenal and don't need to play other people's work.

I turn back to the girl with the long dark hair. The band is halfway through the set and I've heard enough for now. Bryn can stay and let me know what he thinks.

The door opens and I snap my eyes open to see Bryn's tall figure fill the doorway.

"Fuck, Jem..." He pulls a face and turns, blocking the way for the people behind him.

The girl with her mouth around my dick pulls away. Nice bloody timing, Bryn. *Again.*

Worse than that, I catch a glimpse of a girl with bright red hair next to Bryn. Our gazes lock briefly and she pulls a look of disgust and turns away. Guess I chose the wrong room, the bags dumped around must be Ruby Riot's stuff.

The door closes and I sigh. Well, it's not the first time I've been caught with my dick out. Kneeling on the floor in front of me, Sara evidently isn't used to the situation because she has her head in her hands.

"Oh, my God, who was it?" she asks the floor.

I stand and shuffle my jeans back up. "Bryn." I zip them. "He's seen it all before, don't stress."

"Don't want to finish then?" She looks up at me and giggles, pushing her dark hair out of her face. She's drunk, of course. Sober girls in my experience don't go down on random guys. Occasionally me, but that's because of who I am, perk of the job.

"Kinda killed the mood, getting spectators." And seeing Ruby. Why the fuck does that matter though?

Sara's shoulders slump slightly. "Is that it? You want me to go?" The girl pulls herself from the floor and perches on the edge of the sofa.

She's cute. Definitely not innocent and judging by the skill of her blowjob, she'd be worth a go in bed. She no doubt knows the score too; nobody expects more than a night with me. Harmless fun.

Someone hammers on the door. "You done, Jeremy?"

Jesus, Bryn. "No, but come in."

"I hope you've got your jeans on. I'm scarred, man. Nightmares for life."

"Like you haven't seen it before," I call back.

Sara looks at me in confusion and in the brighter light of the room; I catch sight of her pupils. Crap. She's not just drunk; she's high. I catch myself from asking what she's on, as if it's my business.

I pull the handle and yank the door open. Bryn's leaning against the frame. "Not all the addictions are dealt with, then?"

The girl whose lipstick is probably decorating my genitalia now slumps back against the sofa, head against the plump cushions examining the ceiling. Something weird twinges, I didn't deliberately take advantage of this girl but, crap, I'm glad I didn't fuck her.

Ruby barrels past, the real reason I'm glad I didn't. She refuses to look at me, grabs her bag from the floor, and storms out again. The lead guitarist cranes his head around Bryn and spots the two of us.

"Oh. Hey, Sara. I see you met Jem," he says with a knowing smirk. "I told you I'd introduce you, looks like he beat me to it."

Sara giggles. Her giggling is really starting to irritate me. "Yeah."

"I want to talk to you guys," I say gruffly, then look at Sara. "Not you. The band. Sorry."

Sara blows air into her cheeks and exhales. "'Kay." Staggering slightly, she stands. "Nice to meet you, Jem."

"Yeah. Same."

"I hang around with the guys," she informs me and I rub my head trying to figure out why she's telling me this. "So, might see you later."

"Maybe." She steps toward me and I back away.

Sara huffs and heads to the door. "Catch you later, Jax?" She strokes his cheek.

"Umm. No. Sara, get someone to take you home."

I tip my head at Jax as she leaves the room. "Close friend?"

"Once-over." He winks.

Great. At least I don't have to worry about upsetting Sara if she's a free spirit kind of girl. I don't judge, nothing about what she does makes her worse than me because she's a chick. I don't get the impression she'd let people use her. I reckon she gets what she wants. If you don't do relationships, what else can you do? Become celibate? I don't think so.

"I'll be with the guys," says Jax, indicating the bar. "Leave you to chat." He backs out of the door and closes it.

Bryn watches him go then turns to me. "You're right about the band. We should definitely let Steve hear them."

"Apart from them murdering "Rising"..." I mutter.

"Nobody's ever good enough for you."

"No, nobody plays my music like I do."

Bryn shakes his head at me. "I reckon they've a lot going for them, don't judge them because you're in a bad mood about not getting laid."

"That's nothing to do with it. Yeah, I'll talk to them."

The venue empties, a few stragglers hang around the band and one guy in particular hangs around Ruby. He's taller and slimmer than the dickhead she dates and she's not impressed at his attention. I recognise the stance as the same the day I tried to hit on her - sour face, tightly crossed arms. This guy likes a challenge.

I approach. "Ruby, I want to talk to the band. Together."

"Right." She doesn't look at me, staring over the shoulder of the guy she's with. "In the Green Room?"

"Here's fine, once everyone else has left."

The guy looks around. "Hey! Jem Jones!" His interest in Ruby fades. "Dude!"

Dude? "Yeah, but don't ask me for my fucking autograph."

"Blue Phoenix, man..." As the longhaired kid launches into reverential stories about the band, Ruby smirks into her drink, catching my eye briefly. Her smile disappears as she does.

Then Ruby walks away from me.

I unsubtly tell the kid to get fucked, irritated by the events of the last hour, and leave him open-mouthed as I pursue Ruby. She's settled into a leather booth seat in the corner, and chats to Bryn. I don't know what he says to her, but she laughs a sound that tears jealousy through me. Bryn and his sense of humour that everyone loves, even uptight red-haired chicks. The brothers, Will and Nate, look over expectantly when I approach. They remind me of the cartoon animals in that kids' film - the two hyper, over-eager brothers. Harmless and excitable. I guess they don't do aloof, rock star.

"Where's Jax?" I ask, pulling out a stool.

"Smoke," replies Bryn. His response kicks in my nicotine craving.

"No, I'm here!" says Jax, appearing on the stool next to me, the smell of cigarette smoke on his clothes not helping my resolve. A week now since I had a smoke, *go Jem*. "Hope you didn't start without me."

This guy is going to rock the star status. He has the tousled blonde-haired, blue-eyed thing going on with just the right amount of edge and cockiness. Jax isn't along for the ride though; he drives the band. That I know from the constant hassle he gives me for an answer as to what I intend to do. I admire him for that; I did the same with every talent scout I came across in the early Phoenix days.

Ruby picks up a beer mat and taps it onto the table, edge by edge. "So? You got an answer for us yet?"

"I got a question."

"What?" asks Jax.

"Whose idea was it to play "Rising" tonight?"

Jax rubs his mouth and chin. "Mine. Why?"

"I told you we shouldn't have fucking played it!" snaps Ruby.

"We know it though! Always played it in the early days," says Will, darting a look between the two hostile band members.

"I said we should've played all our own stuff." Ruby fixes her darkened eyes on me. "Right?"

"Correct," I say.

"Shit!" Ruby drops the mat onto the table and grabs her bottle. "He hated it! Nice one, Jaxon."

"I've heard you play a few times now, one shit cover of my song isn't a deal breaker. Just don't play my songs around me again."

"He's very protective of his children," says Bryn. "If he had his way, nobody but Blue Phoenix would play them."

"Sorry, man," mutters Jax, glancing at the furious Ruby.

"Have I heard all your work?" I ask.

"Think so," replies Jax.

"When's your next gig?"

Everyone looks at Ruby who shifts in her seat, avoiding looking at anyone.

"We have one booked in a couple of weeks, Ruby needs to check if she can get time off work," Jax says.

"How long since you booked the gig?"

"Couple of weeks," says Jax.

The brothers have gone quiet and the atmosphere shifted to unease.

"How long does it take you to book time off work?" I ask Ruby. "What do you do?"

"Work at a coffee shop." She takes a swig from her bottle.

"So you can't plan your shifts a few weeks before?"

Jax stiffens next to me. "Things are complicated for Ruby."

She shoots him a death stare. "Shut the hell up, Jax."

"It's true. We have issues planning gigs because of your complicated lifestyle."

"So find another fucking singer!" She stands.

Shit, this girl's fuse is short. "No, you're the singer," I say quietly. "I'm interested in you guys as a group and how you are now."

Until this point, Ruby has avoided my eyes; but at my comment, she turns to me. Again, the weird something that's causing problems reaches between us. Truthfully, if the singer wasn't Ruby, this would be easier. There'd be no temptation to touch her, no need to get any closer to the girl who not only triggered off the dreams about Liv; but who also reminds me too much of myself. But in reality, if the singer wasn't Ruby, the band would be a different creature and I wouldn't be interested.

"So you're keen?" pipes up Nate.

"Yeah. I'll give you guys a go, help you get some more gigs and watch how you cope."

"Whoa! Really?" Will rubs a hand through his spiky black hair and practically bounces out of his seat.

"Yeah, but if I'm gonna commit some of my time to you, you

need to be a hundred per cent committed, too. I haven't got time or patience for wannabe kids."

"Fuck, yeah!" enthuses Nate, and he and Will high-five each other.

But all I see is the stress on Ruby's face. Her phone beeps and she jumps, checking the screen. "Dan's here. I have to go."

Without another word to anyone, Ruby picks up her bag and heads to the door at the back of the bar.

"That's the complication, isn't it?" I ask Jax.

Jax doesn't look at me. "Yeah, in more ways than one. Two secs." He jumps up and follows. "Hey, Ruby!"

She pauses and they talk quietly for a couple of minutes, Ruby picking at the strap of her bag.

"Everything okay?" I ask Jax when he returns.

"Yeah, reminding her about the party at ours tonight." He smiles slowly. "Wanna come?"

"Sure," I say and Bryn pulls a sour face. "What?"

"Is that a good move?" he asks.

"I'm sure with you to hold my hand, I'll be fine."

Besides, sober amongst a drunk group of college kids sounds like an amusing alternative to going home and fighting the nightmares about Liv.

Sara comes with us to the party. *Great.* Hopefully, some other guy will pick up the slack once Sara realises she was a mistake.

We bundle the group into a couple of taxis and arrive at the old Victorian terraced house in Mile End, where the guys in the band live. Ruby leaves the club with the dickhead I saw pushing her about the other night and they follow us in his car. If she doesn't live with the guys, does she live with him?

Not my problem.

Déjà vu hits me when I step into the narrow hallway of the house. In the tatty lounge room, a strong smell of cigarettes from the finished beer bottles full of fag ends, and the unmistakable scent of weed emanates through the smoky room. Bryn is aware too and glances at me. Test of my strength right here. Sara hangs onto my arm; Jem Jones is her prize for tonight. There are a few single guys here checking the chicks out. If I'm lucky, and leave her long enough, she might hook up with one of them.

Will appears and slings his arm around my shoulder in an over-familiar way.

"Jem! Wow! Love that you came here!"

I peel his arm off and he holds his hands up in apology. I'm not into people touching me and tonight I'm smothered.

"Yeah, okay." I bump my rear onto the dilapidated green velour sofa and question my logic in coming here. Bryn flops besides me and rests his feet on the scratched wooden coffee table. "Time warp, huh?" he asks, as we watch the kids around.

"I feel fucking old, man."

"Y' know, I love it," says Bryn. "They don't give a shit who we are."

A small part of me hates that. What if Steve's right? What if Blue Phoenix out of the spotlight, equals Blue Phoenix disappearing down the drain? Here I am creator of some of the biggest songs in recent history and nobody cares; apart from Sara attached to my lap.

"Bryn, get me a beer," I say.

"Nice try."

"One?"

"I'll get you one!" pipes up Sara.

"Don't you dare," growls Bryn

Sara doesn't look fazed. "Okay. I'll get myself one." She detaches herself and wanders out of the room.

"Why the hell is she still hanging around you?" Bryn asks.

"She's a friend of the band's, I think. Not sure, we didn't talk much."

"Mmm. Guess that's a bit tricky when she's got her mouth full."

"Whatever, man."

Before anyone comes over to me, or Sara gets back, I head to the back of the lounge room and squeeze through the tiny kitchen full of bodies toward the garden. Outside, white plastic chairs rest on the cracked pavers and I pull one into the shadows to sit on, trying to figure out why I came here tonight.

The cool summer evening chills my bare arms and I curse the fact I left my leather jacket back at the venue. Will it be there if I go back or is my jacket now the prized possession of a souvenir hunter? The smell of cigarette smoke drifts toward me from a couple in the corner of the garden. Out of all my addictions, this one proves the hardest to kick.

I stare at my combat boots, obsessing about asking for a smoke when the door to the house opens and someone slams it closed. Ruby flops herself against the wall of the house and drags a pack of cigarettes from her pocket.

"Can you move?" I ask her.

She peers through the darkness and pauses in her lighting of the cigarette. "Jem?"

"Yeah. Can you move away? You're too tempting."

"I am?" Her voice is quieter than usual, hand shaking as she lights, the orange glow of her cigarette indicating where she is.

"The smokes." I indicate what I mean. Did Ruby again think I was hitting on her?

"Oh. Right. Weirdo." A breath full of smoke heads my way.

"For fuck's sake," I mutter.

"Where's Sara?" she asks.

"Haven't got a clue. Hopefully she's found a new friend."

Ruby snorts softly to herself. "I've lost a bet then."

"What?"

"I bet Sara you'd fuck her."

"Why the hell do that?"

"No reason."

I'm pissed off, wish I'd never touched the girl. "Do you think I'm some kind of man whore?"

"You tell me."

"Think what you like, most people do."

"I will."

I'm tempted to walk away but this is the first time I've been alone with Ruby since the first night I saw the band. She's not moving either.

"Where's Dan?" I ask.

"Inside."

"Wow, he let you out of his sight?"

"What the hell does that mean?"

So much. I want to tell her to get the hell away from him, that I've seen this too many times but I can't get involved. Not again. My involvement is helping Ruby Riot on the path to success, then she might see the light and kick the guy to one side.

"I mean he's possessive."

We both know what I mean. I saw what he was doing and she continues to pretend I didn't. "He loves me," she says quietly.

This softly spoken girl in the dark is different to Ruby. Hidden in the shadows, she could be someone else. The girl beneath the persona.

"Can I ask you something?"

She blows smoke in my direction and I laugh at her attempt to get me to move. "Yeah, I might not answer though."

"You said Ruby wasn't your real name. What is it?"

The couple finishes smoking and head back into the house, door closing behind. She jerks her head round in alarm, but nobody else appears. We're alone with the plastic chairs and rusting metal and glass table.

"Tuesday."

"Your name is Tuesday?" I can't help my incredulous tone.

"Yeah, but nobody calls me it and that includes you."

"Your parents had some weird ideas then."

She scoffs. "My mum. Ironic thing, I was born on a Thursday."

I laugh and hear her giggle, too. "Sit with me?"

She drops the cigarette butt and hesitates. "I should go inside."

"Why? Because of Dan?"

In response, Ruby drags a chair and sits opposite me, crossing her skinny legs. The light from the house casts across her face, her red-painted mouth, and the eyes that are the window to a place of hurt we share. She chews one of her short, black-painted nails and meets my scrutiny.

"You're not what I expected," she says. "Or you weren't until you fucked Sara."

"I didn't, remember?"

"Only because Bryn interrupted."

"What did you expect me to be, Ruby?"

"A condescending dick who'd have his hand up my skirt at the first opportunity."

"I like the band. If I piss you off, I have to start looking all over again."

"So this isn't your natural respect for me?"

"Nope. I'm a condescending dick who preys on women."

"You're not."

"Recently." The turn of the conversation disturbs me and I shift in my chair. Two can play at this. "You're not what I expected."

"What did you expect?"

"A strong girl who wouldn't let a dickhead screw her around."

Ruby jumps to her feet and the light plastic chair falls over. "Fuck you!" she hisses.

"Wow. Okay. Sorry." *That escalated fucking quickly.*

"You don't know a thing about me!" she continues. "Don't judge!"

And she's back, the girl from the shadows gone. I stand too, blown away by the split second shift in mood. "Sure, whatever. But you can't hide from what's happening. Not forever."

Ruby steps closer me, her height in the thick-soled boots places her close to my eye level. "None of your business, Jem Jones."

I want to grab Ruby's shoulders and shake common sense in, pull her off the destructive path she's on. Ruby's glare softens to confusion and she briefly glances at my mouth before stepping back.

"Leave me alone," she says quietly, and then heads back to the house.

As she opens the door and the light shines on her, Ruby's frailty hits me. In her Ruby persona, the weakness is masked behind the attitude. I heave in a breath. I walked the destructive path and I know nobody can pull you off the road you're destined to take; changing direction is a decision only she can make. I wish I knew who put Ruby on the path she's on.

"Goodbye, Ruby Tuesday," I sing softly to myself and laugh.

5

Tonight I'm home before Dan and cook instead of heating up ready meals from the supermarket. He likes pasta so I make spaghetti and hope he didn't eat already. Even if Dan has, I'm expected to have a meal ready for him after work.

Tonight I tell Dan; I'm running out of time.

I sit at the table, chewing my nails and jump up as the front door closes. Dan appears and sweeps me into a tight embrace, before he looks over at the boiling water.

"Hey, angel." He kisses me gently on the mouth. "You cooked, thank you."

Why does he thank me if I'm in trouble when I don't?

"I hope it's okay."

"Sure it is! Smells good. I'll get changed."

I busy myself arranging the bowls and the salad, straightening the cutlery into order and perfection. Dan returns in a clean checked shirt and smart jeans, and sits at the table. I open a beer and place it next to him.

"You spoil me," he says. "Any reason?"

"No."

Meal served, I attempt to eat; but the sickly pasta sticks in my throat. Dan eats plenty, always does. He has two more beers in the course of our silent meal and sweat beads along my back. Dan doesn't need alcohol to make him nasty, but it doesn't help.

We talk about work, his mainly. He's a personal trainer at a local gym and a gym is the last place you'd find me. Some days Dan doesn't have time for his own workout and they're difficult days because he brings home the frustration with him.

The half hour we eat is excruciating because I try repeatedly to broach the subject but can't. Even by the time we're finished and I'm washing dishes, the words still choke me.

"Something's bothering you, angel, what's wrong?" Dan asks quietly.

I drop the cup back into the water. "Ruby Riot has another gig this week." He doesn't respond and I don't look round, rubbing soapy bubbles between my fingers. "I don't want to let the guys down."

Dan sighs. "You shouldn't get so involved. You know the band will fall apart soon, you're pretty crap."

I turn and rest against the sink. "But Jem Jones..."

At the mention of his name, Dan's features harden. "Jem Jones. Still telling you you're talented?"

"Yes," I say in a meek voice.

"Why?"

"He likes our music."

Dan flicks his tongue against his teeth. "Has he touched you?"

"No! And I wouldn't let him."

"Keep it that way. I don't know what his game is but seems strange he's getting involved with a crap band like Ruby Riot."

Dan stands and approaches me at the sink. I gauge his body language, no anger but some tension. I mentally calculate how I need to behave to lessen the chances of a meltdown.

"I know this means a lot to you, angel, and that's why I let you join in. But you do know this won't last forever? If this interferes too much with us - your life here - you'll have to give it up."

I grip the sink, cool metal biting my palms. "I know. Like you said if Ruby Riot is no good, things won't go anywhere so you don't need to worry."

"Where's the gig?"

"Oxford."

Dan's forehead creases. "Oxford? What the fuck? When?"

"Friday night."

"I hope you haven't said yes!" he growls and pulls his phone from his pocket. "I might be busy."

"You don't need to come..." The mistake in those words is apparent when he stiffens.

"You saying you don't want me there?"

"No, I meant if you were too busy."

The switch has flicked and even though the calm is on his face, it's not in the air around. "You don't want me there."

"No, Dan, I do, it's just..."

The darkness sweeps across his face. All it ever takes is one wrong word. Half the time I don't know which words will be wrong, so I don't speak. I wince as he grabs my hair. "Which band member are you fucking?"

"Dan, no, I'm not. There's only you." His grip tightens and my eyes water. "I wouldn't."

"You know you're mine, right?" He hisses into my ear. "You know without me you're nothing." His fingers dig into my arm.

Nothing. Always nothing.

My uncle smacks me across the head and I see the stars that come with the pain. I don't know what I did wrong. I want my brother to come home but I don't know where he went.

"You're fucking useless! Even you mother hated you enough to piss off and leave you!"

I reach for the stars spinning in front of my eyes and focus on them as the pain hits my back. He's careful not to touch my face.

If my brother doesn't come back, I don't know what I'll do

"I know, Dan. I'm sorry. I do want you there. I always want you with me." The lines are so rehearsed now I'm sure one day he'll realise I'm lying. I think he already does.

I remain trapped in the space with Dan, focusing on breathing and willing him to calm down. Tonight he called me angel. Dan only calls me that when he's had a good day. I don't dare meet his eyes, yielding is my best option.

Dan's grip loosens and he drops my arm to pull out his phone. I hold my breath, waiting for a response and hoping to hell that's the end of the fight. "Looks like I'm free Friday. We can go." His voice is light, anger blown away.

Tonight I stay away from the stars.

I drop by the boys' house the next day on the way to work. An exhausted looking Nate lets me in then sinks back onto the sofa. Looks like they had a typical hard night boozing. The small house is littered with bottles and rubbish, the normally dirty carpet now filthy. I walk into the kitchen, where Will rests against the counter eating a bacon sandwich. He's shirtless, the beginnings of his latest tattoo, a huge red and black dragon, outlined on his chest. He rubs his bleary eyes as he notices me.

"I came to see Jax; is he around?" I ask.

"In bed still." I turn and head to the stairs. "Not on his own."

"Right." I stomp upstairs.

"No, Ruby! Wait!" calls Will after me through his mouth of food.

I hammer on his door. "Jax! I need to see you."

No response.

I bang again, maintaining a rhythm until he swears loudly. I hear a low voice of a girl too. Of course.

"Can't this wait until later?" he calls.

"No! I need something from you."

The door flies open and Jax stands in his boxers, tousled hair, and toned physique. This guy never looks like shit, even after what was probably a very late finish. "What?"

I resist the urge to look around him to see who his latest conquest is. "I need some cash."

His eyebrows tug together. "Why?"

"Dan took mine again," I say in a low voice.

"Shit, Ruby. When are you going to end this?"

"Gonna get me some or not?" I demand.

"Key." He holds out a hand, palm upward and I pull out my purse. Inside is the small silver key I keep hidden at home. I place it in his hand. "I don't want her to see." I indicate the girl behind.

"Oh, sure, so I kick her out of bed and say what? She's gonna think I cheated on you."

"Like you give a shit. C'mon, I'm at work in half an hour."

Jax goes back into the room and I rest against the wood-chipped wall at the top of the stairs. There are raised voices and a few minutes later a blonde girl storms out in crumpled 'last night's clothes' and holding her shoes. She tries a withering look on me but my own expression is enough to stop her saying anything.

"Well that saves an awkward goodbye," Jax mutters, appearing in his jeans, holding a black tin.

I barge past him into the room. "Jax, please."

"I'm not doing this much longer, babe." He unlocks the black metal tin.

"Don't call me babe."

"Okay, honey-pie." Inside the tin rests a pile of banknotes and a piece of paper with a figure written on it. "You've almost got enough now, haven't you?"

"Yeah, apart from I keep having to take from it when he takes my wages."

"I don't know why you don't open a bank account."

"You know why. Last time Dan found out and took the whole fucking lot." I pull a few notes from the box. "Soon," I promise him.

Jax catches my arm where my sleeve has ridden up as I stretched my arm out. He pushes up my jacket. Yellowing bruises mar the skin on my forearm and he inhales as he sees them. "Him?"

I snatch my arm away. "Stay out of this."

"How the fuck can I? I'm storing money for your escape and I see you several times a week for rehearsals."

I ignore him and shove the notes into the back pocket of my jeans.

"Have you told him Jem wants to book us some more gigs?" asks Jax.

Jem. My stomach spins at his name. I want to hate him, want him to be the guy I'd formed in my head but he keeps looking at me as if he cares. There's no getting away from who he is, the face of the man who wrote the music that got me through dark times. I've followed his life through the media's eye, even went to Blue Phoenix gigs so, as with a lot of girls, I closed my eyes and imagined myself with one of the band. When I started playing guitar, Jem became halfway to a hero. Only halfway because as well as being talented, hot as hell, and at the forefront of the band, he's an asshole.

Or I thought he was. I'm not sure anymore.

Obviously, he's not an asshole to Ruby Riot but look at him with Sara a few days ago, picking her up like that. No, he might have kicked the drugs; but he's still Jem Jones. And whatever the weird something that hovers unspoken between us, he's bad news. Dan is convinced Jem's motives with the band include wanting to screw me. Maybe, maybe not. Not going to happen. Jem's been to three of our gigs so far and when I see the enthusiasm on his face for our sound, I can't help but surge with pride. Dan's wrong; we are good. Jem's approval almost makes me believe I'm worth this. That I can become something special.

Almost.

"No, I haven't told Dan yet."

Jax drags a hand through his thick hair. "Please don't tell me you're going to back out. Shit, Ruby."

"No! No fucking way. He'd have to lock me in a room if he wanted to stop me going."

What flickers across Jax's blue eyes scares me. Jax believes that's a possibility.

6

Jem

No Bryn tonight. Things have been tense the last few days; my moods piss him off but people in my face telling me what to do pisses *me* off. After a couple of weeks of clashing, he's gone home. Bryn hides it but I can tell he's surprised at my continuing sobriety.

This leaves me alone with Ruby Riot again.

They've played a few gigs over the last month, even going as far afield as Wales and I teased the band that Cardiff counted as a European tour. Liam saw them for the first time when we were over there and I think he was impressed. We were both distracted by chicks that night, haven't had a real chance to talk to Liam about his opinion. Dan the Dickhead comes with us to every gig. I act as if he isn't here; the fucker doesn't know how lucky he is I didn't smack him that time in the alley. He's extra loving to Ruby when I'm around, which grates. I've seen bruises on Ruby. I tried to talk to her before the gig in Cardiff, but she shut me down. I only tried once; the longing to touch Ruby that seizes my logic whenever she's close means staying well away is the only option.

Each time I watch Ruby perform, every second I spend around her, the harder it is to shut her out. There's something about this talented, too tempting woman with her strange personas. The make-up and ink hide some of who she is, the first line of defence against the world. If that doesn't work in keeping people out, Ruby's foul mouth and attitude are turned full volume. Thing is, this doesn't work with me. I can outmatch her because I've had years more practice than she has. So when her defences fail, Ruby's lost around me and retreats to a third persona. Not Ruby, not Tuesday, but somebody fighting to find her way through. I catch glimpses of this girl; I suspect I'm the only one who does. Every time this Ruby appears, she backtracks as if she can't allow her to be seen, and definitely not around me. The hidden girl is the one I'm freefalling toward, the other girl of my dreams. Dreams about Ruby meld with the nightmares about Liv and that fucking terrifies me.

The frustration with the situation doesn't help when the band piss me off too. I book Ruby Riot a decent sized venue they'd never play if it weren't for my influence, and they refuse to give me a definite yes until two days before. Apparently, Ruby hasn't felt well the last couple of weeks and they were waiting to see how she is before committing.

Bullshit.

The reason is with them now; Dan the Dickhead watching everyone set up the equipment, keeping Ruby in sight. In line. Under control. I don't get it, can't figure out how this sharp, smart girl allows her life to be dominated by someone else. Why the hell do women do this?

Not my problem. I can't fix them. The mantra continues, but weakens.

Jax corners me as usual, his hero-worship flattered at first but is bordering on annoying now. He wants to show me a new song he's written and asks for input. Jax is determined, the driving force behind the band and reminds me of myself. A less fucked up version. Jax seems to have his head screwed on the right way, probably had a calmer start in life. I relent and give him the nod to show me. I guess I annoyed the crap out of people pushing Blue Phoenix onto everyone back in the day.

Jax drinks from a bottle of water. He's learned I'll pay more attention if he keeps alcohol away from me, then plays what he's written and I'm impressed. He's a talented guy.

"I'm going to sort you guys a tour then some studio time," I tell him.

Jax's face transforms from rock-star cool to open-mouthed astonishment. "Fucking serious?"

"Yeah. We need a proper set of tracks to play Steve. The couple of songs you have on Bandcamp aren't enough. We gotta get you out there." I pause. "Needs a bit more commitment though."

"Fuck, yeah! I'll drop everything - time out for a few days."

"Not just you. You've got to all be able to commit."

Jax nods vigorously. "We're committed."

"Ruby?" I set down my guitar. "And her 'health problems'."

The sharp look he gives me is an exchange of understanding. "She'll be cool. She wants this as much as the rest of us."

"I don't doubt that." I pause. *Shouldn't get involved.* "What's going on with her?"

"What do you mean?"

"Ruby. Cool chick, ballsy but she doesn't look well. Is she using? That'd be a deal-breaker for me."

"No," says Jax firmly. "We don't. None of us."

"She looks ill."

"She's had a tough time the last few years."

Not going there. "Okay. Obviously not a healthy lifestyle though."

Again, a look passes from Jax, the need to know but not want to hear. "She's trying to change the things in her life doing damage, but it's tough for her."

"Yeah?"

Jax sets down his drink. "Listen, Jem, I keep out where I need to and help where I can. Don't push this. It's complicated and not our business. I've tried to help but she won't let me."

"She's your friend."

"Yeah and how bloody frustrating do you think it is? But what can I do? I'm there when she needs, if she needs. You? As soon as it interferes with your project, step in. Otherwise back off," says Jax then stands. "I need to help set up before Will gets the shits with me."

My project. Pull back, Jem. Keep out.

I follow Jax and sit at the back of the small theatre, feet on a chair in front and watch how the band interact setting their gear up on stage. How did Blue Phoenix get so lost? The Ruby Riot easy-going relationship is apparent. The synchronicity performing onstage is always matched by offstage, as the brothers laugh at Jax's attempts to boss them around. There's a couple of chicks hanging around today, grungy girls in flowery dresses and sloppy cardigans. No Sara, thankfully. Ruby doesn't speak to them, and they stay clear of her.

Dan skulks at the edge of the stage; with his muscles he could join in and help set up but I suspect the band tries to keep him at arm's-length. He's been at each of the last couple of gigs, watching over Ruby's every move. The guys rarely speak to him.

Ruby has trouble tuning her guitar and Jax goes over with his, the pair of them attempting to get the sounds in sync. Then they kneel on the stage together, looking over a set list and Ruby scrawls through with a pen, rearranging the order. I can't hear their conversation but see Ruby getting agitated and Jax's attempts to calm the situation by touching her hand isn't helping. I straighten as her voice rises. This isn't going well.

Dan sits forward, elbows on his knees as Ruby and Jax continue their head to head. Jax pushes Ruby's hair away from where it splays across the paper taped to the floor in front of them, and she freezes, catching his hand. She remains holding it for a few seconds too long for my liking. Is there something going on here I'm not aware of? And if there is, why is my heart sinking?

Jax cheers as Ruby hands him the pen back and calls a triumphant 'yes' before he grabs her by both cheeks and kisses her mouth. Ruby shoves him hard in the chest and, as he's squatting, Jax lands on his back. He lies for a moment laughing and Ruby gets up and storms from the stage area.

Dan follows.

RUBY

Shit.

I stride toward the Ladies, almost breaking into a run. I know Dan will follow. If I get their first and wait inside, will Dan be calmer by the time I come back out, or more wound up?

What the hell does Jax think he's doing?

Dan catches up, his heavy footsteps on the tiled floor behind. Fingers dig my arm as he drags me to one side. Gauging his mood isn't needed; his heavier breathing and reddening face tell me all I need to know.

"You said you weren't screwing anyone else," he growls. "What the fuck was that?"

I attempt to control my own breathing, fighting to keep the oxygen disappearing from my lungs. "Jax messing around."

"You can't let other people touch you."

"I know. He knows. I think he forgot."

"You see now why I have to watch you? See why I don't believe you?"

The pressure on my skin increases; I'll have new bruises on my upper arm later. "It's true, Dan. There's nobody else. I don't need anyone else."

Dan glances around then moves closer. "You're an ungrateful bitch. I take care of you, put a roof over your head, and what do I ask for in return? Nothing. Have you forgotten that without me you're nothing?"

"Sorry," I curl my fingers around his. "I'll tell him to leave me alone."

"Do you forget where you came from?" he asks, voice low and grip firm. "Where do you think you'd be now if I hadn't helped?"

"I don't know. Somewhere bad." *But not as bad as this.*

"I don't know why I bothered with someone as worthless as you; sometimes I wish I hadn't. If your brother had warned me what you were like, I'd never have helped out."

And if Quinn had known what you were like, he'd never have asked.

"Dan... I'm sorry. Please. Don't be angry." I touch his smoothly shaven face, looking directly into his glittering eyes. "I'll make it up to you."

"You better bloody had!" He drops his grip and pushes me. "This is the last night for you and these guys until I can trust you. No more gigs."

I open my mouth to protest but the dark mask is on his face, the other Dan who can hurt me. *Be nice. Get away.* "Can I go for a smoke?"

Dan crosses his arms. "I'll come looking for you in five minutes if you're not back. I need a word with that asshole who had his hands on you."

"Okay. Thanks." I sidestep Dan and, swallowing down my panic, I head to the back door before he changes his mind, hoping he doesn't have a showdown with Jax.

Outside, the full moon is partly obscured by the clouds, low and bright. Stars fight their way through the clouds and I gaze up at them as I light my cigarette with shaking fingers.

"Hey, Ruby Tuesday!"

I pout at my big brother calling me this and he ruffles my hair. "How's my little sis?"

Say nothing. "Okay. How's uni?"

"Good. Sorry I haven't been home for a while, everything going okay? School okay?"

"School sucks. Same old."

Quinn's brow puckers. "Sorry, I wish I was around more."

"S'okay, enjoying your new student life?"

"Yeah, but I worry about you. Are you okay?"

Big brother sixth sense? No, I'm not. I never am when you're not here.

Things are only calm when Quinn's in the house. He's bigger than my uncle and would hurt him, hopefully, as much as my uncle hurts me. Now Quinn's gone.

"I'm okay."

Say nothing. I inhale the smoke and hold it in my lungs, closing my eyes as I calm myself. Lost in thoughts of Quinn, and how unfair it is he's not here anymore, I'm unaware of someone else close by until I open them. Jem rests against the wall opposite, the orange glow of a lit cigarette in his hand as he regards me. Did he see what happened with Dan again?

"Shit! You scared me." Is that really, why my heart rate has picked up again? Alone with Jem in the dark; close to the man who's creeping into my dreams and my stupid body reacts, the tension of my encounter with Dan replaced by desire for Jem's attention. *Stupid body, stupid girl.* Screwing Jem would be a mistake for a million different reasons, and I'm beginning to get the impression that's what he wants. Yet at the same time, I'm unsure. The way he usually looks at me isn't desire, if anything he's attempting to avoid looking at me much of the time. There's something going on between us but I can't figure out what.

"You're on in ten," he says.

"Yeah, doesn't take me that long to smoke." I throw my half-finished cigarette to the ground and step on it, preparing to leave. "Done now. See?"

"How much do you want this, Ruby?" he asks in a low voice. "The band, the music. Success, if I have anything to do with it."

I hesitate. "A lot."

He makes a soft sound in his throat. "That's not enough. You have to need it. Music has to be a part of you, something essential every day to survive. Something you'd give everything for." He pauses. "Change everything for."

"It is. I do."

"But will you walk away from what you need to?"

Jem did this before, attempted to talk to me about my screwed up situation but there's no point. How would Jem Jones understand how complicated my life is? Like most people, he'll think I should walk away from the situation with Dan and look down on me because I don't.

I fold my bare arms across my chest, skin goose bumping in the evening breeze. "Did you walk away?"

Jem steps from the shadows, closer to me than he's been since we had a similar conversation in Cardiff. "I'm not talking about me. I'm asking you."

"Music is the only thing that keeps me going day to day," I tell him. This is one thing Jem will understand. This is why he's here. Music is his life, saved him at his darkest times too.

"It shouldn't be the only thing in life you live for, just a big part of it. You need more than music to keep you happy or you'll burn out."

He's further into my personal space than anyone gets apart from Dan and occasionally Jax and I *feel* it. The energy from Jem reaches between us, surrounding us. I shuffle away. "Very philosophical."

"You think I'm philosophical?" He snorts. "It's true, believe me." He moves closer again. "I'm not interfering in your personal life, that's your call. But if Dan has to follow you to weekend gigs, what's he going to do if we go on tour?"

"On tour?" I straighten.

Jem takes a drag from his cigarette and pauses before exhaling the smoke. "Not a done deal unless the whole band agrees, but something I'm willing to help with."

"Why?"

"Because I can remember being you," Jem says quietly. "I remember being consumed by the music, by the belief Blue Phoenix were fucking good. All I wanted was a chance to prove that to the world but nobody would help. I want to help you guys do that."

"Why though? Why us?"

"I just said, you remind me of Phoenix." He throws his half-smoked cigarette to the ground. "You also know what's happened in my life recently. I need a distraction. A project. Music is what allows me to cope; and if I can't do that with Phoenix, I'll do it through another band. Preferably yours."

The mystery surrounding Jem Jones intrigues me. I've watched his rise and fall over and over, read stories about how these guys treated women in the past. Objects, playthings. Will Ruby Riot be his plaything? Is Dan right? Is part of his agenda screwing me? Is that why he's closing in on me physically right now?

"Yeah, we can talk about this. I can't believe you have such faith in us though..."

Jem shrugs. "I know something good when I hear it."

"Thanks." I smile.

The curious look Jem gives me sends my alert system haywire. I spend a good deal of time not meeting his eyes, because when I do, I feel exposed. Jem sees into a place nobody does, through Ruby and to the edge of Tuesday. He rubs a finger along his lips and pulls something from his back pocket.

"I want you to have this." He holds out a small card in his long fingers.

"What is it?"

"Blue Phoenix's publicity company. I want you to chat with them."

"What about?"

Jem shrugs. "Dunno. PR shit. I can only do so much. I've spoken to them about you guys. Arrange a meeting."

"Okay..." I hesitantly take the card, and as I do Jem's fingers linger against mine. The gesture is innocent enough, but to me loaded with the weight of realisation he's never touched me before, not even accidentally. If he had, there's no way I'd have forgotten the shock of his calloused fingertips against my skin or the effect on my heart rate. I curl my fingers around the card and drop my hand.

"Get rid of him," Jem says in a low voice. "Don't let him destroy Ruby; she's actually a nice girl when you get to speak to her."

My normal response would be a retort at him to back the hell off; but I'm aware I'm reaching a point where I need to make my choice, between being who I am, or who somebody else wants me to be. I don't know if I'm strong enough to choose.

Without another word, Jem ducks back into the building and I wait a minute before following. The Jax situation was bad enough; arriving back with Jem wouldn't be wise. I flip the business card in my hands as I head back to where we're setting up for tonight and catch sight of something written on the back. In black scrawl is a Notting Hill address. I stop and stare at the words.

Jem gave me his address.

Shoving the card in the back pocket of my jeans, I keep walking. Another man interfering in my life isn't what I need.

7

Ruby

The days slide through my fingers as I try to catch time and slow it down. I'm not ready to face Dan yet. Ruby Riot is rehearsing several nights a week now, up from the one Sunday afternoon session. Dan only knows about Sundays, the day he comes with me. He works some evenings and I match the extra rehearsals to those; that way Dan doesn't know I'm going and we don't argue about it. Jax is pissed off with me at rehearsals because the anxiety over whether Dan will find out is affecting my performance.

What can I do? Dan said no more gigs after dickhead Jax decided to touch me in front of him, so what choice do I have? I have to take the risk and do this behind Dan's back even though I'm terrified he'll find out. He won't. Dan's work timetable is rigid and he spends more time there than at home anyway. Jem will give up on us if we don't maintain extra commitment; I'm sure. Then the band would hate me. And if I lost Ruby Riot, I've lost everything.

Our rehearsal space is a room above a pub in Box Hill, a

popular place for small student bands; it's where I met the Ruby Riot boys a little over a year ago. The band was the three of them back then, and Jax was lead singer. After the gig, he hit on one of my friends and invited her back to the guys' house. Because we didn't know them and I wanted to make sure Cathy would be okay, I went too.

This was back when Dan wasn't as bad as now, his controlling behaviour insidious. I was allowed out alone in the evenings without an argument, although he'd come up with spurious reasons for me to stay home with him. No threats, just careful manipulation. It was when I became involved with Ruby Riot that things took an ugly turn.

That night, Jax inevitably picked up his guitar and turned on the charms for not just Cathy but the other girls. He's a good-looking guy and had already sweet-talked Cathy, so add in the guitar playing and he had a circle of admirers. Jax's swagger amused me so I picked up the spare in the corner of the lounge and outplayed him. Instead of being annoyed, Jax switched his attention from Cathy to me, which pissed her off. I informed him I had a boyfriend and Jax told me he didn't care because I wasn't his type of girl. With that out of the way, we spent the next two hours straight talking about music.

Jax calls it fate that the band was named Ruby Riot, and in walks a Ruby who completed the band. I laughed, was flattered, but he was dead serious. We arranged for me to get together at their rehearsal the following Saturday.

That evening, it was as if someone opened a window and fresh air rushed in. I gave up music shortly after I moved in with Dan; I didn't have time to rehearse with the guys from school anymore and they replaced me. Before Dan, music was my sanctuary but he pushed me away from that side of who I was, slowly, until so many days passed I forgot about playing. I switched off the essential part of who I was, to be who Dan told me I should be. One evening with Jax and the twins, and the buried Ruby reappeared, a new reminder that this girl from the past is who I am.

Time ran away and I was late home.

That was the first night Dan moved from verbal abuse to physical.

A week later, when I met the guys, the bruises had faded but the yellow marks on my arms were there. So was Dan. He agreed to come and check out the band and told me if he approved I could go ahead. I'd never performed in front of Dan, or anybody for a lot of years, but I did what I always do; closed my eyes and tuned into the sound around, tuning out everything but the music rippling through my body. I see sound like colour. When I'm playing, I'm on another plane, one where I visualise the interaction of the bars and notes, the procession of colour melding into a rainbow of melodies.

Dan disappeared downstairs to the bar after half an hour, muttering about how shit I was but he was alone in his opinion. The three other people in the room told me I was talented; Ruby Riot wanted me and the possibility I was worth something flipped a page on a new book in my life. Now I can fill the pages or tear them out.

"Ruby, what the fuck?" Jax shoves me, dragging me to the here and now. Rehearsals. Time's short. Need to get home. "You missed the intro again."

"Sorry," I mutter.

"Get in the right headspace; Jem's coming today."

Nate taps the drums in a quiet rhythm while Will matches the bass as they tune out the inevitable flare up about to happen between us.

"Jem?" *Shit.* He's going to ask about the tour. He'll want an answer.

"Yeah, the guy putting himself out for us. Remember?"

I scuff my boot along the scratched wooden stage. "Yeah. Forgot."

"I take it from your paler than usual face, you haven't told Dan you're going away?"

I chew a nail and refuse to meet his eyes. "Soon. I have to pick the right moment to ask."

"For fuck's sake! Not ask him, bloody tell him!" Jax rips the strap from around his neck and props the guitar against the speaker, storming across the room. I stride after and catch up to him in the narrow hallway to the stairs.

"Jax!"

"What is with you? Why can't you get away from him?" he snaps, face lined by anger. "You're stronger than this! Just leave!"

His words knock my breath. I thought he understood. "I can't."

"Bullshit! You don't want to!"

"You think I enjoy him treating me like he does?"

"I don't know? Do you? Why else would you stay?"

"I have to!" I yell. "I owe him!"

"Again, I call bullshit, Ruby. You're choosing to stay. Which means you're choosing him over yourself."

For the first time in a long time, I want to cry. I want Jax to understand that it's not as easy as packing up and walking out of the door. Jax knows I'm trying to change things but I'm scared. Scared of what Dan would do to me and terrified that Dan's right, nobody else would want damaged goods.

Dan loves me.

"You don't understand!" I yell. "I thought you understood."

"I understand you might be fucking up Ruby Riot's big break just because you're a coward!"

My frustration matches his, but as usual, I have a harder time controlling mine. I shove Jax hard in the chest and he stumbles backward, banging his elbow on the wall. "Fuck you!" I yell.

"This looks familiar," says a voice from the stairs. Jem walks slowly up the narrow wooden stairs that lead down to the pub. "Musical differences or lover's tiff?"

Jax makes a derisive sound and rubs his elbow. "No way I'd get involved with Ruby."

How much did Jem hear? He knows the truth about Dan because he's witnessed it, but I want him on the edge of my personal life. Jem can't know the full story. Again, Jem gives me the look, the one I hate, the one with more understanding than Jax.

"She's right. You don't understand," he says quietly to Jax.

"What the fuck do you know about my situation?" I snap at him but the address on the card he gave me already answers my question.

"I'm not blind, Ruby. And I know more about this shit than you realise."

His admission silences me, but doesn't quiet the adrenaline fuelling my system. I turn away and stomp back toward the stage.

"Come on!" I yell to Jax.

A couple of minutes later, the pair appears. I don't know what Jem said to Jax but he gives me an apologetic smile before retrieving his guitar. I mouth 'sorry about your elbow' between verses in our first song. He winks and mouths back 'no problem.'

Jem Jones said something, explained to Jax what I couldn't. He understands.

Jem's getting too close.

8

Ruby

I check my calendar for the fifth time. A week to go. Yesterday I lied, I told Jax and the guys that Dan knows about the tour. I didn't miss how Jax swept a look over my visible skin; like me, he expects Dan's reaction to leave marks. I change the subject, preventing the guys asking me to elaborate.

We haven't seen Jem since the tense rehearsal last week, although Jax chats to him on the phone most days. This irritates me and, the fact it does, annoys me further. I'm used to Jax dealing with all things Ruby Riot but I want Jem's attention too. Why? Validation? Something more? I'm in a fucked up place in life and my head; I don't need to look elsewhere.

Returning from a rehearsal, buzzing with the endorphins the music floods into my system, I step into the house that's my self-imposed prison. Ruby is on day release and comes home to become Tuesday again. I can spend my whole life denying Tuesday exists, but I'm lying to myself.

Each day that Ruby Riot step closer to being my waking life is an extra step away from this Hell with Dan. Every gig is a push in the direction of the belief I deserve more, that I can *be* more. And every penny I put in the tin Jax has hidden in his bedroom is the means to taking the final move.

Lights are on in the house but Dan isn't around. Anxiety grips, tightening my chest. Did I leave them on this morning or is Dan home? I hold my breath. No sound of the TV. Kicking my boots off, I creep along the hallway, warily listening and checking rooms.

Nothing.

With heart-thumping relief, I head to the bathroom. As the shower runs, I undress and study myself. The other day Jax commented that I'm getting skinnier and I told him to piss off, but he's right. I never noticed; I don't obsess about my weight the way I once did. I forget to eat because I have little appetite.

The brightness of my ink matches my hair, the tattoos symbolic of my attempt to cover up the girl beneath. Some people have tattoos because they're significant, I went for the brightest pictures I liked because I wanted a rainbow of colour to cover my life. Two blue and red birds are inked on my collarbones, pointing inwards to a winged heart. Jax loves the winged heart so much; he decided to use it as Ruby Riot's logo. My newest tattoo is a string of red roses and thorns, spread across my lower belly.

Inked along my rib, beneath my small breasts are words from the Rolling Stones song "Ruby Tuesday", a homage to the name I wish I didn't have. As I study the tattoos, the bruises stand out too. They have their own dull pattern, from black to purple. The place I plan to tattoo next are my upper arms; that's the place rings of fingermark bruises circle my skin. I want a sugar-skull there, black to hide the marks.

Dan's increasing violence and shift away from psychological abuse worries me and is gradually pushing me toward the decision I need to make.

The girl who steps from the shower is make-up free and bare to the world. I rub steam from the mirror and brush out my hair. The colour's fading and her eyes are too; Ruby is slipping away. Wrapping a long, blue towel around my body, I head to the bedroom.

Dan sits on the end of the bed in the dim light, his large figure straight and hands resting on his knees. Waiting.

I hesitate in the doorway, unease setting the hairs on my arm in alert. "I didn't realise you were home," I say lightly, and cross the room toward my chest of drawers.

"Where've you been?" he asks in a low voice.

"I was having a shower. Have you eaten? Do you want me to fix you something?" With shaking hands, I pull a pair of cotton panties from the drawers and quickly put them on. I know he's watching me, but there's nothing sexual in the room with us. I drag a faded blue tee over my head, ridding myself of the vulnerability of being naked in front of Dan.

"No, where have you been tonight. I came home earlier and you weren't home. Why weren't you home?"

The light from the hallway casts shadows across his face and his thin mouth tells me all I need to know. Some situations I can't escape and this is one of them.

"I… I went to a rehearsal," I say quietly.

"You never asked."

"I didn't think you'd mind."

"So why not tell me? All you had to do was text me," he says, voice dropping the room temperature.

Not true. Dan would've dragged me home again.

"I didn't want to disturb you."

He stands. "Didn't want me to know more like!"

"I'm sorry; I didn't think you'd mind." I pick up my jeans but Dan grabs them and throws them on the floor between us.

"Rehearsal? Is that where you were the other times I came back and you weren't here?"

The room lurches. *Not only tonight*. How many times? "Other times?"

"Yeah. Twice last week and this is the second time this week."

I tuck my trembling hands beneath my arms. "I didn't know... Weren't you working?" My meek voice betrays the fear I don't want to give him the satisfaction of causing.

"It's that blonde fucker isn't it?" he growls. "You're screwing him."

As he moves toward me, I edge back, glancing at the open door and running through my options. Where are my shoes? Car keys? "No! We've been rehearsing! I promise!"

Dan kicks the bedroom door shut and seizes my arms, slamming me against it. "You dirty whore. Did you think I wouldn't find out?"

I wince at the force of my back against the wood, at the fingers digging into the bruises I examined ten minutes ago. "I promise. It was rehearsals. You said you didn't want me being with the band so I didn't want to tell you. I'm sorry; I should've said."

Dan snorts and holds his face close to mine, his hot breath fast against my ear. "Do you expect me to believe that? You'd rather risk me finding out and thinking you were fucking someone else?"

The smell of beer explains where he went after he came home and discovered I wasn't here. "No! I promise!"

Pain sears my cheek as Dan backhands my face. "Is that why you were showering? Trying to clean away your behaviour?" He seizes my throat with both hands. "I hope he was worth it."

I'm violently pulled forward by the neck, pushed, falling on the floor. My hand slaps on the bare tiles as I try to break the fall, t-shirt riding up, exposing my belly. "Why would he want you? Look at you! You're nothing like a real woman. You've got no tits or ass; why anyone else would want to fuck you, I don't know." He kneels and grabs a fist full of my hair, yanking until my eyes water. "No wonder I need to go elsewhere."

"What?" I dig my fingers into his hand, attempting to disentangle them.

"I fuck other women, Ruby, because you're no good." His voice is soft, teasing, and a tear threatens to leak from my watering eyes. *Don't cry. Don't cry. Don't argue.*

"No, you don't. Tell me you don't."

"You fucking hypocrite!"

The strength of his next slap sends me reeling back, head hitting the polished tiles, the pain jarring my teeth. I close my eyes and cover my head, curling into the stars. This is my place, where I can go and nobody can hurt me. If I focus on the stars, I won't feel anything until he stops. His words fall around me, as the pain of his assault continues. Words I can barely hear through my ringing ears are pounded into me, reinforcing his programming that I'm worthless without him.

But I can't reach the stars this time, my mind won't let go. This is different. He's harsher and he's never accused me of having sex with another guy before.

And he screwed other women.

"What do you think about that?" I catch the end of his rant and blink away tears, head pounding.

I can't find any words. Please. Stars. Come soon. A pain rips through my chest and my first thought is don't hurt me enough to need the doctor. He's broken ribs before, but this time he didn't kick hard enough. The pain is still sickening, worsened by him yanking me to my feet and smacking me back against the wall. My head hits the plaster. *Stars. Finally*. I attempt to slump to the floor but he holds me in place by the chest with one broad hand.

Through the dizzying dark of pain, the jangle of his belt buckle crashes me back to reality.

His zip.

No.

"I fuck you, Ruby. Nobody else."

"Dan!" I struggle against him and he shifts his hand back to my neck, pressing his bulk against me. "Don't do that! This is what you stopped from happening! This is what you protected me from!"

"And look at how you rewarded me. By screwing another guy."

"I didn't. I promise!" *No tears. No tears.*

The scrape of his fingernails across my hips and the fingers yanking at my panties pulls me further from the stars. This would break me. This would be the end of Ruby; I have to fight for her.

"No!"

Struggling with his grip, I twist from side to side and he

battles to hold me still. I won't be her, I refuse to be the girl he claimed he was saving me from becoming. I slam my head against his mouth, the impact on my forehead barely felt through the numbness.

"Fucking bitch!" He staggers backward and steadies himself on the end of the bed frame, hand at his mouth.

Grabbing my jeans from the floor, I pull at the door handle with my sweating palms. Out. Get out. My bag is by the front door, if I get there first...

I'm slammed to the floor, landing face first as he tackles me from behind.

"Let me go!" I scream, immobile under his bulk and I'm rewarded by a punch to the head.

"You whore!"

Never this. He's never been like this. But I deserve it, don't I? I shouldn't have lied. I made this happen. I lift my head and stare at the blood from my mouth on the white tiled floor.

I can't move so I slump back down. Dan's weight lifts and he pushes me onto my back, dragging my legs apart. I kick out again, my foot collides with his face, and he grabs my leg, forcing it to the floor. I don't know this Dan; the man's face looking back at me is contorted with a hatred I've never seen.

"Dan! Don't!"

"You move and I'll fucking kill you!"

His surety I'll weaken at those words is his downfall because the fact I believe Dan triggers my next move. I focus on relaxing, letting him think he's won and when Dan shifts enough to free my legs I push both knees up and slam them into his balls as hard as I can.

Dan lets out a strangled yell and falls backward to the floor, hands going to his crotch. "Fuck!" he attempts to yell, but the sound is hoarse.

I should've fought back weeks ago.

I pull my shaking body from the floor, grab my jeans and stagger to the front door. Blinded by the pain, I seize my bag from the hallway and crash through the front door, into the drizzling rain. Not looking back, I run barefoot to the car, as I rummage in the bag for my car keys. Climbing inside, I central-lock the doors just as Dan charges into the street. My hands tremble and I struggle to get the key in the ignition, but I'm safe.

"You can't go! I'll find you! I know where you'll be!" he shouts and slams his hands on the driver's window.

The angry mask of Dan's face is the monster who's held me captive, convincing me he was the best I'd ever get; that I was worthless to anyone else. The growing realisation this isn't true, and the increase in his physical abuse, has broken that control. Where once I was convinced he loved me, this switched to fear convinced he'd hurt me. This last attempt at violating me and breaking the frightened girl for good is just that. His last.

Focusing the rationality I have left, I manage to start the car and get into gear. Dan steps to one side as I rev the engine; he's no longer in control now there's a ton of metal between us. Slamming my foot on the accelerator, I drive.

For an hour, the rain on the windscreen and tears fight over which blurs my vision the most. I swallow down the urge to vomit, tasting the blood from my injured mouth, and focus on the road as I squint at the headlights beaming from cars travelling toward me on the opposite side of the road.

I can't go to Jax. Dan will come for me.

I drive for another half hour. Rain. Tears. Pain.

Fear.

A lurching realisation.

I have nowhere. Nobody.

9

em

The intercom buzzes into my dreams, pulling me from the edge of the nightmare. I stayed up late attempting to finish a song I'm working on, and frustration hit when the notes wouldn't gel. The time spent recording the Phoenix album last year is lost in my drug-addicted haze; I was dragged through the process by the guys. Not our best work. These days, the songs wake me in the night, months of buried creativity pushing to the surface and consuming. I'd kill for a session with Dylan, to be in the recording studio with the guys.

I grope the side of the bed for my phone and squint at the display, three a.m. Who the fuck comes here at three a.m.? No missed calls, so whoever it is doesn't know me well enough to try calling first.

Muttering expletives under my breath, I head out toward the intercom. The sticky weather has broken and rain pours outside.

"Yeah?" I snap at the intruder.

"Jem?" A woman's voice. Fucking great, I thought late night groupie visits had stopped.

"Who's this?"

The intercom crackles again. "Ruby."

Her name jolts me to alert. "Ruby?"

"I didn't know where to go."

"Wait there. Gate's opening." I hit the button to unlock the security and pull my jeans on.

My confusion follows me downstairs, through the carefully restored Victorian house to the original but now heavily secured doors. Unlocking and sliding back the bolts, I pull open the front door.

Ruby stands on the porch, soaked. The security light shines on the red hair flattened by the rain, water running down Ruby's pale cheeks. Tears or rain? A thin blue t-shirt and jeans are glued to her body, and the expression on her face rips my heart out. Ruby often looks lost; but this girl is terrified.

"What happened?"

"Sorry, I didn't know where to go," she repeats.

I step back and gesture to the doorway, Ruby walks in and drips rain onto the floor. "Sorry."

"Stop apologising. Why else do you think I gave you my address?"

Her face is messed up, a cut below her blackening eye. She shivers and I don't know what the fuck to do.

Ruby misreads my hesitation. "I can go."

"No. Upstairs." I gesture to the polished wooden staircase and she slowly climbs, unsteady on her bare feet. This is bad.

Again, Ruby hovers, this time in my lounge room, staring around at her surroundings when I flick the lights. She squints against the spotlights so I swap them for a lamp in the corner of the room.

Towel. She needs a towel.

I grab a grey bath sheet from the linen cupboard and return, handing it over. Ruby stares at it blankly.

"You should get dry."

"Oh. I should." She pulls at her t-shirt, and then let's go, as the damp item becomes part of her skin again.

"I can give you a t-shirt, but I don't have any women's clothes."

Ruby giggles. Then snorts. Gripping the towel, she descends into a cross between laughter and hysterics that blows my mind considering the silence since she arrived. "No, I don't suppose you do."

Unsure whether to be insulted or happy she's snapped back to the living, I rub my head. "I'll get you a t-shirt."

I root around in my drawers, pulling out the first one I find then go back to Ruby. What the fuck happened? I can guess and bet she has more than a cut face. At least she's upright and conscious because I laid bets the time Ruby fought back that I'd be visiting her in hospital.

"Can I use your bathroom," she asks, frowning at the t-shirt. "I don't um...undressing." Ruby hugs the towel to her chest.

"Oh. Yeah. Sure. Over there." I indicate the direction she needs.

Ruby disappears and I slump onto the sofa. The nightmare I was on the edge of is replicating itself in front of me and I don't know how to deal with this.

The girl who reappears in my Guns N' Roses t-shirt isn't the Ruby I know. She's quiet and wary. Bare legged and skinny, the fabric hangs off her slight frame and because Ruby's tall, the t-shirt isn't as modest as it could be. As I take in the sight of this broken, frightened girl I ache, confused by the strength of my need to comfort her.

"Did he hurt you?" This is a bloody stupid question considering the state of her face.

"I'm okay."

"I didn't ask that. I asked if he hurt you."

She closes her eyes and inhales, before opening an eye again. "I was going to ask if you had anything to drink."

"Not in this house. Best I can offer is something to warm you up."

Listen to me, I sound like Bryn. *'I'll make you a nice drink and we can chat about how your boyfriend just assaulted you'.*

"Water's fine."

"Are you hurt?"

"Water's fine." She perches herself on my white leather sofa, sitting forward with her elbows on her knees.

In the kitchen, I resist slamming cupboard doors and getting pulled back to the anger over men who assault women. I've been an asshole, done some shit stuff around women; but apart from that fucked up incident with Dylan I barely remember, I've never done anything close to assaulting one.

From the doorway, I watch Ruby, her rigid figure and unmoving eyes are those of someone elsewhere. I've fantasised about this woman, but now all I see is a lost soul.

"Ruby." I approach and hold the glass out.

Bruises circle the wrist of the hand she takes the glass with and anger flashes into my mind, ramped up when I see the darkening marks on her neck.

"What the fuck did he do?" I say, stronger than I intended.

"I can't go back."

"You should've left a long time ago."

"I don't know where to go. I don't have anywhere. Last time Dan was the place I could go."

I swallow. "Last time?"

"I could share with Jax and the guys, but Dan will find me."

Ruby isn't listening; she's locked in her place of safety where nobody else is allowed right now, talking through her thoughts. I touch her hand and Ruby jerks it away, eyes growing as she looks at me.

"Do you want me to leave you alone?" I ask.

"Can I stay?"

There's no way I'll have a reasonable conversation with her, not until she rejoins the world. "I said yes."

"Here?" Ruby pushes herself against the sofa arm.

This fragile girl pushes into my past and drags up things I don't want to think about - not just Liv, but before. Bruised and crap knows what else, she came to me. *Me.*

This isn't fucking good.

10

*uby*

The girl in the mirror isn't the same as yesterday, and not just because of the bruises and cuts. Dan's attempt to tear apart the Ruby I created, the one who could walk away, has backfired because now she's more determined than ever to push out and leave Tuesday behind. I won't be the frightened mess of a girl who blindly arrived on Jem's doorstep last night; nobody is going to see her again.

The blackened bruises around my neck and arms are bad enough, but there are dark marks on my legs where he gripped my thighs. The bile edges into my mouth, how close he came to breaking me completely. The person who, three years ago, offered a safe place is the one who nearly ended who I am.

The nausea I feel about last night's events isn't just Dan's abuse, but the vulnerability I showed to Jem. Nobody but Dan has seen me so powerless; and although the barrier is back, Jem has seen behind. Nobody gets to see the reality of who I am or control me again.

Dan failed.

They'll all fail.

But Jem saw Tuesday. Now he has access to the vulnerable girl, will he try to take advantage too?

I turn on the shower, step inside, and wash the rest of Dan off my body. Forever.

The coffee machine splutters as I attempt to figure out how to use it and as I wipe up the mess with a kitchen towel, Jem appears. He pulls a t-shirt over his head as he walks into the room and the cotton slides down his hard abs, over the jeans sitting loose on his hips. I ignore my body's reaction, telling myself the attraction is because he was kind to me last night. His brown eyes are reddened, betraying his tiredness at his early hours visitor. Amusing, I spent the night with Jem Jones but not in the way my suppressed fantasies ever imagined. I'm vulnerable in just Jem's t-shirt. I wish it covered more of me, or that I hadn't left my wet clothes screwed up on Jem's bathroom floor last night.

"How're you feeling?" He pulls his thick brown curls into a ponytail and snaps a band around them.

"Do you want a coffee? I made a mess so may as well make it worthwhile." I pull another cup from the cupboard, fielding his question.

"Yeah. Thanks."

Silently, I prepare the drinks with shaking hands. Jem passes me the milk from the fridge, as if this is a normal morning, two people living together and following their routine. When I pass Jem the cup, his fingers linger on mine long enough to indicate comfort. I pull my hand away. "Thanks for letting me stay. I'll call Jax later, see if I can use his couch until next week."

"Stay here if you feel safer," he says quietly, brows tugged. "You need to go to the police."

I touch my swollen lip. "No."

Jem's face hardens. "Why?"

"Leave it." I sip my coffee. "At least there're no issues with Dan stopping me touring now."

Jem slides onto a black stool next to the counter and rests his elbows on the edge. "I care about more than whether you can tour, somebody attacked you."

"Don't bother. Are we meeting the guys to firm up the tour later?"

"You turn up at my house in the middle of the night after being assaulted by someone and tell me not to bother?" presses Jem.

He's not going there, his involvement stops now. "Looks like it. I'll go if you want; my car's outside."

"You don't want my help?" He's unable to disguise his incredulous look.

"No. I can deal with this." A memory of last night seeps in and my heart rate spikes. Can I?

The silence re-joins us and I debate whether to leave him and find my car keys. "Why did you come here?" he asks eventually.

"I don't know. After... it happened, my head was a mess. I got in the car and drove and somehow ended up here."

"Because it's me. Because you know you can trust me."

"No, because Dan would go to the guys' house to look for me. You think I'll trust you because you helped me when I needed it? Newsflash: I trusted the last guy who helped me and last night he tried to rape me."

Jem's face reddens and he sweeps a gaze over me. "He did what? Fucking hell, Ruby, you should be on the phone to the police!"

"He didn't and he won't get the chance again." I finish the drink, forcing the hot coffee down so I can get out of the room. "Maybe it's a good thing Dan did this."

Jem's mouth parts. "You're fucked up! It's a good thing a guy tried to rape you?"

"Yes! He finally stepped over the line far enough that I have the strength to walk away."

Coffee sloshes from the cup as Jem crashes it onto the counter and leaves the room, slamming the door behind him. I stand in the kitchen, and let go of the control I've held onto by my fingernails.

Just a few words to Jem about what Dan did unlocks everything, the fear shaking through my exhausted body. Tears spill and I bite hard on my injured lip, the familiar metallic taste of blood on my tongue intensifies the memory.

"If you fucking think..." Jem reappears through the door then halts as he catches sight of me.

I spin around to face the sink before he sees any more and rub my face on the shoulder of the t-shirt.

Jem mutters expletives under his breath and I wrap my arms around myself, holding in the need to keep crying, willing him to leave.

I'm unsure whether Jem has gone, until he speaks again. "I understand you don't want another guy trying to control your next move, but stay here. Do your own thing until you get your head together; I'll leave you alone." There's a clatter as keys hit a table. "I'll give you the alarm code."

Jem's behind me, I don't need to turn, hairs on my neck standing up at the awareness of his presence. He's close enough to touch and I tense, but another part wants to sink back, allow Jem to hold me and tell me things will be okay. The stupid, trusting part that screws my life up.

"I'll back off; but if you go back to Dan, I'm cutting my ties with Ruby Riot," he says quietly.

I hold my breath until the door closes again. Smart guy. Jem knows he can't push me into anything, so he goes for my Achilles heel. The one thing that's kept me going for the last year, the dream I've kept alive in the midst of the nightmare: success for the band.

If I screwed that up, I don't know where I'd go, or what I'd do.

Placing my bag on the floor, I catch sight of a note on the kitchen counter. Scrawled in black marker pen is a list:

No drugs

No alcohol

Don't ever wake me up

Don't touch my stuff

With amusement, I read the list several times. I guess this is Jem Jones's equivalent of a housemate agreement.

Is that what I am? What is this situation? Once we figured out Dan was working, Jax took me to grab some stuff from Dan's place. Tucked in the holdall is my black tin, the savings for my escape plan. I'm going to need it sooner than I expected. I count and I have enough to see me through the weeks where I can't work due to the tour. Then after the tour, I can look for a place to live. I almost have enough for a deposit on a room.

Jem suggests I stay for a couple of weeks until Ruby Riot goes on tour, so I can take time to get my head together. His behaviour is weird and the niggling feeling Jem wants something worries me. The idea Dan could find me at the guys' place is a bigger worry, so I accept Jem's offer and settle into the spare room he gave me last night. There's dust on the drawers and the place looks untouched. I guess Jem doesn't have regular guests. The wardrobe is empty and I don't bother hanging anything up, dumping my holdall on the floor instead.

When I head back into the living area, I spot Jem sitting on a stool in the kitchen, flicking through his phone.

"Hey," he says, barely glancing at me.

I attempt to take in the sight of bad boy Jem Jones tucking into something the opposite of his old image.

"You're eating yoghurt," I say.

"Yeah? Why? Did you want some?"

I giggle. "Jem Jones eating yoghurt."

He slams the pot on the counter. "Why is that fucking funny?"

Okay, so the temper is still there. "Sorry, it's just strange."

He scowls and I grasp for a subject change. "I got your housemate agreement."

"My what?"

I pull the A4 sheet from under a pile of mail and push it toward him.

"That? Just a list of shit." Jem focuses on his phone again.

"I wouldn't bring drugs into the house; you didn't need to write that."

He rubs his nose. "Cigarettes."

"What?"

He points at the list with his spoon. "I didn't write those down. I'm trying to stop, so no smoking in the house." He catches my look. "I have a garden. Go out there."

"Right."

Jem scrolls back through what he was looking at and continues to eat. At least I don't need to worry about him interfering; currently it appears he wants nothing to do with me. I should be happy this allays my fears, but the girl who craves attention lurks close by.

"I need to shop if I'm staying. Did you want anything?"

Jem blinks at me. "What do you mean?"

"Shopping. Groceries." I point at his tub. "More yoghurt."

I cringe. I shouldn't have teased because pissing this guy off isn't a good idea when he's helping me. Jem makes a soft snort of amusement and shakes his head. "I'm good. I have plenty of yoghurt."

Conversation over, I head out into the fresh summer air, dizzied by the surreal situation and on edge in case Dan lurks nearby. When I return, Jem's no longer around and music filters from upstairs. The house has three storeys and Jem's living area appears to be at the top. The second floor, where the other bedrooms are, also holds the kitchen and a lounge area, which includes a huge TV and the sofa I slept on last night.

I unpack the few groceries I bought. I don't eat a lot, more than I did when I counted every calorie and obsessed about my weight, but now I'm skinny because I don't have an appetite. I forget to eat much of the time rather than choosing not to. Alcohol fills the gaps, but I won't be drinking any of that if I'm here.

I retreat to my room and pull out my guitar. Time to lose myself in my other world; in the place, I'm safe from Dan.

11

Ruby's lived here three days and I hardly see her. We cross paths in the kitchen or lounge and exchange pleasantries, but it's bloody weird. I'm aware she doesn't leave the house much unless Jax is with her, but if I so much as touch on the subject of Dan, Ruby closes down. If Dan came here to find her, I'd break his fucking legs.

I don't go out much either, I'm enjoying the down time and peace. I never thought I'd say that, but I've finally listened to my body and the professionals insisting I do. After a morning in the upstairs lounge, the place nobody goes, I head downstairs to grab something to eat. For once, Ruby's out of her bedroom and in the lounge, watching TV and eating a bowl of noodles. I head over and sit on the sofa arm next to her. Ruby watches me cautiously. The cut on her lip is healing but the dark bruise still covers her cheek, the others around her neck yellow.

"You feeling better?" I ask.

"Yeah. How are you?"

"Yeah."

Awkward conversation over, she returns to her noodles. The familiar smell of spice and salt hits me. "Are you eating the instant crap? I lived on those. They taste like shit."

She swallows the mouthful. "Are you discussing eating habits with me, Jem Jones?"

"Just saying. At least you're eating." She frowns at me. "You look better."

Ruby's face has lost the gauntness. A couple of days eating properly and she looks better, even if she's still skinny as hell.

"Right." Pink tinges her cheeks.

"You don't have to stay in your room all the time when you're here. I don't mind you trying different rooms in my house as long as you keep out of my space."

She turns her blue eyes to mine, and licks the sauce from the noodles off her bottom lip. *Those lips. Fuck.* "I'm happier on my own, too."

"Oh. Okay. Well, just saying." I stand, is she trying to drop a hint?

"No, I hope you don't think I'm being rude though." Ruby puts the bowl down and stands too.

"Nah. I've never lived with a chick before so I'm not sure what to do."

Ruby stares at me as if I have something sprouting out of my head. "Really?"

"No. Or anyone. I guess I like being on my own. Touring, I have my own room. Sometimes I stay with one of the other guys, but I've never done the whole house share thing."

"Oh. Sorry, I won't stay much longer."

"That's not what I meant. You're cool to stay here. It's not like we're really living together, is it?"

"Definitely not. You hide in your room; I'll hide in mine and we'll get along fine," Ruby says with a smirk.

"Yeah." I tuck my hands beneath my arms. "That way we can avoid not knowing what to say to each other."

Ruby nods and sits back down, curling her legs under and resuming her shit meal.

Thing is, I want to sit with her. But I don't.

12

Jem

Ruby's creeping into my life; the way the morning sun shines through the curtains and crosses the bed until eventually the light shines in your face and you can't hide anymore. The brightness is outside, waiting. You just have to get up and let the warmth in.

Her presence in the house isn't just the scent of her perfume that drifts toward me when I walk through the door; but little things like somebody else's food in my cupboard, bits and pieces of her life spread across the kitchen counter. Ruby tidies after herself, attempting to minimise her impact, but however hard we hide from each other and stick to minimal contact, we're clearly sharing the same space. The last person who stayed here was Bryn and that was for three days. Ruby's been here over a week now.

Usually, I'm out until the evening, but I arrive home early from a meeting and come across Ruby sitting on the floor of the downstairs lounge with paper surrounding her, lidless coloured marker pens spread across the table. Her guitar is slung over her skinny shoulders, hair pulled on top of her head in a loose bun. When she looks around in surprise, the thing that hits me the most is her face is clear of make-up.

With her pale lips and eyes free from heavy eyeliner, Ruby's vulnerability shows through. She looks her age for once; but in her eyes, she's older. We're caught in one of our moments, and this time I can see more of her because she's only half Ruby. Is this Tuesday? She rubs her long fingers across her lips and, as ever, I wish I could taste them.

"Sorry, I'll clear up." Ruby pulls her guitar from over her shoulder and gathers the pens from the table.

"You don't have to, I was going upstairs anyway."

"To your den?" she asks with a smile.

"To my den." I pick up a red marker. "Sweet pens. I didn't realise you liked colouring."

"Ha, ha. I'm writing." Ruby lifts up a piece of paper containing unintelligible lines in different colours.

"Secret code? Cool."

"I guess it is."

I take the paper and examine the markings. I know what this is; and if I'm right, this is something else I wish wasn't part of Ruby. "I can decipher this."

She looks at me doubtfully. "Sure you can."

Sitting on the leather sofa, I pick up her guitar. Ruby opens her mouth to protest, as I would if somebody picked up one of mine. They're an extension of myself; touching them is like touching me. "Pass me a sheet," I say as I loop the strap over my neck.

Ruby's way of writing the notes is different, the scrawl harder to decipher because her colours are different. I play a couple of notes attempting to figure out which colours they match. The chords fall into place and I strum the opening lines of the song she's writing.

"How can you know that?" she asks quietly.

"This is music. It's a bit tricky because your E chord is yellow, that's the colour of my C," I tell her. "And your C Minor is orange, mine's green. Some of our notes match though."

Ruby lowers herself onto the glass coffee table and continues to stare. "You have synaesthesia? You see music as colours?"

I nod and concentrate on playing. "This is half-decent. Did you write this today?"

"Yeah."

"Do you always write music like this?"

"The only way I know how, I taught myself."

Now it's my turn to stare. "You are kidding me?"

"No. And thanks, a compliment from you means something."

"Sure does, I don't deal them out much."

The look that passes is too heavy with the unsaid, the opportunity to talk about what else we have in common. I'm not sure what Ruby sees in my eyes, but she looks away.

Ruby carefully places the lids on the remaining pens. "But, really? You have synaesthesia, too?"

"Yeah, all the best musicians do, you know. For instance... me."

"Sure, Jem Jones." She shakes her head. "I thought I was weird, seeing colours when I listened to music until someone told me what it was."

"I guess that makes us both weird then."

I can't. She's pushing at the edges of my world, another part of Ruby slipping through and joining me.

"I've never met another like me before," she says.

"Oh, I'd say we're unique people."

"I doubt that's the word most people use."

We know the truth here, we're unique; but so similar it threatens. If she were Dylan or Jax, I'd grab my guitar and join her in playing, write a song with her. But not Ruby, no more. The pale-faced girl came here because she needed to escape, needed my help and protection. I'm not tangling with another broken girl.

I hand Ruby the sheet and pull her guitar off me. "Cool, well, I'll look forward to hearing the song when you're finished."

The thread of connection snaps, springing back and Ruby attempts to hide her disappointment that I'm not staying to chat.

"Back to hiding?" she asks.

"What do you mean?"

She points upwards at my bedroom. "In your den."

"Oh. Yeah."

"It's safer there." She gathers her pens. "Nobody can touch you."

Of course, she understands.

In my room, I sit on the edge of the bed and stare at the sun streaming through the window. The sound of Ruby's song travels upstairs, through my open bedroom door, following me. I close my eyes and lie back on the unmade bed. Individually, the notes have the colours from her sheet; together the song has another, a rich purple that fills my mind.

Why does she have to be so much of who I am?

13

The bass from music playing thumps through the house and into my dreams until I can't ignore the noise any longer. My phone illuminates two-forty-five a.m., not the most thoughtful time of day for Jem to play music so bloody loud. Half an hour of shifting in bed, attempting to cover my ears with a combination of pillows and duvets, and the last remnants of sleep are gone.

Giving up, I pad along the polished wooden hallway floor into the kitchen. I pour a glass of water and rest my tired head on the counter as I consider what to do. I don't have any right to go upstairs and tell Jem to turn his music down, but I'm working in five hours and need my sleep.

The music stops.

Did I psychically do that? I hesitate in case the music starts again; but after a few minutes, the house remains silent. *Yes.*

Heading out of the kitchen, I almost walk into Jem who's coming in.

"Shit!" I say in surprise.

He's shirtless, the curls hanging in his face unable to obscure the confused look. "Forgot you were here." Jem pushes past.

"Obviously," I mutter.

"What does that mean?" Jem snaps.

I turn to retort but he's scowling at me. Edgy. Unpredictable? "Nothing. You woke me up. Night." If I get back to bed now I can get an extra couple of hours.

"Shit. Sorry. Ignore me." Jem crashes around in a cupboard, swearing under this breath.

Jem Jones apologising?

"It's okay. This is your house."

"Yeah. Couldn't sleep." He grips an empty glass as if confused over what he needs to do with it. His pupils are dilated. Is he high?

"You okay?" I ask tentatively.

For a long moment, Jem stares at me unblinkingly, face pale. No, not drugs, something's upset him. "Doesn't matter."

When he turns away to fill his glass, I edge away.

I'm in bed less than five minutes when a crash jerks me awake. When this is followed by several more crashes, I climb out of bed and head back into the other part of the house.

In the kitchen, Jem rests his hands on the bench, head bowed, breathing deeply. Broken glass surrounds him on the floor and blocks his path out of the room.

"Jem?"

"Do you know where my keys are?" he asks, not looking round.

"Your car keys?"

"Yeah. Can you get them?"

I chew the edge of my mouth and point at his naked feet. "How will you get out of the kitchen to leave?"

"I don't want to get out of the kitchen," he growls.

"Then why do you want your car keys?"

"Just fucking get them!"

"No, I fucking won't if you swear at me."

Jem throws his head back and stares at the ceiling continuing to swear under his breath. "Phone Bryn," he says to the ceiling.

"Phone him yourself! I don't have his number anyway."

"I need to talk to someone, you stupid girl!"

I straighten; scalp prickling at his behaviour. "I doubt anyone wants to talk to you if you're behaving like an asshole!"

He looks over his shoulder. "Get me my keys and my phone." I arch an eyebrow and he huffs. "Please."

"Where are they?"

"Upstairs. By my bed."

Jem's inner sanctum. Huh. Who'd have thought? Days of curiosity and I get to take a look.

Jem's room is tidy, apart from the scrunched up bedclothes on the king sized bed. The main reason it's so tidy is there's barely anything in it. He has a guitar by the bed; one I'd love to inspect but don't. A set of keys and a phone rest on the black bedside table so I grab them and head back downstairs.

When I get back to the kitchen, Jem is sitting on the counter and he's arranged mugs into a line, ones he keeps shifting to make the painted patterns line up.

"Catch."

I throw him the phone and I'm about to throw the keys when he shakes his head. "You keep them. Don't give them to me."

"Then why ask me to get them?"

"Because I don't want to leave the fucking house!" He tears a hand through his hair. "Shit! Leave me alone!"

I'm too tired for this shit and, to be honest, scared. I've lived with my share of unpredictable men; and at this point, I question if staying here with another was the right decision.

"Don't worry, I will." I stalk away and get as far as the lounge before Jem's phone sails through the kitchen doorway and lands near me.

"Did you just throw that at me?" I yell.

"No! I can't see you! I want you to use it."

"What for?"

"Bryn's not answering! I need to speak to him!"

I step back into the doorway, relieved the broken glass is between him and me. "Maybe he doesn't want to be woken up at three o'clock in the bloody morning!"

Jem jumps down from the counter straight onto a pile of glass and I wince for him. "Shit! Fuck!" He jumps back up and pulls a shard of glass from his foot, grabs a tea towel and presses it to the wound.

"What's going on?" I ask.

"I couldn't sleep."

"This isn't a normal reaction to insomnia. What's with the attitude and the glass?"

"If I leave this house, I won't stay sober. So take my keys and fucking leave me alone, if you won't phone Bryn."

I drop my shoulders; suddenly aware I'm in the room with an ex-addict who needs help. "What happened?" I ask gently.

Jem shakes his fringe from his face. "This is nothing to do with you. Just throw my phone back and go away." The hostility has dropped from his voice, replaced by a tired defeat.

What do I do? Should I try to call Bryn, too? Do I wait with Jem and make sure he doesn't do anything stupid?

I sit on the floor and cross my legs.

"What are you doing?" he asks.

"Talk to me. And if you don't, I'll sit here anyway." Jem's eyes narrow until they all but disappear beneath his heavy brow. "You helped me the other night. I want to help you."

The response is a short bark of a laugh from Jem. "Right."

"Your foot is bleeding through the tea towel." I point at the seeping blood on the beige cloth.

"Don't care."

"Doesn't it hurt?"

Jem inhales. "Yeah. Everything fucking hurts."

"What's wrong, Jem? There's at least three broken glasses on the floor here. Did you need me to call someone; do you have a counsellor or something?"

"He's no use. I want to speak to Bryn."

"We'll keep trying him; he'll answer eventually."

"We?"

"I'm staying here until I'm sure you won't walk across broken glass to attack me for your car keys, then disappear somewhere to get high." I cross my arms over my chest in what I hope looks like determination and not an attempt to hide the shaking in my hands.

"Fine."

Silence descends, apart from Jem's tapping on the counter and the slow movement of an occasional car outside. I pull my knees into my chest and rest my head on them, listening to the blood whooshing through my ears.

"How long are you going to sit there?" he asks.

"Until we get in touch with Bryn."

"Why?" asks Jem.

I want to say because I see your pain as readily as I feel it; because I know he needs someone here even if he wants to be alone. Jem shouldn't live on his own and whatever's triggered this need to get out of the house and relapse, it must be significant.

"Because I'm worried about the manager of Ruby Riot," I reply. "I don't want to go back to square one and look for another."

Jem meets my eyes and the understanding passes. His mouth curls into a half-smile but he doesn't respond.

If the broken glass didn't cover the kitchen tiles between us, I'd go to Jem, pull him back to reality, and tell him I understand. We're connected, existing on the fringes of the world. Two shattered people with broken glass surrounding us; we're unable to step out, or risk hurting somebody else by allowing them in.

"I'm fucked, Ruby," he says hoarsely. "Totally fucked."

"No, you're not. You're here and sober, not wasted and on your own somewhere."

"The dreams..." He says through gritted teeth. "They don't stop!"

"What dreams? Is that why you're awake now?"

"Just dreams, Ruby. Just dreams." He shakes his hair away again and leans down to retrieve his boots. I want to push him, ask more, and help the guy because he helped me.

"Jem, if you..." I'm interrupted by a sharp ringtone, the sound shocking me in the quiet of the house. "Bryn." I say as I look at the caller ID.

Jem holds his hand out and I throw the phone across the small space. His gruff responses to Bryn are accompanied by shifty-eyed looks to me. Unsure what to do, I stand and watch.

Jem holds the phone away from his face. “Bryn has keys. You can go. I’ll wait here for him.”

“You sure?”

“Go back to bed, Ruby.” His dismissive attitude pains me as much as the panic of the last few minutes.

The more time I spend around Jem Jones, the more aware I am that he’s a lot more complicated than the image he presents to the world.

14

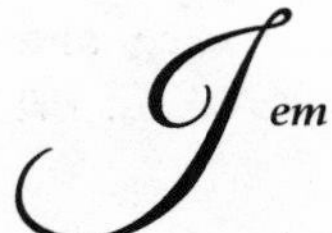

Jem

The club Ruby Riot plays in tonight is a smaller venue in Camden, another I recognise from years ago. Bryn's in town claiming he wants to see how the band is doing; check up on me, more like. This evening, Ruby left the house as soon as Bryn arrived, jumped into the waiting van the guys use when they gig, and they drove away. I arrive with Bryn an hour before they're due on stage to find Jax and Ruby huddled together, running through the set list as they usually do. Their relationship bothers me, especially now Dan isn't around. Whether they're a couple or not isn't the only thing that bothers me; it's the fact she's comfortable with him. Ruby's not comfortable with me.

I'm not surprised following what she witnessed a couple of nights ago. My stomach turns over when I think about Ruby seeing me like that; but in a weird way, it equalizes us, vulnerabilities shown on both sides. Considering her history, Ruby should've run as far as she could from an irrational man throwing things around the house, but there was no fear in her eyes, just concern and understanding.

The incident hasn't been mentioned since and we both behave as if it never happened.

Bryn pushes through the bar and we head toward the main hall of the old theatre. "You still haven't explained why Ruby was there the other night. What's going on?"

"Ruby's living with me."

He halts. "Define 'living with you', Jem. I thought we'd agreed you avoid relationships for a few months?"

"We're living in the same house. Sharing a kitchen but not a bed. Platonic."

Bryn chokes back a laugh. "Right. For how long?"

"I don't intend fucking her anytime soon."

Bryn arches an eyebrow. "I meant how long is she staying. Your response suggests you're thinking a little too much about the non-platonic part."

"Shut the fuck up," I mutter. Am I that transparent?

"She's not bringing anything into the house that can screw around with you, is she?"

"Ruby knows not to." Bryn's lips purse and he keeps walking. "Her ex beat the crap out of her, okay?"

"That's even worse!" says Bryn, turning back to me. "Liv, much?"

This edges my thoughts every day, but I don't acknowledge it. "Not 'Liv, much'. So piss off if you haven't got anything useful to say."

Ruby sits on the edge of the stage drinking water between growling at the brothers. The more stressed Ruby is, the snappier she is, as I'm beginning to learn.

I can guess why.

"If Dan comes, I'll sort it," I tell her as I approach.

Ruby slowly screws the lid onto the bottle. "Don't care if he does."

"I do." Ruby frowns at me. "I saw him threaten you when you were together; what the hell do you think he'll be like now you've left him?"

"Now?" Ruby hops off the wooden stage. "I'll tell you what Dan will be like now. He'll be like you."

Too stunned to reply I step back. Ruby leans closer, face impassive. "He'll be super nice. Apologetic. He'll offer to help me but say he doesn't want anything in return. Like you."

"Are you comparing me to Dan?" I ask in a low voice.

"No, I'm saying I trust people too easily. I trust you when I shouldn't," she replies as quietly.

"I never asked you to. All I did was give you somewhere to stay. Feel free to leave when you want." Infuriated that she's comparing me to Dan on the smallest level, I turn and walk away.

Ruby doesn't realise, but I know exactly what she's doing because it's a favourite trick of mine. Piss them off, push them away, and they won't disappoint you.

Tonight is Ruby Riot's first performance since Ruby left Dan, and there's a new energy around her on stage. The connection between Ruby and the rest of the band is sharper. At past gigs, she was lost in her own world, part of the group but at the forefront and alone. On a couple of occasions tonight, Ruby even cracks a smile at the other band members. She and Jax joke around, Ruby interrupting his playing with hers and he sings over her in return.

Ruby Riot grips the crowd by the throat and drags them into a place that nobody in the room can escape from. This is the kind of performance people will talk about in years to come because this band is killing it.

I leave before the encore and head to the Green Room; Bryn's already back there nursing a beer.

"You okay?" He swaps the beer for water as I walk in, and sets the bottle out of sight by the brown sofa. "You look pretty pissed off for someone whose pet project just raised the roof."

"You can drink around me, Bryn."

"Doesn't feel supportive when I do." He throws me a bottle of water and I catch it. "So, what's up?"

I flop next to him. "Missing the guys. Watching the band tonight reminded me of the other high - the legal one that was good for me. That's the thing I crave."

"I get that. A few months and we're back on tour, yeah? This isn't over, Blue Phoenix aren't done."

But we're not Ruby Riot. We don't have the thrill of striving to make it; the high of the electric connection to the crowd you can only get in small venues. Blue Phoenix will still be a machine.

"Yeah, I guess." I prop my feet on the plastic chair opposite.

"Ever thought of getting them into the studio?"

"Yeah, I'm arranging that."

"Cool. You could offer to session for them."

"No. They need to establish their own sound. I don't want to be part of them; they make it on their own terms not because Jem Jones played on their debut."

Bryn sits forward and peers at me from under his fringe. "You're edgy again, man. Is Ruby Riot really doing you any good? If this starts to stress you, back off. You know what your counsellor said..."

"Okay, Auntie Bryn, I know. I've been here three times, yeah? This time I'm done for good, no more drugs. I know my triggers and music isn't one of them."

The door opens and Ruby walks in, perspiration gleaming on her body, face glowing with heat and happiness. She runs a hand through her damp hair and turns a smile on me, which blows my mind, a smile where her eyes are alive and focused. A smile for me. Ruby's back in the world and that world is a brighter place because of it. When I don't return her smile, she approaches me. Ruby doesn't get far because Jax appears behind and wraps his arms around her waist, spinning Ruby around and off the floor.

Ruby laughs at him, the sound as powerful to me as her singing. Ruby from a week ago would've slapped Jax; this one joins in. He hugs her tight and kisses the top of her head and my stomach drops.

What the hell?

Bryn kicks me and I look around sharply. "You've got a trigger right there, Jem."

Will and Nate appear, straight to the fridge for beers. A whirlwind of activity swirls around my dazed head as they pour drinks and talk excitedly, Will constantly trying to pull me into the conversation, desperate for reassurance I still think Ruby Riot is awesome. I join in as much as someone drinking water in a room full of alcohol-fuelled people can. Ruby and Jax continue to talk, squashed together on the sofa. Where her leg meets his and their heads touch are images imprinting themselves on my brain.

I shouldn't feel like this. Jax is doing me a favour. He's saving me from myself by stopping me trying to save Ruby.

15

Satisfied that Dan isn't going to make an appearance and unable to sit in a room full of temptation, I leave. Perceptive as ever, Bryn follows and suggests coming home with me but I inform him I want to be alone. Things descend into an argument over how I think he constantly assumes I'm about to go home and start using, as if I have a secret stash somewhere. Bryn puts up with a lot of my shit and is a solid friend, but he needs to back off.

Still wired from the evening, I pace around the house attempting to deny I'm jealous of Ruby and Jax for more than their musical relationship. The jittery energy stops me sitting still for long or able to focus on playing. I run through my scrawled list of distraction techniques and lying on my bed staring at the ceiling conjuring images of Ruby's mouth on Jax's don't help.

Ruby isn't home. I guess she went back to the guys' house. Pouty Jem wonders why the hell she didn't just move in with them anyway. I'm sure Jax would've shared a bed with her.

Shit, Jem, get a grip.

Exercise is my other release. I've learnt I can run off stress and get a kick of endorphins this way, with the added bonus that it keeps me in shape. However, two a.m. sessions on the treadmill indicate when things are slipping. Tomorrow I'll talk to someone.

The gym is in the basement and when I emerge calmer and ready for a shower, a light is on in the kitchen. Poking my head around the door, I see Ruby grappling with the coffee machine. Her lack of co-ordination amuses me, like one of those fake drunks you see on TV. Coffee beans cover the bench next to her and Ruby swears as she fails to attach the porta filter for the third time.

"Want some help?" I ask.

Ruby jumps then turns to me. "I wanted coffee. Your machine's broken."

I laugh at her. "Sure it is."

I take the beans from Ruby and the smell of booze assaults me. As I put the machine together and switch it on, I'm aware of her scrutiny.

"On your own?" I ask.

"Clearly. Who would be here?" Her words slur at the edges.

"The rest of the band."

Ruby wrinkles her nose. "I don't invite guests to your house."

"I never said you couldn't."

"Right." She elongates the word. "So I can bring random people to Jem Jones's house?"

"I trust your judgement."

The aroma of fresh coffee subdues the smell of alcohol and Ruby pulls out two cups. "Coffee, Jem Jones?"

"Why do you always say my name like that?"

"Like what?"

"Like you're taking the piss."

"Sorry, I'd have thought you'd like people around you to be reverential."

She rubs her lips together and focuses on my mouth, before touching my naked chest. I step back, someone's fingers on my skin is unusual recently and sends a shock through my body. Ruby traces the outline of the stars tattooed on my bicep.

"Your ink's cool. I have some. Do you want to see my favourite?" Ruby switches to fumbling with her baggy black top, pulling the side up so the edge of her lace-covered tit is visible above her ribs.

Fuck.

"Yeah, nice." I take the merest glance at the black words tattooed below the lace and look away. "I'm going for a shower."

"I have more!" she giggles again. "Secret ones."

As she bunches her skirt higher up her thighs, I grab her arm. "Stop."

"Don't you want to see?" Ruby stumbles closer.

"You're drunk. Sort yourself out. And I don't want to see, no."

"Do you want to kiss me?" she whispers, moving her mouth close to mine.

"What the fuck, Ruby?" I hold her shoulders and stretch my arms so Ruby's as far from me as possible, so those lips are out of temptation's way.

"I feel like you want to. I've seen that you do." She moistens her lips and touches my arm. "Jem Jones looks at me like he wants me."

Jem Jones. Ruby has a perception of who he is and despite over a week living here, and several weeks of knowing me, she still sees me as Jem Jones and not Jem. Yeah, several months ago and in the same intoxicated state, I'd be screwing her on the kitchen counter by now. I can't control my dick's reaction to her, but I can control what I do with it.

"Move away," I say in a low voice. "You're pissing me off."

"But you're so good to me; I want to do something good for you." Ruby's attempt at a seductive look is tempered by her inability to focus properly.

"Is that what you do? You think a guy wants something in return for helping you? Because by doing this you're comparing me with that piece of shit you left."

She scoffs at me. "Like Jem Jones knows how to treat girls. Remember the second night I met you and you had some girl's mouth wrapped around your dick? Classy."

My shoulders stiffen. "Stop talking. Make your coffee and go to bed."

Ruby lowers her eyes to my crotch. "Is that the problem? You don't do kissing? I can do other things."

When her fingers go to the waistband of my sweatpants, I grab Ruby's arms and push her away. "Get the hell off me, Ruby!"

Ruby slumps against the counter then slides slowly to the floor, rubbing her face. This girl is a fucked up mess. Bryn's right, she's several steps removed from Liv, and I'm trying to help. Again.

Before any more damage is caused, I leave.

Time for a rethink.

I don't think I can have Ruby living in my house.

There's a pile of girl on the white leather sofa the next morning, tangled red hair obscuring her face, and an untouched mug of coffee on the floor next to her. My anger from last night fades to pity. Leaving her alone, I mooch around the house and plan my day. Maybe I should step away from all this, go to the States for a bit, spend some time in my Manhattan lifestyle, and look up some old friends. Too late, I'm committed to helping these guys on tour now and that kicks off in a few days.

I call Jax to check if he's arranged the band's accommodation yet and he sounds as disconnected from the world as Ruby currently is. "Is she okay?" Jax asks as soon as he answers.

"Ruby? She's passed out on my sofa."

A girl's voice in the background asks Jax something and he covers the mouthpiece for a muffled response. "'Kay. Just worried a bit when she got the text from Dan."

"Dan? When?"

"Not sure. Ruby started knocking back the drinks and I was umm... busy with a chick. When I came back Ruby was really drunk. She waved her phone at me and there was a text from Dan saying he wanted to see her. Then she started freaking out big style, so I put her in a taxi."

My intention to ask Ruby to leave and go live with the rest of the band evaporates. Why the hell didn't she say something last night?

"You there? Jem? What were you calling for?"

"Oh, yeah. Meeting. I need to catch up with you to finalise the dates." I'm zoned out now, and I walk through to look at Ruby asleep on the sofa. "Listen, I'll call back later."

"No problem, I'm busy right now." The girl in the background giggles.

I end the call, annoyed by my relief that Ruby and Jax aren't a couple.

I pour a glass of water and head to the lounge, poking Ruby with my foot.

She groans and squints at me. "What do you want?"

"I think you need this." I thrust the water and painkillers at her. "I need to talk to you."

"Later." She twists her head and buries it into the sofa. Several attempts at getting another response fail, so I give up.

There's a cafe close by and I can go there undisturbed most days. Recently, anyway. A few months back, when life was a huge ball of shit and I was in the middle of it, leaving the house was hard enough. No longer trapped, I can walk the streets in peace and usually sit and chill at a coffee shop. Small pleasure but ones missing from life until recently. Inevitably, someone takes my picture but there's no story to attach. A couple of hours later I head back to the flat.

Ruby's now curled up under her duvet on the white sofa watching old movies on TV. Her damp hair is piled on her head, accentuating her pale, drawn features and the huge black marks under her eyes. A half-empty two-litre bottle of coke rests on the table.

"Morning, sunshine," I say. "How are you?"

"Feel like shit. Sorry. I hope I didn't wake you up when I got home last night."

"Gotta love alcohol memory blanks." *Or not.* "I wasn't asleep."

Ruby massages her temples. "I hope I wasn't full-on Ruby with you. I was a bit aggressive with people last night."

"Let's not go there. I want to talk to you about Dan."

At the mention of his name, her hand curls around the duvet and she shifts her focus onto the TV screen.

"We haven't talked about him since you moved in. I spoke to Jax and he said Dan texted you. If you want to stay here, you need to do something about him."

She pulls herself to her feet. "I'll leave. I can stay with Jax."

"There's a reason you didn't go there originally, isn't there? I know you feel safer behind my security gates."

Ruby moves to pass me, and I gently take her arm. "He's a threat to you. Go to the police. I'll help."

She drags her arm away. "Help? Why do you keep trying to help?"

Crap, my big mouth. What do I follow that up with? The wide-eyed girl waits my response; and the push-pull of wanting her with me, and also wanting her somewhere I'll never see her again, tightens a band around my head. Be professional. "Because I don't want the lead singer of Ruby Riot ending up in hospital!"

"That's all?" I can't tell from her tone whether she's annoyed or disappointed but her dull eyes tell me she's not happy.

"That's all and I don't want anything from you in return apart from go out, perform, and be awesome. This shit with Dan will interfere. Draw a line. Move on."

"Just like that," she mutters and sits back on the sofa.

Does Ruby know that I'm piecing together her story slowly? Or that the more jigsaw pieces that fit, the harder I need to try to convince myself this is business?

"Yeah, I'm putting money into you guys. Faith. Attaching my name means something."

"Gee, thanks, Jem Jones," she snaps.

I sit in the chair opposite. "I'm not interested in fixing your fucked up life, Ruby. Sorry."

"I never asked you to."

"I tried to fix someone before," I say quietly, "and she died." Ruby's eyes widen. Of course, she knows the story; the whole fucking world knows the story. "So that's why I'm not going to try to fix you and why I won't ever see you as more than Ruby. I don't want to know about Tuesday."

"Don't call me that. Don't ever call me that!" she says, tone rising.

And *this* is why I don't want to know. "Do you understand why I won't interfere beyond what's best for the band?"

She nods and the tears are fighting through; Tuesday is fighting through and I don't want to see her. I can't see Ruby weak.

The frail girl pulls at the edge of the duvet and I consider how many sides she has. There's Ruby, the obnoxious girl covered in thorns; and underneath a broken girl, Tuesday, who has secrets I don't want to hear. But with me, in this house, she's neither of those people. Instead, this girl is somebody who acknowledges she's neither but both. This Ruby doesn't hide, but she doesn't attack.

Ruby's demons moved into my house too and although our demons don't get along, they sure as hell recognise each other.

16

*uby*

I push open the door to the hotel room, guitar case on my back and rucksack over an arm. The neutrally decorated, narrow room barely fits the furniture and heavy brown curtains block out all natural light. I push the keycard into the slot and the lights come on revealing two queen size beds. *Great.*

Jax barrels in behind me and leaps onto the nearest bed, flopping back and looking at the ceiling. Will hovers in the doorway, chewing on his lip piercing.

"This it?" asks Will.

"What did you expect?" I ask. "The Ritz? Most bands our size don't have a sponsor and have to sleep in the van!"

"Dunno, it's... small," says Will.

"Yeah, that's what I heard the chick saying about you the other day." Nate pushes him out of the way and walks in. "Seriously? We're not spending much time here anyway."

"I know, but what about the after party?" says Will.

"It's going to get a bit cramped if you invite more than one person," I reply.

"I bet Jem's room is bigger; reckon he'll let us party in there?" Nate asks.

"Sure, Nate. The recovering addict would love his room full of drunk and high kids. Great idea. Maybe we should ask him to dump us now if you're going to piss him off! Dickhead," I retort.

Will laughs. "Ohhh! Listen to you. You live with a rock star and now you're his bestie?"

"Fuck off." I prop my guitar against the wall. "Who's sleeping on the floor?"

"Why does anyone have to sleep on the floor?" asks Nate, lying on the other bed and resting his hands beneath his head.

"Two queen beds, four people, three guys, one girl." I raise a questioning eyebrow.

Nate smirks. "You're not a real girl, Rube, not to us anyway."

"Yeah, but I don't want to share a bed with any of you guys."

Jax throws back the covers. "Me! You can sleep with me and we can work on the lead singer and guitarist relationship." He pats the bed.

"I don't think there'll be room for me and your conquests," I retort.

"You could share with me and Will, and then..." begins Nate.

I narrow my eyes. "One comment about threesomes and I'll kick your ass."

"If you're in my bed why would I need to pick up other chicks?" continues Jax.

"Shut the hell up." I'm uncomfortable with his words. Jax is the only guy I've ever trusted and that was because he had no interest in me outside of my music; there's never been any attempt to hit on me. Once over, I didn't think Jax ever saw me as anything, but the band's honorary guy; but recently I'm not a hundred per cent sure. Our banter is full of innuendo, always was, and Jax has never looked at or touched me in a way to make me question that. But comments like that niggle and have me on alert for any extra meaning behind his friendly kisses and hugs.

"I reckon she's going to sweet talk Jem into sharing his room," says Nate.

"Yeah, what's the deal with you guys?" Will pokes around in the bar fridge. "Hey! Look at this! Beers!"

"There's no deal. I'm just staying at his house."

Will pulls one out. "Have you done the dirty with him yet?" Jax throws a pillow at him. "What? I'm only asking what we all want to know."

"What do you mean what you all want to know? Have you been discussing me and Jem behind my back?" I slam the hotel room door shut and glare at Jax.

"Aw, c'mon, Rube. You've lived with him two weeks and he's Jem Jones. I even saw you on the internet as 'Jem's new girl'."

The day I saw myself blasted on social media as Jem's latest chick, it pissed me off. Jem said he didn't give a shit; I could be eighty years old and they'd still accuse me of being more. The guys loved it because it was more publicity for the band; and as they're right, I put up with the rumours and bite my tongue.

"Jem and me don't interact a lot; and I sure as hell won't be asking to share his hotel room, too!"

Nate whispers something to Will and they snigger. I'm ready to lose it, for the first time I'm aware that as the only female band member there's connotations.

"I'll sleep on the floor, Ruby," says Jax and I glance at him. He knows me better than I realise, his awareness of my moods helps with band diplomacy on my bad days.

"You'll pass out on the floor anyway, so nothing for me to worry about," I tell him.

Jax climbs back off the bed. "Let's grab the rest of our gear from the van. We haven't got much time until we need to be at the venue to set up." He stops as he reaches me. "Next time we'll ask for four singles."

The smile he gives is apologetic but also concern. Jem doesn't want to know about Tuesday, but Jax has spent time trying to get me to talk about her. In the early days, Jax attempted to talk to me about Dan, too. He soon learned it wasn't worth it; I wouldn't allow anyone to interfere and hid as much as I could. Jax recognises when Tuesday's around, but has given up trying to understand her.

A couple of hours later, Jax and me sit on the edge of the stage chatting as the brothers finish setting up their gear. Will and Nate contain enough excitement for all of us. They've always amused me, their enthusiasm for life infectious. On my dark days, spending time with the brothers helped. Their positivity radiates to those around, and multiplied by two, the twins always bring a great vibe to anywhere they go. This reflects in their music, and is why Ruby Riot's music could never have a downbeat sound.

What would it be like to have a twin? Will and Nate are identical and telling them apart isn't helped by their decision to rock the same image. I tease them sometimes, saying they should get their names tattooed on themselves since they have plenty of others. They made a concession – both have pierced eyebrows, but Will's is the left and Nate's the right. Their identical spikey black hair doesn't help; the only option is to get close enough to see. The pair plays on this with chicks that take an interest and I've heard them offering to show girls other differences in their appearance, differences not visible when they're clothed. I laugh, at their idiocy and at the girls who fall for it.

Jax shows me the latest viral videos on his phone, not-so-hilarious footage of guys our age doing stupid things. Gluing their mouths together with superglue is funny, why? I feign interest but keep checking the time on my phone. Every night we're due on stage, I freak out for a few hours before. My mouth has a mind of its own and I'm best avoided altogether because when adrenaline courses through me, things never come out well. The guys tend to leave me alone or ignore any outbursts. They know what to expect, and I'm heading in that direction again.

I haven't seen Jem since this morning when we left his house and weirdly went our separate ways to travel to the same place. I piled into the hired van with the guys and Jem said he had something to do before he started the trip to Manchester. I don't think Jem's sleeping again because recently the door bangs waking me in the early hours to indicate he's going down to the gym, and then when he comes back I wake again. Some nights I hear him playing in the early hours. What concerns me is I worry about Jem.

We both hide but parts of us seep through.

Things cooled between us when I refused to go to the police on the day after Dan tried to get in touch with me again. Jem insisted but I was too hungover and not in the mood for him to interfere. I didn't appreciate his comments about fixing me, or the weird look he gave me when he told me he wanted to help. That's too reminiscent of Dan's 'help': taking control.

Jem's face is a pissed off red when he stomps into the stage area. I don't miss the fact his look lingers on where Jax's arm is around my shoulder, or how he avoids meeting my eyes. This is the other thing that concerns me. I can't deny I'm attracted to him and I'm aware of something between us that was there but never mentioned in the time we spent alone in his house. Unless I'm imagining it. I don't know.

"What's up, man?" asks Jax, dropping his arm.

"I'm not used to dealing with this shit," Jem says. "I usually just play and don't have to deal with venue managers and crap."

"Why? What's going on?"

"They're screwing around over door sales percentages or something. I don't understand this side of things." Jem's half-talking to himself. "And why the hell are you two sitting there?"

I stiffen. "What?"

"Will and Nate are sound-checking. You guys think you're too good to join in?"

"We're done, they had some sound issues they wanted to double-check," I retort.

"You do this as a band!"

"We do this how we always do it!" I say and stand. "We have our way of doing this."

Jem glares at me. "You have to do things my way when you're on tour with me."

I straighten. "What the fuck? Since when?"

"I know what I'm doing. I've been doing this a lot longer than you."

"And we don't?" This isn't helping the pre-show anxiety.

"You have a lot to learn, sweetheart."

Sweetheart? Since when did he call me such a condescending name? "Fuck this!" Relieved that my self-control manages to limit me to just those words, I stomp away to the Green Room. I need to get ready anyway, I'm still in my scruffy track pants and loose flannel shirt, and I'm not performing in those.

I'm midway through getting changed when Jax appears, walking through the door without knocking. He halts and stares, I only have panties and a thin black vest on.

"You could've knocked!" I snap.

Jax has seen it all before. In the early days, I changed in filthy toilet cubicles but soon swapped to half-stripping in front of the other guys when getting ready for gigs. I'm not shy, and they're used to it now. I'm not exactly curvy and I doubt they find me attractive, as evidenced by the 'semi-guy' comment in the hotel room.

"You okay?" Jax asks.

"He'd better not be like that at every gig."

"This manager gig is new to him, but we should listen to him. He knows what he's doing."

"Yeah, but I don't like being spoken to like I'm a kid." I dig around in my bag for my black dress.

"Well, we are to him and you kinda behave like one sometimes."

I glare, choosing to ignore the dig. "He's only five years older!"

"And wiser."

I make a derisive sound. "Not really."

Jax runs a hand through his thick blond hair and fixes his pale blue eyes on mine. "Don't fuck this up. Be nice."

"Nice? You're asking me to be nice? This is Ruby Butler you're talking to here."

"Very true." Jax catches sight of something and points. "You got new ink. When was that?"

The short vest exposes my stomach, revealing the pattern of

red roses and thorns stretching across my lower belly. "It's not that long since you saw me almost naked! I got it a couple of months ago."

The door opens and Jem walks in. Instantly I hold the short dress against myself, and Jax steps back tucking his hands under his arms. Jem's eyes widen and in them, for a split second, is the reason why being semi-naked in front of Jem is different. I'm not imagining Jem's attraction to me; the desire just flickered across his face.

"What's going on?" Jem asks.

"Nothing. I was admiring Ruby's tattoos," says Jax.

Jem narrows his eyes.

"I'm getting changed, if you don't mind." I pull the dress over my head.

"Sorry. Okay." At least he has the decency to be embarrassed.

"Then I'm going to have a smoke, if that's okay with you?" My hair sweeps forward as I grab my combat boots and shove my feet in. "Don't worry, I'll be present and correct, ready to go on stage, sir."

Snatching my cigarettes and lighter from the pocket of my discarded pants, I leave the room.

Jem

Jax launches into one of his Q&A sessions about my early Blue Phoenix gigs and all I can picture is Ruby semi-naked with him. Ruby semi-naked with me, and my hands on her skin. I fight the memory of Ruby revealing her tattoos in the kitchen – and what else she revealed with them. I've spent a few nights fighting my overactive imagination's attempt to picture what would've happened if things had gone further, but my subconscious took hold and pushed her into my dreams. Big pat on the back for not taking advantage, but *shit* that night hasn't helped my fantasies about this chick.

Now this, and in the pit of my stomach seethes an emotion I'm unfamiliar with recently. Jealousy.

For years, I've felt nothing and then in this last couple of months the whole range of emotions has assailed me. Anger, despair, grief, and a shitload of guilt over people and events from the past. The suddenness and strength with which these emotions can overwhelm are what pull me backward. I know why the dreams about Liv began again, the one thing from my past I can't go back and fix.

After rehab, I had apologies to give and amends to make. It was fucking hard, but I went to Dylan, and we worked through all the crap of the last couple of years. I apologised to Sky for how I treated her and we've reached a wary stalemate. Liam was cool apart from another lecture about how Dylan's and my behaviour screw around with the band. Bryn just shrugged me off and said the real apology will come from staying clean, because this time I almost killed the thing I love the most. Blue Phoenix.

Now Ruby stirs other emotions beyond the physical lust I'd have for girls before.

I worry about Ruby when she goes to work in case Dan appears. I care whether she's okay when she spends half a day in her room without coming out. I'm happy when we sit together, even if it is in silence.

And I'm fucking jealous when I see Jax's hands on her.

I've fooled myself that Ruby in my house for a couple of weeks meant nothing; that she was hanging out until we safely went on tour. I allowed Ruby a glimpse into myself and I saw a different girl, one who has triggered a desire for somebody else to share my new life with. Bryn's right, this is heading in a direction bad for my grip on sobriety. I can't get attached to a girl like her - or any girl currently. Back in her life with the boys, Ruby's relaxed and at home, the distance has reformed and I need to keep things this way. When we finish this tour, she needs to leave my house.

17

Jem

As the days pass, the tightness of Ruby Riot places me further on the edge of Ruby's life. This allows me to back off, which will make asking her to leave a ton easier when we get back. Two weeks and ten gigs, the band holds up well. This is what I needed to see. There's no real friction apart from what comes out of Ruby's mouth before she goes on stage and the guys are used to that. In a weird way, Ruby breaks the tension.

Liam and Bryn came to a couple of the gigs and their approval reinforces this is the right decision. Only Steve's thumbs up is needed now. He hasn't been in the UK recently. His wife has him tied down to their house in the States so he's asked for a full demo. The excitement on the guys' faces when I tell them I have studio time booked after the tour is priceless. Even Ruby cracks a smile.

Tonight Ruby Riot played their last gig of the tour to a crowded venue in Oxford. Their sets get tighter, the audiences bigger. There's a weird fatherly sense of pride toward them, although my feelings for Ruby remain increasingly un-fatherly. The bad thing is, the more I resist my brain's attempt to develop an emotional attachment to her, the more I want her in my bed. Yeah, I want her out of my house but in my bed; I'm still a selfish bastard.

Guys hit on Ruby after gigs every night and I watch with a combination of jealousy and amusement, depending on how she responds to them. Curiously, Jax intervenes most nights and gives outsiders the impression the guitarist and lead singer are an item. I've heard her thank him for getting rid of unwanted attention and he shrugs it off but this gnaws at me. I know the four of them share a room at each hotel; and who knows what happens following the late night, drunken sessions I keep out of. At least those thoughts reinforce that my dumb, sober brain needs to find someone else.

Yeah, right, apart from she's cock blocking me, Jem Jones passing on groupies who inevitably pass themselves onto the other guys.

Heading back to my room after the gig, I find Ruby sitting on the floor in the hallway, resting against my suite door with her eyes closed. I pause, wishing the sight of her didn't fire up the irritating mix of desire to screw her with the longing for her attention. We've barely spoken in days. Ruby's plain grey top is scooped across the neck and has slipped on one side, past the ink to the top of her black lace bra. *Not helping*. Her amazing legs stretch in front of her, wrapped in black yoga pants; barefoot, toe nails painted bright red to match her fingernails. I pull the room's keycard out fighting the usual image of those legs wrapped around my body.

"You okay?" I ask.

Ruby opens an eye. "I'm too tired to deal with people. The guys are really going for it tonight and I want to sleep."

I laugh at her. "It's ten p.m."

"Two weeks of this and I'm fucked. No idea how you guys tour for months on end and don't burn out."

"The current state of Blue Phoenix answers that question." I slide the keycard and push open the door. "I'll get you a drink and you can hide out here for a few hours."

"Thanks." Ruby stands.

I hold the door like the gentleman I'm not and catch her fresh-showered scent as she passes, rewinding me to our days alone in my house.

"Shit, if I'd know your rooms were this big I'd have asked to stay before," she remarks as she crosses the penthouse to look over the skyline. "This is an apartment, not a hotel room!"

Stay?

"I like my space," I say as Ruby sits on one of the sofas opposite the bedroom.

"Yeah, I noticed."

Was that a loaded comment? "Did you want a beer?"

She looks at me curiously. "No, I don't like drinking around you. Hadn't you noticed?"

I hadn't but now she mentions it, this explains why she avoids me after most gigs. I convinced myself she avoided me for other reasons.

"Yeah. Okay. Coke?"

She nods and I return with a can from the fridge to where Ruby's stretched out on the cream cushioned sofa, legs crossed at the ankles. Resting her head on one arm, Ruby's scarlet hair flows behind almost touching the floor as she gazes at the ceiling.

"It's been a while since we talked," I say.

"I see you every day."

"I mean, since we chatted, me and you."

Ruby twists her head toward me. "I guess not. Maybe because you're hiding behind Jem Jones again?" she suggests.

"And you're Ruby again."

"There's our answer." She looks back to the ceiling.

"You look healthier even if you do feel burnt out," I tell her.

She twists her head toward me. "Healthier?"

"Not as skinny."

She pushes to sit. "How much attention do you pay to my body?" she asks in a low voice.

"It was just a comment. Don't get so defensive!"

"I'm not! I'm just saying, don't make me worry that you're perving on me." She adjusts her top, pulling further toward her neck.

"Jesus, okay, I was saying you look better after all the shit from a few weeks ago."

She pulls a sour face. "Again, don't."

When we disagree, there's a weird thing that happens, a clashing of wills as we stare at each other waiting to see who'll back down or get the last word in. I've given up trying. Apparently satisfied she's reprimanded me enough with her stern look; Ruby shifts her gaze to the open door behind where I'm standing.

"Oh! Your guitar!" Ruby points at the acoustic leaning against the end of the bed. "Is that a classic Martin?"

Thank fuck for that. I thought we were going down the route to things that shouldn't be said.

"Yeah."

"Wow, I bet it's a rare if you own it." How many people could identify a guitar from a distance?

"OM-18," I say with a small smile. I have a collection; this one isn't exactly my most expensive, but I love the sound. I may not be in the band, but my music comes with me.

"Serious? Can I try?" She looks at the acoustic with an amusing awe.

"Sure."

Ruby heads to where the guitar rests against the wall in the bedroom. Picking it up as if this is a precious heirloom, she perches on the edge of the king-sized bed and hauls the strap across her shoulder, then balances the guitar on her lap. "You got a pick?"

I toss her one from my pocket. I have never been in a room with a chick who's more impressed and excited by the sight of my guitar than being with Jem Jones. But she's no ordinary girl. This is Ruby, the mind-blowing woman with her amazing voice, talent, and a body that dances into my dreams on a too frequent basis. The twinge in my chest grows, as she strums the opening chords of a Ruby Riot track, "Shellshock". I could push the hair from where it falls across Ruby's face, brush her skin with my fingers, kiss her. *Crap, Jem.*

"Who writes your lyrics?" I ask and cross to sit next to her on the other edge of the king-sized bed.

"Me and Jax, mostly him." Her focus remains on the guitar but she stops playing. "Huh. I don't often play acoustic. One day I'm going to get myself a really rare Gibson. I bet you have a crap load of guitars. I know that's what I'm spending my money on if I get cashed up."

"One or two, and I'm sure one day you'll have a collection of your own." I smile and lie back on the bed, tucking my hands behind my head. "Play me a song, Ruby Tuesday."

"Why did you call me that?"

"It's who you are, isn't it? Play me something." Ruby taps the edge of the guitar. "Go on. Then I'll play something for you."

She purses her lips. "Okay, but only because I want to play this awesome guitar."

I smile to myself when I hear the opening chords to "Rising"; typical of Ruby to do this when I told the band never to play my songs again. Only this time the sound reaches inside my heart. The memory of the day I wrote the song, of Phoenix being as new as Ruby Riot joins the images. "Rising", the first real song we wrote. I knew at that moment we'd be big and I'd sacrifice anything to get there. I didn't realise the sacrifices came later.

Aware Ruby's stopped playing, I sit up. "Don't stop."

"Your breathing's funny, are you okay?" She removes the strap from her shoulder.

"Just rewinding in my head. You're making me feel old. I wrote that song eight years ago."

"I thought Dylan wrote Blue Phoenix's songs."

"Lesser known fact, I wrote "Rising."

"Really? Well, I listened to it on repeat for weeks. The first song that ever spoke to me," she says softly, rubbing the neck of the guitar. "Did it help you?"

"No, but it sounds good, hey?" She doesn't want me to meet Tuesday so she's not going to delve into my mind either. I won't share the pain that lies beneath the song.

The intensity and softness in her expression kills me. The song weakened and hit me further with what I deny: Ruby is the epitome of myself. She's here and her eyes are acknowledging what I repeatedly see: we're from the same place and we don't want to be there. I can't hold Ruby's look; I'm sitting on the bed with this woman and the buried need to hold her resurfaces. Kiss her. Touch her. Inhale her, until she's part of me.

"Why are you looking at me like that?" she asks.

"Because you blow me away. You're amazing."

Ruby carefully places the guitar on the floor and shifts on the bed, tucking her long legs under her. "Can I be straight with you, Jem? Get this out in the open so we can lay it to rest?"

"Be straight as you like, you always are." I prop myself on my elbows.

We half-smile at each other and the understanding floods the physical desire again.

Ruby tips her head. "You know we've avoided each other for most of the tour, right?"

"No," I catch her look. "Okay, yeah. A bit."

"Because something weird's between us, isn't it?"

"Is it?"

"Yeah, I can't get past seeing you as the guy in the kitchen that night; he was pretty scary." I look away. "I wanted to help you when I should've run and that's part of this 'something weird'," she says with a small crease of concern between her brows.

"I'm sorry I scared you. Don't worry; you won't see him again. We'll keep things professional."

Ruby drags her hair from her face and holds it as she studies me with pursed lips. "Not just that but all the parts of you I saw in that week. I felt a weird connection to you and it worries me. Especially when you say shit about how I'm looking better, as if you're thinking of me."

"Okay, I won't say anything. I won't come near you if you don't want."

She's so hypocritical. Ruby came here tonight; and we're sitting on my bed together, talking about guitars and music and wrapping our world back around our shoulders. All that's left is to reach out and admit this.

Ruby indicates herself and me. "URST."

"Erst?"

"Unresolved sexual tension. It's a thing on TV and movies. Two people attracted to each other but can't or won't do anything about it for whatever reason. It follows us too."

I shrug. "Right. If you say."

"Seriously, Jem? You're saying there isn't any?"

"Are you asking me if I want to fuck you?"

"No, I'm not asking; I don't want to have sex with you. I'm saying there's an attraction and it's awkward, yeah?"

I guess Ruby doesn't have an issue with the topic; but the word 'sex' should not come from that mouth, otherwise I'll be forced to kiss it away and show her what the hell she's doing to me.

Deep breath, Jem.

"So what if there is; we don't need to act on it. I get why you're saying this and you should know by now I'm not going to do anything that'll cause problems. You're an attractive chick; yeah, I'm not screwing this up by hitting on you."

"Okay," she says doubtfully. "Because I don't want anything messing up the other relationship we have… the musical one."

"I think you need to worry more about you and Jax if the concern is messing up musical relationships."

"Me and Jax?"

"Your URST or lack of, if you're an item."

"We're not an item! Jesus!" Ruby laughs. "No way, never Jax. He models himself on you when it comes to women. If I was with him, would I put up with the girls he scouts out after every gig?"

"I don't see much of him doing that."

"Yeah, you're not around. You come back to your room and sulk. This whole tour you've behaved like a grumpy old man apart from when your Blue Phoenix buddies have been around."

Does she do this deliberately? Each time we tentatively relax around each other, she says something to push me away. And each time it gets my back up. "I am not an old man! Besides, how do you know that's what I'm doing? I might have groupies of my own, sounds like I have a reputation to maintain."

Ruby's mouth thins. "Never thought about that."

"Did you think I was up here thinking about you and our URST?"

The chilled out feeling switches, the barriers re-erecting on both sides and she shifts away from me.

"I don't know, Jem Jones, were you?" she says, coldly.

"Don't flatter yourself."

"Huh! Fine." She swings her legs to climb off the bed. "I'll go, leave you to your sulky old man life."

"Grow up, Ruby," I snap.

She pauses, her back to me, and I will Ruby not to walk out of the door. The first time alone with her for almost two weeks and this happens. So, it's clear sex isn't on the agenda, but I want to spend more time with the person who brought my world to life.

I temper my tone. "Sorry, you just pissed me off. I'll play for you like I promised. Stay."

She glares at me as I pick up the guitar and indicate she should sit back down.

"Serenaded by Jem Jones? Aren't I a lucky girl?" Her voice is edged by sarcasm.

"Yeah, you are. I don't normally play for a crowd less than ten thousand."

"Fine, but I'm sitting over here." Ruby heads back to the sofa, the dark sky in the wide windows behind her.

"Sit where you like."

"I will."

"I know." With a small laugh, I shake my head and scour my mind for the right song. There's only one I've been dying to play her since she first told me her name, the one that goes through my head when she's around, "Ruby Tuesday." I smile to myself and position the guitar.

I hardly get past the intro when she stands abruptly. "Jem. Stop. Don't play that."

"Why? It's your name." The song is her. To me. To the world. I continue.

Ruby heaves in a breath. "Don't. You can't." As her voice cracks, I stop. Tears fill her eyes and she shakes her head at me, causing one to spill.

"Shit. Okay, I thought you'd like it. You know, your name. What's the big deal?"

"Tuesday. You said you don't want to know who Tuesday is, and then you try and pull her out of me!"

I'm witnessing another of Ruby's flips from calm to panic, her switch so easily triggered by the smallest, unknown thing. I've come across complicated chicks before but this one wins the 'what the fuck?' stakes hands down.

"No, I'm not trying to find Tuesday; I have no interest in her. I just played a song I love that makes me think of the real you."

Her eyes widen, pupils dark. "Think of me? Don't think of me, Jem!"

"Why not?"

"Don't, just don't..." Ruby heads for the door. What the hell is going on? She talks about us and what we're hiding, then instead of sorting things out pushes me away. We need to have this conversation; she's right. Put this to rest. Move on. I jump off the bed.

"Don't leave, I'm sorry," I say.

"I have to go."

"Forget the song, let's deal with this other shit, then we can draw a line and move on."

Ruby's teary eyes meet mine. What did I do?

"How do we fix this? What happens on the TV with this URST crap?" I ask.

"Nothing for about three seasons. Move." She attempts to open the door and I place my palm on the smooth wood to prevent her. "Please."

"Three seasons? We can't go that long. What happens after three seasons?"

"I want to leave, Jem." Ruby's hand trembles and she pulls at the handle.

"What happens?" I repeat.

She turns a furious face to me. "They kiss. They fuck. Then the world jumps in and pulls them apart. Either that or they marry, have beautiful children, and live in a house in the country. Either way, things are dealt with. Move."

I touch her hair, pushing a tangle from her face and she slumps against the door as my fingers linger on her cheek.

"Kiss?"

"Jem, please don't."

This is torture, not whatever the hell stupid name she calls it. I hold Ruby's face in both hands, rubbing my thumb along her cheek where the tear fell, inhaling the warmth emanating from her. She closes her eyes as I move my mouth to taste her lips.

"Don't do this. Don't take us there." She twists her head away the moment my lips skim hers. "Stop, Jem!"

Her words, the shortness of breath... What a dick move, cornering a girl who's recently escaped an abusive ex. I step back. Ruby's wary but thankfully, there's no fear in her eyes. Worse, it's disgust.

"Back off. I'm not going to fuck you," she says.

"I don't want to fuck you."

"You just tried to kiss me." Her eyes harden.

"Last I knew they were two separate acts."

"In my experience, one always leads to the other." She takes a ragged breath. "I come here because I think you're my friend and then..." She waves a hand. "All this!"

"This?"

"You. Being nice then trying to kiss me, playing songs to serenade me into your fucking bed! Well, you chose the wrong song! And the wrong girl!" Ruby drags her palm across a cheek, wiping a new tear.

"That's not what I'm doing. You were the one talking about sexual tension."

"Because I hoped we'd deal with it and move on. It wasn't a fucking invitation."

Whoa, this girl is on a short, and very confusing, fuse. "Fine. I get that."

"So I can leave now? You won't stop me?"

"I wouldn't ever stop you doing what you wanted, Ruby."

"Good. Then leave me the hell alone!" She drags the door open.

As it slams behind her, I'm dazed at how quickly her mood shifted. And annoyed with myself for screwing this up. Sometimes,

I need to learn to listen to the part of me that screams 'stop what you're doing or everything will go to shit'.

Ruby

I slam through the open door of my hotel room straight into a suffocating mix of people, alcohol, and a sickly smell of weed. The music blares from one corner, a dozen or so people crammed together in the room. Jax is on the bed, shirtless, with a petite blonde girl wrapped around his naked chest.

"Ruby!" He waves a half-empty bottle of bourbon at me. Jesus, he's buying into the cliché.

What do I do? The headspace Jem just dragged me into isn't one that can include other people. As Jax disengages from the girl and heads in my direction, I'm aware of others staring at me. *Crap. Tears.* I scrub my face and head for the brightly lit bathroom. Jax appears.

"What's going on?"

"You've got drugs in here! If Jem knew, he'd lose his shit. Do you want him to drop us?"

"He won't know. Anyway, it's only a bit of weed."

Something Jax has evidently partaken of, judging by his pupils. "Is it?"

Jax shrugs. "As far as I know. Couldn't vouch for what everyone else has taken."

"Shit!" I turn on the tap and splash my face with cold water.

"Where'd you go? What happened?" he asks.

"I'm fine."

"No, you're not. Who upset you?" I dry my face on a white towel. "Ruby?"

"I said I'm fucking fine!" I yell and push past him.

"Come here." Jax takes my elbow and guides me around the

bodies on the floor, and into the empty hallway. "Where did you go?"

Leaning against the wall, I stare at the worn carpet. "I went to see Jem. I didn't want to come back here for another party, so thought things would be more peaceful with him."

Jax straightens. "What did he do to you? I've seen him watching you. Did he come on to you?" He sweeps a gaze over my figure. "Did he do something you didn't want?"

"Nothing! He didn't do anything!" The tears return, threatening to spill.

"You don't cry for no reason." Jax continues. "You never cry."

"Well, clearly I do." I move away as he tries to touch me again. "Jem wouldn't do that; he doesn't want to screw things up with the band."

Jax rests against the wall next to me and says quietly, "Yeah, I get that. Relationships inside the band would screw things up whether it's the manager and the singer or the lead guitarist and singer."

"Exactly, and he..." I stop. "Lead guitarist and singer?"

Jax screws his face up and rubs his temples. "Shit, forget it. I'm drunk and a bit stoned."

I cross my arms tightly. "Don't you dare! Don't you fucking dare throw this crap at me! There's nothing between us."

"Ignore me. It's just I care a lot about you. I've seen the shit you've been through; and even though you pushed me away and refused to let me help, I still kinda feel protective."

"Protective?"

"And yeah, I probably like you a bit too much, but I ignore it. Thing is, I can't if I see you with someone else."

Ohmygod. Talk about things going from bad to fucking worse. "Shit, Jax!" I shove him in the chest. "Don't do this! Stick to screwing your groupies; there's plenty willing."

He catches my arm. "Yeah, I get that you're not interested, but you're special. Too special to be screwed around by Jem Jones."

My chest constricts as the sob attempts to find its way out. "I am not special!"

"And that's the other reason, Ruby. You're a mess. It's not your fault. I know. But you can't get self-esteem boosts from guys like him."

"You don't understand at all!" I half-yell. "You and your perfect middle-class upbringing. Your loving family who pay for you to live in London and follow your dreams. There isn't one thing you struggle with. So don't judge me! You don't know me!"

"I've known you over a year and I've stood back when I shouldn't. I'm not doing it again. Don't get messed up by someone else who's fucked in the head. Underneath, Jem's no different to the other asshole you got involved with."

"Fuck you!" I yell, the sound echoing along the corridor.

"He's probably right, Ruby." I turn to the familiar voice. Jem stands a few feet away, lines creasing his forehead as he looks between us. "I shouldn't have tried to go there with you."

"I knew it! What did he do?" Jax straightens; face hardening as he watches Jem.

"Nothing!" I snap at Jax.

"Everything's too hard. I can't get involved with anybody else's drama." Jem crosses the hallway and hands me the keycard to his room. Our hands touch and I jerk my fingers away. I could've kissed him. I wanted to, was so close to giving in, and giving myself. "I'm driving back to London tonight. Use my room, Ruby. When you get back tomorrow, we need to talk about a few things." He looks to Jax. "All of you. I'm not stupid. I can smell the drugs in that room."

Jax stares at his bare feet like a scolded child. "Sorry," he mumbles.

"Yeah, decide on your priorities because I'm not managing a bunch of stoners. Your music should come first. See you tomorrow."

Jem pulls his phone out and scrolls through the screen as he walks away. I stare after his retreating figure, stunned by the turn of the evening.

"What a fucking hypocrite," says Jax. "He's the biggest stoner of them all!"

I itch to slap Jax, at his immature understanding of Jem's situation as a recovering addict. "Maybe take his life as a warning."

I head away from him. Nothing would persuade me to go back into the hotel room I share with them. "And have some respect!" I call, not looking back.

Jem's room is empty apart from the guitar I played before. He left it for me. This lances pain into my heart because it means Jem heard me play at night when I was staying with him and I couldn't sleep, and is aware tonight will be difficult. He's wrong. I'm exhausted; the events of the evening dragged the remaining energy from me. I don't touch the guitar; instead, I crawl into the soft bed and wait for sleep.

He was right. I'm wrong. Sleep doesn't come easily. I'm in the bed Jem once slept in and I breathe in the scent of him. Jem came so close to kissing me; if I hadn't turned my head, I'd have given in to the hidden desire for Jem I deny every day. I can't let him in; he'll take advantage of my vulnerability, use me, and break apart the pieces I'm gradually slotting back together.

18

The trip from Oxford to London the next morning is short but the journey drags. The toll of the last couple of weeks on the band shows. When we left to go on tour, the atmosphere was jovial and full of apprehension; now it's replaced by exhaustion on all sides, which emerges as irritability. An exhausted, irritable Ruby makes the usual Ruby appear laid-back in comparison.

One thing's for sure, I need to leave Jem's and move on with my life. The two weeks I spent living with him were the safest I've felt in years, but incidents like last night show how wrong it is for us to spend time together. If we're on the edge of an invisible line separating us physically, running away from the situation is the best option. What a glorious fuck-up screwing Jem Jones would be.

I ask Jax to help out and he agrees; I'm uncomfortable with Jax sounding relieved considering his drunk words about hidden feelings. Will and Nate give the okay for me to stay with them for a while, that period of time undefined but the impression I get is they want it short. We've already lived on top of each other for a few weeks. There's muttering about where I'm going to store my stuff in their small house, considering my room will be the sofa in the lounge, although it's not as if I have many possessions. Dan owned most of my things, the way he owned me.

Jem isn't home when I arrive at his house the next day so with relief I bundle what I left behind when I went on tour into bags. The quicker I do this, the better.

I'm scouting around Jem's lounge room for anything I might have left lying around when I hear the front door close. My insides turn in on themselves as Jem's heavy footsteps ascend the stairs and I attempt to judge his mood from the pace.

Jem pauses when he sees me, frowning at my rucksack. My heart turns rapid fire, memories of how close we got last night flaring into my cheeks as I'm caught in the attraction I have to this hot as hell guy from my fantasies.

"You're leaving then." He indicates my bag.

"Yeah. Thought it was best."

"Yeah, probably a good thing." He fiddles with his keys, avoiding my eyes. So much for the 'things to talk about'.

"I can't fit everything in my car though, is it okay if I come back later?"

"Leave things here as long as you like." He lifts his eyes to meet mine. "Going to stay with Jax?"

"That's a loaded comment if ever I heard one."

Jem scowls. "I'm not arguing with you, Ruby. I'm too old for little girl games."

Before I get a chance to retort he walks past into the kitchen.

I debate following him and giving him a mouthful for patronising me; to point out he's behaving like a big kid too. We're not exactly being mature about this, are we? Placing his house keys on the coffee table nearby, I leave the house.

Our conversation outside the hotel room isn't mentioned by Jax; hopefully, he was too high at the time to remember his words, but I'm on edge around him now. I replay any physical contact we've had; looking for signs, Jax saw our relationship as more than musical. How Jax ever thought I could be added to his list of conquests, I have no idea.

I won't get undressed in front of him again.

Life returns to normal after the tour, or as normal as my life ever gets. We have a break from official rehearsals but often evenings at home turn into a few drinks and a fair bit of music. The four of us discuss what's coming next, planning our future.

I don't see or speak to Jem. Tour over; he backs off for a while. Jem's away, we're not sure where. The States I think. We have our studio time booked for when he returns. Whatever stress Jem entering my life has given me, the fact Ruby Riot are on the path to becoming a success makes everything worthwhile.

But Jem consumes my thoughts. As a housemate, he was weird, and I kick myself that the easiness we had together was ruined by the step into something more, the night at the hotel. I question my sanity – at pining for an ex-drug addict, the unstable Jem Jones from Blue Phoenix. Yeah, he's just what I don't need. The 'no relationships' rule I have when it comes to the band should more than obviously apply to our pseudo-manager. Besides, I need to spend time outside of a relationship before I dive into another, and stop attaching myself to men who claim to want to help me.

Yet I continue to miss him. Jem understood and didn't judge, and he looked at me in a way that saw beyond Ruby. And for the first time, I didn't care. Someone offered support and wanted nothing in return, an unusual situation in my life. I hope in a small way I returned that.

Dan.

Since the text that freaked me out before the tour, he's been silent. On tour, the nightmare was distant but back in my normal life I'm on edge again. Maybe Dan's with one of the girls he said he was fucking. The thought turns my stomach, not because he was having sex with other girls; but the possibility he might not have used condoms. I get tested and thankfully, I'm clean. That would be one last kick in the guts if he'd given me an STD.

After a week of sleeping on the sofa at the boys' house, I up my attempts at finding a new place to live. Sharing with three guys is okay but none of them has any clue about hygiene, let alone tidiness, and I'm used to living with clean freak Dan. Living and breathing Ruby Riot is okay, living and breathing Jax, Will, and Nate, not so much. A room comes up in one of Will's friends' house. My tin of savings covers a deposit and I gladly move out.

A week after I take the room, life settles. I share with two uni students, Alison and Kate. They're nice enough, but we have nothing in common. I don't do small talk so I'm not sure living here will work out long term. I mostly keep to myself and fit into their house routine so at least the atmosphere is calm. The one problem is Kate is a serious student who studies more than she parties. She has a 'curfew' of no noise after eleven p.m. and she isn't a fan of my guitar playing. So inevitably, I end up spending time with the boys anyway.

Ruby Riot's studio time is booked for next week and I've swapped as many shifts at the café as I can to early mornings and late evenings, freeing up my afternoons. Ben's not happy with my unreliability, two weeks away touring, and now this less than a month later and I'm concerned I'll lose my job. I have a little left over from my Escape Fund but not much. I don't care if I lose my job. I'll find something else. This is my big chance – our big chance – if Jem Jones has faith in us, I should too.

This Ruby is worth something, now all I have to do is believe she can be who she wants.

The evenings darken as summer heads to autumn although the late summer heat isn't going anywhere. I head home from my shift at the café. I've arranged to catch the guys at the pub later, so Kate needn't worry about the noise tonight. The narrow house is squashed together with other terraced homes, the majority filled with students. Ours is easily spotted because for some weird reason Kate likes to tend the square metre patch of grass below the window and there're pansies growing there. I'm willing to bet our house is the tidiest on the street inside and out.

Inside, Alison lounges on the sofa eating ice cream, blonde hair pulled into a ponytail, and watching some reality TV crap.

Alison looks up when I walk in. "You've got a visitor." She indicates the kitchen with her spoon. "Hot guy - how many do you have tucked away?"

I drop my messenger bag on the floor. "You mean Jax?" I doubt Will or Nate would match her tastes, but Jax appears to be everyone's taste, and he loves it.

"No, Dan. You never mentioned you had a boyfriend."

A sharp spike of panic launches into my body. "What?"

"Dan. He's in the kitchen with Kate." Alison frowns at me. "What's wrong?"

The room shrinks as I'm sucked into the fear I've not missed in the last few weeks. "Dan."

"Yes. He said you'd asked him to come over."

The dizziness grips, the weak girl fighting through. "Make him leave," I say hoarsely. "Tell me when he's gone."

"Oh, God, I'm sorry. Is he an ex? I didn't know. He seemed so nice and friendly."

I fight the urge to charge out of the house. "Make him go. Please."

"Ruby, that's not very nice," says a familiar voice. I snap my head up and Dan stands in the doorway, holding a mug of coffee. The friendly, smiling man is a world away from the bastard who threatened to rape me last month. Physically, he's imposing and he frightens me, but Dan also knows how to charm and use his looks into sweet-talking girls into doing what he wants. Evidently, this worked with Alison and Kate.

I swallow against the memory of the last time I saw Dan. His hands on me, hurting, violating. The words, threatening what he'd do when he found me again, echo in my ringing ears. I can't talk over the lump in my throat.

"You never told me you were back," he continues. "I've been wanting to chat to you about our misunderstanding."

"Misunderstanding?" I choke back the words. He can't see my fear; he feeds off that. "I don't want to see you, Dan."

"Just a chat?" he offers.

"No."

Dan is dressed for a night-out in a crisp black shirt and jeans covering his long legs. His blue eyes are one of the things that captivated me years ago; the friendliness in them is a charade though. Good-looking guy with a rotten core.

Kate appears behind Dan, cradling her mug. "Everything okay?"

"No, it's not. Why did you let him in?" I keep my gaze trained on Dan, refusing to break eye contact. I'm stronger than the girl he attacked. I'm not her.

"I couldn't leave him on the doorstep!" protests Kate. Dan gives her a grateful smile and she returns it.

"Yes. You could."

"Maybe we should leave you to talk?" suggests Alison.

"No!" I clear my throat. "Dan's leaving."

No. Three times, I've said 'no'. Dan's mouth twists further into anger each time. *No*. The word I should've learned years ago.

"Ruby," he says, tone cajoling.

"Get the fuck out!" I shout, pushing away the weak Tuesday threatening to invade. "I don't want to see you!"

If I climb the stairs to my room, will he follow? My housemates look at each other awkwardly.

"Maybe you should leave, Dan," says Kate. "Sorry, Ruby, I never realised you didn't want to see him. I did think it was a bit strange; I thought Jax was your other half."

I widen my eyes. What the hell did she say that for? I glance between her and Dan whose expression scares me.

"Me and Ruby had a bad fight because I thought that about her and Jax too. You haven't replaced me, have you, angel?" he asks.

At the word 'angel', I want to vomit. I cross my arms and step to one side as he moves closer, pissed off with myself that his bulk and presence intimidate me. If I keep replying, we stay engaged, and then the further he worms his way into my new headspace.

"Okay, I see this is a bad time. I'll catch up with you later. I could drop by the café after work and take you for a drink? Or I've seen you at The Lions Head with the guys; maybe I could come and see you there?"

His hardened look accompanies the veiled threat: 'I can find you'.

"Don't bother! I don't want anything to do with you!"

"I'll come and see you when you're on your own, then we can talk properly." Dan smiles in a way that chills my soul and I'm frozen in the moment as he says his polite goodbyes to my housemates and strolls out of the house.

Just like that.

Aware the fear coursing through my body will lead to outbursts at the two girls that could get me kicked out of the house, I run upstairs before any words escape.

I close my bedroom door and lean against it. What if Dan changes his mind and comes back to the house? Comes for me? This man has been part of my life for five years in one way or another; how did I think I'd get rid of him so easily?

19

A week of looking over my shoulder, but Dan hasn't reappeared. Every day I expect to see him at work or at the house but he never comes. Instead, Dan sends texts, taunting me with clever hints that he's watching me, telling me where he's seen me each day. Dan's threats and my fear are enough to maintain some kind of control. Has he decided that's enough for now?

Shuffling shifts around to fit in with recording this week means I finish later and leave work at dusk. Jax knows the situation and insists he'll meet me after work and take me home. I want to tell him not to but a small doubt niggles. No, if Dan has backed off again, I'm sure I'll be okay. Psychological fear was Dan's favourite weapon and he knows how effective it is on me.

I don't want to think about Dan. He's the past and today I'm one step closer to my future. Another piece of my dreams just became reality: Ruby Riot is in a recording studio. My impression of recording studios comes from movies and this one is nothing like I imagined. It's bigger and the technology is beyond my understanding. Nothing like the little place we hired to get a couple of tracks to upload to Bandcamp, the online place Ruby Riot has music for download.

The large mixing desk dominates the room and the sound engineer runs through something on a laptop screen. Will and Nate have settled themselves onto a nearby sofa taking selfies and uploading to Instagram and Facebook. Our pages have a big following since the tour and their constant updates recently make us masters of spam.

"Don't forget to get Jax in a shot," I say, indicating the lusted after guitarist tuning his guitar. His blonde hair has grown, falling into his face. I'm relieved that his confessions haven't changed our relationship; but if I were at all interested in this guy, I'd be fighting off other girls who want a piece of him too. Judging by his popularity on tour, they'll be forming an orderly queue for Jax next.

I don't notice Jem appear as I absentmindedly compare Jax to other guys, but when I do, the reason I'm not interested in Jax is abundantly clear. The moment we look at each other, my heart skips into my mouth and I realise exactly how much I've missed him. Jem returns my look, eyes expressing the reality of what we are. This isn't just about clumsy attempts to deny physical attraction; our similarities slowly bind us.

Why does he have to be Jem Jones?

He tears his gaze from mine and greets everyone in his typically gruff fashion, ensuring no special welcome for me. My stupid heart retreats back to my chest.

We spend half the morning working through the ins and outs of the studio, what we're planning, and a couple of practice tracks. Jem's different from on tour last month, looser than he was when I stayed with him. I haven't seen him for almost three weeks. As Jem sends a text, I surreptitiously study him. He's bulked up a little too and lost the edge of skinniness that hovered around his wiry frame. Aware of my scrutiny, Jem looks up, eyes shining. Has somebody rather than something breathed life back into him?

We break for lunch and this includes beer for the boys. I despair at their continued lack of thought about Jem's situation and mutter something to them before walking away. Jem sits next to me, sinking into the brown sofa, and opens a bottle of water.

"It's okay, Ruby. I don't mind. Just because I'm dry, doesn't mean I expect everyone else to be."

"I think it's fucking rude. Dickheads."

Jem snorts. "You and your mouth." I don't miss his lingering look at the mouth he's talking about. "How's things?"

"Yeah." I can't say good; Dan's made sure of that. "How's things with you?"

"Better. But you're not." He drinks. "You've lost weight again."

"Checking me out already?"

He sighs. "No, Ruby. Don't start getting bitchy with me. What's going on? Is it Dan?"

I slide a look to my bitten fingernails. "I'm fine."

"Your singing's shit when you're stressed," he remarks. "No point paying for studio time if you're not up to par."

I jerk my head back up and fight against launching into an unhelpful string of expletives. Of course, Jem's concern isn't for my welfare. I told him not to care about me, so what do I expect?

"I'm tired. Tomorrow will be better."

"Where are you living?"

"I moved in with a couple of girls. Students."

He tips his head to the guys. "Not them?"

"Not Jax."

I can't fathom the look Jem gives me. We're not close enough to touch accidentally, but the hyper-awareness of the proximity is intensified by the memory of the night his mouth briefly touched mine.

"As long as it's not Dan," he says quietly and stands.

When Jem walks away, I'm pissed off by the limit of his attention. Almost trysts in hotel rooms on tour mean nothing to Jem Jones; I'm long forgotten and back to being part of his project.

Jem

I'm bloody furious. Wall-smacking furious. I rub my sore palm from where I've hit the exposed bricks in the small hallway between studio rooms. I'm lying to myself. Lying that my anger is the effect the Dan situation has on Ruby's performance and not because the effect on her worries me.

Ruby's haunted again. The girl hidden behind the mask slipped out when I talked to her at lunch. I cornered Jax and asked him to fill in the gaps. He told me about Dan's return, his borderline stalking, and Ruby's refusal to do anything. As far as Jax knows, she's spoken to Dan twice and now avoids him. Jax has been picking Ruby up after work; that's how fucking frightened she is.

Life in the States was a world away from Ruby Riot. I told myself the distance would help scrub Ruby from my mind; that spending so much time around her was the problem. Wrong. The chick haunts my thoughts and dreams wherever I am; and since I returned a couple of days ago, the urge to contact her has increased. Even though I surrounded myself by people and hooked up with an old friend, there was an emptiness. Those people are from the old Jem's life and are already alien. This is what Ruby has done; she's removing the last parts of him and pulling me into a fresher reality.

Liam was around in LA, weirdly, he's still with Cerys, the chick from school, years back. She's a bit of a transformation in taste after Honey, but who am I to judge? At least Bryn hasn't joined Dylan and Liam and entered the realm of the lovelorn yet, so there's hope for the band.

Lovelorn. Since when did the guys change from lust to love when it comes to chicks? How do they know when that shit happens? When I was still suspicious of Sky, I asked Dylan to explain exactly what he meant about 'loving her' but his words make no sense. To me, 'love' sounds like needing someone too much and that never ends well. People take from you and hurt you; and if you try to love them, they fuck off.

Or die.

One thing Dylan said sticks uncomfortably, his words about looking into Sky's eyes and seeing himself - his heart and soul. I'm unsure I'd go that far, but I do see something in Ruby's eyes. It can't be my heart because I don't reckon I have one when it comes to emotional shit. My heart's a muscle that pumps blood around the body, including to the part of me I normally think with when it comes to girls. That's all. My soul? What the hell does soul mates even mean? That you both need each other so much you're scared to leave? Makes my head spin.

A chick walks by with a coy smile thrown my way. Long legs, glossy brown hair, and a killer ass moulded into her skinny jeans, she heads to Jax. I watch in amusement as Jax ramps up his semi-star status, loudly showing her around the studio. As usual, Will and Nate have disappeared to continue their drinking at the pub round the corner, and nearby Ruby packs up her guitar. Her reaction to Jax and the girl is non-committal, but something about them bothers her because she's frowning at the discussion Jax and the girl are having. I heard what Jax said to Ruby outside the room that night, have they acted on it? Jax doesn't introduce the girl to us; maybe he doesn't know her name. Ruby switches to ignoring them, until Jax announces he's leaving, arm around the shoulders of his brown-haired goddess.

"I thought you were giving me a lift home?" asks Ruby, straightening.

"Shit. Forgot. We're joining Will and Nate. I doubt I'll be driving. You can come too?" suggests Jax.

"Thanks a fucking bunch," she snaps. "I have a six a.m. shift, then the afternoon here. I'm not going anywhere apart from home."

"Sorry," says Jax but he isn't; he's too focused on groping the chick's ass and kissing her eager mouth.

"I was waiting for you; now it's getting dark! I'll get the bloody bus," mutters Ruby and grabs her bag.

"I'll take you," I say, happy to find an opportunity to talk to her about this crap with Dan.

Ruby's tense shoulders relax. "You sure?"

"Yeah. It's cool. I'm not busy tonight. How far is it?"

"Maybe twenty minutes from here. At this time, anyway."

Ruby's house is closer to half an hour away. The journey is polite conversation, Ruby keeping the topic on what I've been doing in the States and carefully steering away any questions about her. In return, I don't answer much of what she asks. I pull my BMW up outside her small house. She's chewing her nails and surveying the street. The happier Ruby has retreated since we last spent time alone together.

"Going to invite me in for a coffee?" I ask, switching off the engine.

"You do know that's a euphemism for fucking?"

Jesus, this girl's barriers are high again.

"Yeah, but I actually mean coffee. Decaf."

Ruby allows me a smile. "You really have kicked every addiction, haven't you?"

"Most. So? Do I get my decaf?"

She opens the car door and pauses. "Sure."

Inside Ruby's house, a girl sits in the lounge, ordinary looking chick with short brown hair clipped back at the side, curled up reading a book. She looks up at me and recognition flickers.

"Oh. I didn't expect you to bring him home," she says to Ruby.

"This is Kate, my housemate."

"Hey." I nod and she continues to gawk at me as we head to the kitchen.

"Do you ever get used to people's reactions to you?" Ruby asks, flicking on the kettle that rests on the counter in the narrow room.

"That wasn't a reaction. A reaction is her unable to resist my charms and wanting my attention. She didn't give a fuck."

"That's the Jem Jones I expect," she says quietly and pulls mugs out of the cupboard. "Besides, she's more of a boy band girl."

"Ugh." I pull out a dining chair and sit at the scratched wooden table.

Ruby pulls her phone out of her bag and places it on the

counter before throwing her bag into the corner. "Losing your touch, Jem."

I pull a face and she laughs. I fucking love it when Ruby laughs. She rakes her hair upwards and ties it into a high ponytail. "I wish this weather would break; it's too bloody hot."

I don't listen. I stare at Ruby's mouth, at the curve of her neck, at where her fingers trail through her hair, and I want her. There's no room in my head for anything but Ruby, the daily obsession isn't helped by putting myself in the situation of time alone with her again.

Does she recognise my not-so-hidden thoughts when she returns my gaze? Probably because she looks away. "I want to get changed. I'll be back in a sec." Ruby heads out of the kitchen.

I tap my fingers on the table. Seems Kate isn't the only girl in the house immune to my charms. Since the night in the hotel room and after the time apart, we're back at square one because, despite what I see when I look at her, Ruby has me at arm's length.

Ruby's phone buzzes with a message and I glance at the door before crossing to pick it up. Yeah, I shouldn't but I'm worried about her.

Dan.

<We need to talk>

What the fuck is she doing communicating with the dickhead?

I scroll back through the messages. Dan texts several times a day but she never replies. Veiled threats about waiting for her after work, or coming over to the house. Another text appears as I hold the phone.

<Where were you today? You weren't at work.>

"What the hell are you doing?" hisses Ruby. She reappears next to me and snatches the phone.

"I could ask you the same question. What the fuck is this?"

"None of your fucking business!" She lowers her voice. "I'm dealing with it."

"It is my business. Remember, Ruby Riot's my business."

"Don't pull that bullshit!" She's trembling, cheeks pink.

"You okay?" calls Kate from the other room.

"Yeah. Differences of opinion. It's cool. Jem's leaving once I've put him straight," calls back Ruby and closes the kitchen door. She's changed into a short blue cotton dress covered in a cherry print. With its thin straps and barely skimming her knees, this dress reveals an uncomfortable amount of her body. She might be cooler, but the amount of Ruby's skin on show heats my blood.

"No, I'm not leaving. Not until you tell me why you're communicating with him."

"I'm not! I don't reply, do I? Or did you not get far enough with your spying to see that?"

I inhale and hold the breath, calming myself. "Change your number. He's still in your life."

"I said I'm dealing with it."

"If you let him back in..."

"I won't! Back off!" she interrupts.

"No, I won't!"

"Are you threatening me? Because that makes you as bad as him!"

I drag my fingers into my hair. I want to take Ruby by the shoulders and shake away her stupidity. "No. I care about you."

Shit.

Ruby crosses her arms tightly. "Don't go there again."

Screw it. I might as well admit it now it's slipped out. "It's true. I care about you a lot."

"Well, don't!"

We face off, battle lines drawn again. We're closer than I realised; I'm in Ruby's personal space and she hasn't backed off. The look in her eyes isn't fear or anger, but something I recognise as easily. Confused desire. Ruby parts her lips as she looks at mine.

"Fuck, Ruby. I can't do this anymore. I don't do this."

"What?"

I close the remaining space between us, but she doesn't move. "Games. Dancing around. Holding myself back because I'm scared of hurting you. I'm not interested in your URST crap, I just want to fucking kiss you."

Ruby's breath hitches slightly and she glances at my mouth. Before she can respond, I take her face in both hands and crash my mouth onto hers. I need to feel her lips, see how she reacts, and if she pushes me away, fine. At least I'll have snatched one kiss from the girl who has me wrapped around her finger without realising it. Ruby pulls my hands from her face and her mouth away but doesn't move, keeping her fingers wrapped around mine. Her breath comes in short, hot bursts against my cheek and at each point our bodies touch, my senses shut down against anything but her.

"I missed you," I whisper, lips moving against her cheek.

"Don't, Jem," she says hoarsely. "Don't play with me."

"I'm not." I move my head back and take her face again; she continues to grip my hands. Wide eyes look back, but her shared want is unmistakable. I skim my lips against hers and wait for the reaction, fighting against the need bubbling to the surface, the one pushing out weeks of self-control. "Ruby."

"Fuck it." I want to laugh at her words as she winds her fingers into my hair and presses her lips against mine. I shift, encircling her waist, holding her to me. Parting her lips with my tongue, I claim her mouth, the mouth I've tortured myself dreaming about, and the dreams that keep away the nightmares. The depth of her kiss drags away the last worry that she doesn't want this. Ruby's fingers trail to the nape of my neck, holding my head against hers.

The lust floods to my hardening dick and she stumbles backward as I push her against the door. Ruby drags her mouth away with a gasp so I lay kisses along her neck. I'm desperate to touch her but I'm limiting myself, listening to the tiny piece of rationality surviving the hunger I have for this woman. If I slide a hand up Ruby's naked leg, I'm pretty damn sure I'd get a slap and this would be over.

"Jem. Stop," she breathes, although her body is telling me a different story, arching toward me as I nip at her soft skin. I want her so fucking much, kissing her isn't enough.

Ruby's puts her arms between our chests and shoves me. "Stop!"

I drop my arms and step back. Her pink face reflects my confusion.

The line crossed, reality hangs between us. With that kiss, she jolted the emotions I've pushed and pushed until they were buried in the corner of my mind but without drugs, denying to myself how I feel isn't as easy. Ruby's kiss ripped the hidden corner open and my deepest thoughts and fears flood out, along with the weeks of desire for her pouring into my body. Not physical desire, that's clear and always was; but an ache to have Ruby in my life. Take care of her. Be who she wants me to be. Who she needs me to be.

Like Liv.

Shit.

I take another step back, pulling away from the fusion happening. "Shit. Sorry. I have to go. Sorry, I can't do this."

"What the hell?" she whispers.

I rub my palms across my face. Yeah, what the hell am I doing? "I shouldn't have. Shit, Ruby. I'm sorry."

Ruby's flushed face now pales and I pray there's no tears. "You bastard. I knew you were screwing around with me!"

"It was only a kiss."

Ruby parts her mouth to say something; but instead she turns away, tearing at my heart. Yeah, my heart, the muscle that pumps blood suddenly hurts. No, it wasn't just a kiss. It was a unity. The raw connection I saw and denied the first time we met led to this moment and melded our lives.

And I'm not going there.

I hover for a moment; but Ruby doesn't turn back to me, instead stands with her arms wrapped around herself. I won't be able to give Ruby what she wants because I'm not prepared to give myself to anyone. Ruby deserves someone to love and cherish her, not a fucked-up ex-addict who can't look at her without seeing the girl who died because of him.

When the silence remains, I walk away. What point are words?

20

Ruby

Do I hurt? No. Am I angry? Fuck, yeah.

I'm exhausted when I arrive for my shift the next morning, I spent the night awake replaying Jem's kiss and trying to figure out what the hell he meant by it. Jem said no games and he's playing the biggest one of all. I touch my mouth, firing the memory back through. Nobody's ever kissed me with the passion Jem did, and I've never kissed anybody back with a desire that matches theirs. I avoided kissing Dan unless I had no choice; I could stay disconnected from him that way.

Jem Jones kissed me like he meant it, as if he wanted me. Then seconds later, he kicked me to one side. Did he get what he wanted and then decide I'm not as attractive as he thought once he touched me? Or did he wake up to the fact the whole situation is complicated and wrong? The door to trusting Jem I'd opened is slammed shut, and now the key's hidden. So he's worried my situation with Dan might fuck up the band? Newsflash, Jem Jones, you did.

No, I don't hurt, it's worse than that. I ache more than any physical or emotional pain Dan ever caused, my heart rent into pieces. With Dan, I was numb. With Jem, I feel everything.

After my morning shift, I call Jax and tell him I'm too sick to get to the studio this afternoon and spend the time I would've been with the band hiding under the duvet in my room. Is Dan right? Am I not worth anything to people? Am I that broken? Dan's words circle my head, every cruel thing he's ever said. Nobody would be interested in me. I'm worthless. I don't deserve to be loved.

I didn't expect Jem to fall in love with me but it's clear I invested too much of my self-esteem into his approval, not just for the band but also for myself.

So how can I blame Jem? This is all my fault; it always is.

Evening arrives and I have to face the world again. I shower and dress for work, paint on my disguise. The shift is a blur, my usual poor customer service skills worse than ever. I spill drinks, slide food off plates, and end up reprimanded after a customer hears me call her something unpleasant under my breath.

Ten p.m. and I'm out. The August air is thick with moisture; the horrible breathable weather has hung around all this week. I hope it breaks soon because the oppressive humidity doesn't help my mood - or my ability to sleep. My phone beeps and I freeze in the cafe doorway in case it's Dan.

Jax checking up on me.

I send back a bright and breezy text informing him I'll be at the studio in the morning and he replies with a smiley face. I'm not sure I will, or if I can face Jem yet. My head's a mess.

Jax forgot to meet me again tonight. Steeling myself, I head between the buildings that run from the street the cafe's on to the place where I park my car. I imagine the boys are at The Lion's Head. Will Jem be with them for once?

Get out of my fucking head, Jem. I touch my mouth, pissed off I keep pulling out memories of his lips, his clean scent and the sensation of his rough cheek against mine; the way my body begged to meld with his. Be his. Why did I do it?

Someone slams into me from behind, knocking my breath and I stumble. Pain seers my scalp as my hair is yanked back and I'm pushed headfirst into a wall. Before I can put my arms out to stop, the rough brick scrapes my forehead.

Solid, hard muscle pins me to the wall, the overpowering smell of familiar deodorant. "You shouldn't ignore me."

"Dan," I gasp. Survival mode kicks in and Tuesday comes back. "Sorry. I'll talk now."

Grabbing my hair, he pulls and slams my head against the wall. The stars are back and prettier than ever. This time the night sky comes with them, the darkness clouding my vision.

"I'm over talking to you. I've given you everything. I fucking loved you and look at what you did!" His voice is low and his breath smells of strong liquor.

"You don't do this to people you love," I say hoarsely. "You don't hurt them."

"Yeah, well I don't love you anymore. I know you're fucking Jem Jones. Or Jax. Maybe both, you stupid whore. Do you know how much it hurts that you treated me like this? You deserve to feel the pain I fucking feel."

Hurt him?

I slide down the wall, cheek scraping along the bricks and crumple to the paved ground. Instinctively, I cover my head. He has a pattern. My ribs will take the next beating. Then my head. If I know what's coming I can tick them off the list in my mind until it's finished.

When Dan kicks me in the side, all I can think is I'm glad he's wearing trainers. The pain radiates along my ribs and I clench my teeth, refusing to cry out.

I won't fight back.

I'll wait.

My response to the kicking isn't enough; Dan stops, kneels on the floor, and pushes his hands around my neck. This isn't his usual order of attack. My head spins through pain and lack of oxygen; above me, Dan's face is a darkened mask and his hollow eyes are disengaged.

"Dan. You're leaving marks. People will know," I gasp, putting my hands over his.

"Like I fucking care." He lets go and hits my face, open palmed against my injured cheek and I wince, tears forcing their way into my eyes. "This is over. If we're over, then you're over." His voice echoes, distant in my sky.

I attempt to pull back from the stars. Dan's threat is real. The ferocity of his attack is uncontrolled. We're not hidden at his house. This is in public but he's launching a harder punishment than he ever has before, anybody could see and he doesn't care.

Dan grabs my t-shirt and drags me into a sitting position. Squatting down so his face is against mine, he speaks. I don't hear or respond and my teeth jar as he shakes me, the pain in my head intense. Another smack in the face and my lip stings as the skin splits.

He lets go and I slump back to the ground. "You hit my head too much," I mumble. "I won't be conscious. You want to do this when it hurts me."

Dan pauses, and my heart thumps in my ears as I struggle for energy to get away from him. My heavy head won't coordinate my body and all I want to do is lie here and wait for this to be over. Will I ever escape him? Or does this end now? When I was a little girl, monsters in the dark never scared me. When I grew up, I learned the worst are the ones who live in the bright part of my life. They trick. They lie. They hurt.

"Jesus fucking Christ!" A voice yells in the distant dark and the face of the monster who's eaten away at my life is gone, as Dan reels sideways. A third person is with us and the two figures land on the ground beside me.

I roll onto my side and attempt to focus through the dim of the world. A man kneels on Dan's chest and lifts his arm, thumping Dan so hard I hear the crack of bone. The fear trembles through my body; I vomit, the familiar metallic taste of blood on my lips. The second man remains on top of Dan, pinning him down with a knee on Dan's throat. He turns to me, but I already know who it is.

"Ruby, are you okay?"

Jem. Words won't come as I struggle to stay in the reality I was trying to push away.

"Ruby!" he repeats more urgently.

Dan shifts, struggling against Jem. "You piece of fucking shit!"

Jem snarls. "What the hell have you done to her?" Jem grabs Dan by the shirt and drags his face toward him. "I should fucking kill you."

The world is sideways, everything at the wrong angle and I'm unsure it'll ever be upright again. Throwing Dan back again, Jem rains blows with a ferocity to match that of Dan to me a few minutes ago. Dan has his face covered against Jem's fists and I want to yell stop, but I don't; a vengeful part wants Dan to feel some of the hurt he caused me. I watch as Dan weakens, not fighting back. Not once. He lies and takes the attack the way I did for so many months.

Closing my eyes, I smile at the stars and my brother who's by the second star to the right. My Peter Pan who'll never grow up now and never be in my life again.

Now I have Jem Jones, the man who doesn't want to take care of or protect me as my rescuer. And I bet he hates it.

em

Ruby's face is a mess.

I'm a mess.

Why am I involved?

Guilt took me to meet Ruby after work tonight, I wanted to persuade her to come back to the studio tomorrow. I feel like shit about what I did to her last night, and I've battled with the chaos of thoughts in my head. If she meant nothing, I wouldn't have stopped at a kiss because the physical satisfaction of sex with her would've been my goal. The problem is, in a screwed up way, the jolt of life to my emotions led me to hurt her because I didn't want to hurt her. I don't understand my own logic.

Ruby had left work by the time I arrived at the café and I've no idea what made me scout around in case she was nearby but I did. I'm fucking glad fate sent me there.

I've been involved in a fair few fights in my time and spent too many years solving arguments with my fists, but what I witnessed when I walked around the corner is beyond anything I've seen.

Time stopped when Ruby didn't reply, the fear for her safety intensifying my need to smash the fucker's face in.

How can anybody do that to a woman? Or anybody? He behaved like an animal so I treated him like one. When I realised I might've seriously injured him, I didn't give a shit; a raw anger had me gripped out of control. I wanted to kill him. Only now do I realise how lucky I am I stopped. For a couple of minutes I was sure I had killed him; he didn't move or make a sound when I held the trembling Ruby in my arms. The fury intensified as I sat on the ground with her, not knowing what the fuck to do next.

By the time I calmed myself enough to help Ruby away, Dan groaned and shifted but didn't sit and for a split second I thought: I'll try harder next time.

Next time.

No way.

This shit stops now.

Ruby sits at the table in my dining room staring at the bowl of water and facecloth I put in front of her. Medical supplies aren't a staple in my house - I don't even have any Band-Aids. Uselessly, I hover, head aching from the range of emotions dragged through my system in the past twenty-four hours.

Ruby doesn't speak. Hasn't spoken since she yelled at me for threatening to take her to hospital.

"I'm going to call a doctor," I tell her.

She turns her battered face to me and I can't tell if her eyes are red because she's been crying or from the mess the fucker made of them.

"Call Jax."

"You want Jax?"

Ruby puts her head in her hands then drops them, gingerly touching her face. Her loose red hair hangs forward, disguising her expression. "Yes."

Something strange clutches my chest, an old emotion joining the others. Rejection. But I helped her?

"What do you want me to say to him?" I cross my arms.

"He can come pick me up. You don't have to be involved."

"I am involved. I just beat the crap out of a guy for you."

"For me?" She laughs softly.

"Why's that funny?"

"Nothing. We're a bit fucked now, with this lip I doubt my singing will be up to par."

Her words echo mine from yesterday. "This isn't the right time to talk about the band. Probably not the right time for you to talk about anything."

"Yeah."

She's pale and the amount Dan beat her around the head worries me. "But I think you need to see a doctor."

"No!"

Or the police, but I'll save that suggestion until she's calmer. "What if you're concussed? Aren't you supposed to stay awake or something? Are you sleepy?"

Ruby drags her hair from her eyes. "Your concern is touching. I'm fine, I'm not concussed."

"How do you know that?"

Staring straight at me, Ruby says, "He gave me concussion before. I know the difference."

Rejection. Frustration. Heart-rending pain for this girl. I can't respond and return to the kitchen where I can hide how I feel. My knuckles are swollen and I grab ice from the fridge. I should get Ruby ice too. Should I? I throw the door shut and grip my hair. I don't know what the hell to do. Liv's pain and abuse was before I knew her; Ruby's is current and in my face, her blood smeared on my blue shirt.

"Did you call Jax yet?"

Lost in the memories of Liv, I'm unaware of Ruby joining me in the kitchen. The bright halogen light illuminates the darkening and torn skin across her forehead and the caking blood on her cheek.

"No." I touch her face, a small space my fingers can fit without brushing her injury. "I'm not going to."

She takes my hand and moves it from her face. Ruby's fingers are ice cold despite the warmth of the evening and I curl mine around them, refusing to let her go.

"Why?" she asks.

"Stay here. You're safe here."

"I can't."

"Why?" She doesn't answer but I know why: because of last night. Because I fucked this up. "Besides, Jax is probably drunk somewhere, or in bed with whatever her name was."

Ruby huffs. "Yeah."

But she wants Jax, not me.

"Stay here. Tomorrow we talk about what we need to, Ruby." I rub my fingertip across her cheek and she closes her eyes.

"I doubt I'll be doing much else."

Oh, yes you will. You'll be going to the police and sorting this. Then I can step back.

21

Ruby

I wake the next morning confused where I am, but my mind catches up as soon as the pain hits. My head aches, face sore, and when I sit up, I notice the blood staining the sleeves of my white work shirt. Memories of last night surge, and my stomach heaves. I put my shaking hands over my ears and close my eyes, trying to blank my mind of the looping images of Dan's face and fists invading. Focusing on controlling my breathing, I stand but the room lurches and I sit back down. There's painkillers in my bag, but will they work against the headache I have? I touch my forehead, and wince at the lump.

I survived.

Another thought intrudes: what would've happened if Jem hadn't arrived? I thrust it away; I can't go down that route. I'm here and my injuries aren't as bad as they could've been. In a screwed up way, I'm lucky.

Jem's right. This time I go to the police, take seriously the danger I'm in. I can never damage Dan the way he's pulled me apart, but I can get him arrested and make his life hell. Who knows what will happen, or if any justice will be done, but I'm going to try.

Then I'm going to gather up the remaining pieces of Ruby and put them together.

If I could, I'd run from all of this, go somewhere nobody knows who I am. Not to hide, but to live in freedom for a while. Half an hour in the room and my mind continues its attempt to drag up the horror of last night, and I don't want to visit that place. I head out into the quiet house and call Jax.

Jax arrives and although the shock on his face is bad, the fact he averts his eyes from the mess of mine is embarrassing. "What the fuck happened? You said Dan had attacked you, but *shit*...not how bad."

"Don't say anything, please." I wanted to put make-up on, but the police will need photos. For the first time, I have to show the world what Dan does to me.

"Is Jem around?"

"I don't know." I haven't seen him since last night. I'm not sure what to say or what exactly our position is now. No way can I think anything through currently. "You want a drink before we go to the police?"

Jax looks around the lounge room. Of course, he's never been in the house. I poke him. "I'd give you the guided tour, but I'm not sure I'm allowed."

"Not without the entrance fee." I turn to a smiling Jem who's in the doorway, rubbing his head with a towel. He's post-workout, damp t-shirt stretching across his abs and perspiration glistening on his taut biceps, all of which would be enough to fuel any girl's Jem Jones fantasies. Jem's smile disappears when he looks at my face, the action causing a twinge of pain around my mouth.

"Hey, man," says Jax with a cautious tone.

"Hey," he says then looks to me. "You're coming back here after the police station?"

"If that's okay," I reply.

"Sure."

"Okay."

"Right." Jem heads upstairs.

The amount said with so few words doesn't escape Jax. "What's going on?"

"Nothing."

"I wish you'd come back with me instead."

Last night I was adamant I'd go to Jax and the boys, since waking today, I'm too scared to go far. "I feel safer here."

"Yeah, but why? Jem's the reason you didn't come to the studio yesterday, isn't he?"

"That's dealt with." I head to the open door.

"Is it? Really? The more involved he gets the more likely things will go wrong."

"For me or the band?"

"Both."

Irritation prickles. "I'm really not up to talking about this shit now, Jax. Perhaps you should discuss your concerns with Jem."

Jax rubs his eyebrow, the way I recognise he does when Jax is about to ask something he's not sure he should. I can guess what. "Did you... you know. The other night after the studio when he took you home? Is that why you couldn't face him?"

"Did I fuck him? Just come straight out with it."

Jax wrinkles his nose. "Yeah."

"No, I didn't, and I have no intention of."

"So why avoid him?"

"He kissed me."

Jax laughs. "A kiss? And that was enough to screw around with your head?"

At this moment, I feel like screaming at Jax but his words resonate. Why did a kiss from Jem then rejection have such a big impact? I could explain to Jax that to me there's an intimacy in a kiss greater than sex, that kissing Jem was like opening myself up and letting him across the void between me and the world. How can a kiss be that? I don't know, but it was and that's why it fucked with my head.

"Shut the hell up, Jax," I growl, "I'm not in the mood."

Jax brow creases with concern. "I really don't think it's a good idea for you to stay here if that's how you feel."

"And I really don't want you interfering." I gesture at the door. "Let's go. Get this over with."

"Ah, Ruby..." As he approaches, Jax touches my hand and laces his fingers through mine. "I'm here if you need me. Please be sensible."

Physical contact with Jax isn't unusual and, despite his words outside the hotel room the night on tour, there's nothing between us. No spark of something unknown hovers or any intense desire to keep his skin on mine. He's Jax, a mate, and nothing else. If I mean any more to Jax, he's hiding it.

Jem

Jax taking Ruby to the station is good for two reasons. Firstly, Jem Jones at a police station would have the media and Steve down on me like a ton of bricks. The other reason: distance. If I'm the one to take Ruby, I can't keep the distance between us that I still fool myself exists.

The whole time Ruby and Jax are away from the house I attempt to channel my nervous energy into something constructive and end up on the treadmill. Music and exercise are the only things that drown out the onslaught of memories – from last night and the ones from earlier in my life.

The pair aren't back by lunchtime so I text Jax. No response.

Keep out of it.

I call the studio manager and attempt to shift around the booking. He's pissed off but I don't know why, he's getting paid. I hang up after a terse conversation and the phone rings again immediately.

"What the fuck, Jem?"

"Wow, Steve. Hello to you, too." There's me thinking I could avoid talking to my manager.

"What the hell did you do? Were you high?"

"Stop shouting and tell me what you mean?"

"The chick from the band. Y'know, the one the media likes to hold up as Jem's latest fuck buddy."

"Don't call her that."

"Not my words. I'm surprised you're not at the police station, too."

"She didn't want me to go."

"I bet she fucking didn't!"

"Whoa. Okay, Steve, tell me exactly what this call is about."

"You might ignore the media; but they don't ignore you, and when the girl you're connected to turns up at a police station with her face messed up where'd you think the finger's pointing?"

The phone digs into my hand as I grip it tightly. "You have to be kidding me." No response. "Tell me you're fucking kidding."

"Tell me you didn't. I was enjoying my break from dealing with the shit you guys get into."

The world retreats as my head scrambles to catch up. "I cannot believe you are accusing me of this," I say and launch into a barrage of words I normally only reserve for people like Dan. "I don't attack women!"

"You were accused of killing one less than a year ago."

"Too far, Steve, too fucking far!" I yell and hang up before things get really nasty.

Déjà vu. The cops will be on my doorstep. The media back. I sink onto the sofa and stare at the phone. The world just leapt backward several months. I can't cope if I'm dragged into shit again. I did something good and now it's all going wrong. Why can't the world give me a break?

Ruby

I step out of the police station with Jax, and straight into the blinding sunshine and camera flashes. Half a dozen people wait in the forecourt; a confusing crowd I barely register before I turn my back and meet Jax's surprised eyes. People shout questions about Jem and my aching head can't comprehend what's happening. I've spent half the morning giving statements. I've already had my picture taken more than I'd like in the police station, and I'm exhausted and confused.

"What's happening?" I ask Jax.

"I don't know. Back inside." He guides me through the sliding glass doors and into the station. I sit on an orange plastic chair in the waiting room. A police officer crosses to the door and the middle-aged man glances outside before looking back to me.

"You okay, love?" he asks.

I nod stupidly and he gives me a small smile before walking off and calling for somebody. So many kind and understanding smiles today for the beaten girl.

"I'm going to find out what the hell is going on," Jax says and heads to the door.

I want to protest he should stay out of this, but he's already deeply involved, besides I've lost my ability to cope with much more. A few minutes later, Jax returns, consternation in his blue eyes.

"What is it?" I ask.

He runs his hands into his blond fringe, pushing it from his face. "They're saying Jem did this to you."

"No!" I stand. "Why the fuck would they?"

"I don't know."

"I have to tell them!" As I make to leave, Jax grabs my sleeve.

"Don't. We don't know how to deal with this."

I yank my arm away. "Jem helped me. He never wanted to help me and now he's being accused of this shit. Jem wouldn't hurt me!"

"I know he didn't, Ruby; but the media's waiting for him to trip up."

Tears spring into my eyes, at Jem's life, at the way he's been manipulated, at what he has to fight along with his demons every day. He wants to change, but the world wants to keep him demonised.

"It's not fair! He's a good person." Jax opens his mouth to say something but decides against it. "Jax?"

"I'm not saying anything."

"You don't need to. You think I'm ignoring his bad side, don't you? You don't know him!"

"Do you?" asks Jax in a low voice.

I slap Jax in the chest. "Look what he's done for us. You selfish prick!"

Jax catches my arm. "You're vulnerable. He might take advantage. I've seen how he looks at you, it's predatory."

"Don't be stupid!" I snap.

"Jem Jones uses people and tosses them aside. I don't want you getting hurt by him."

I choke on the words I want to yell, disgusted at Jax accusing Jem of being the cliché too. Instead, without another word, I walk out of the police station away from him. I stride through the middle of the media frenzy, head high. Cameras click as I walk by, but I'm not hiding. There's nothing to hide, they can say what the fuck they want. These people can follow me to the other end of the city if they want, but there's one place I'm going.

22

They're outside Jem's house too, loitering on the wall and eagerly standing to position their cameras in my direction as I climb out of the taxi.

Ignoring the barrage of flashes and questions, I hover at Jem's security gates, waiting for him to answer the intercom, terrified he'll tell me to piss off because I've caused him trouble. The speaker crackles but he doesn't speak.

"It's Ruby."

The gate clunks and I open enough to slide through sideways. Keeping a lid on Ruby is hard but I manage. How I've kept my silence and not screamed at the press, I've no idea. I pause and turn to the reporter closest to the gate. He's young, not much older than me, and practically salivating over his proximity to the new Blue Phoenix scandal. I run a disdainful look over his close-cropped hair and smart attire.

"If Jem Jones had done this to my face, would I be here now?" I ask as the metal gates close between us.

"Hey, money can fix anything. I hope he gives you what you want."

It's a good thing the gate's between us or his mouth would match my injured one right now. I see myself through his eyes, his lack of respect for someone who looks like me. He called me a cheap whore in not so many words.

"Fuck you," I retort and head to the front door.

The door's ajar but Jem isn't in the hallway. I stomp upstairs enjoying the heavy sound of my combat boots; the ones I resisted using on the feet of each media asshole I came across outside.

"Jem?"

"In here."

Jem stands in the lounge room, close to the window; and when he looks over, pain lances my heart because he's the Jem I saw in the kitchen surrounded by broken glass that evening, haunted and confused. *This is my fault.*

I hate myself for thinking this in the moment, but I've seen the thought in Jax's eyes today. Have I fucked up the relationship between Jem and Ruby Riot, the one moving us on?

"I'm sorry," I say.

Jem drags a palm slowly down his cheek. "What did you tell them? The police."

"I told them what happened. I told them it was Dan. They'll question him, not you. I don't know where this has come from."

"I do. It's who I am, isn't it?" He turns to the window and looks to the people below, the defeat in his tone pulls further at my guilt.

I cross and touch his arm. "No, it's not."

"And so it starts again. Not that it ever stops."

"What doesn't?"

"Their control, moulding me into the person they want to see. This last year has been worse, after... Liv, I'm painted as a man who hurts women. Now this."

The whole time, Jem's gaze remains on the window, at the world outside threatening his new peace.

"Jem, you were cleared with Liv. It wasn't you."

"What's the saying? Where there's smoke, there's fire. They want me to fail. They want him back." His voice is the flat. Dead.

"But he doesn't exist, Jem, not unless you let him."

"He does. I've done some bad shit. You have no idea."

"I don't care; he's not here. Don't let them drag him back up."

Jem turns to me and we share another of those moments where we recognise each other's rawness; see the lies we tell ourselves. "You, saying that, almost convinces me."

"To me, you're Jem and not the Jem Jones they say you are. This Jem is a good guy. Don't let anyone tell you otherwise. They don't know you."

A muscle twitches in his cheek. "You don't know me."

"I know enough," I say quietly. "You're good. In here." I place a hand on his chest and he flinches. "Don't you like being touched?"

"If it's you, I don't mind." He gives a small smile and curls his hand around mine.

Jem's words confuse me considering his reaction two days ago. The kiss. His freak out. Now his knight in shining armour routine from last night. I hated him yesterday for how he treated me; but now he's back to taking care of me, looking at me in the way he once did. My head is a screwed. Everything is screwed and I shouldn't be here.

Yet there's no other place in the world I feel calmer or safer right now.

"Just no kissing?" I ask.

Jem's grip on my hand tightens. "I came to apologise about that last night. That's the reason I was there."

"Whatever the reason you were there, I'm glad. And you don't need to explain yourself. I just wish you'd left things and not kissed me the other night. You messed with my head, Jem."

"Yeah, I messed with my own too. I couldn't stand the thought I'd hurt you more by being such a dickhead." With his other hand, he strokes hair from my face. "Did I? If I did, I'm sorry."

I shrug. "I'm used to it."

"Exactly. I spend weeks telling you to believe in yourself, to show you how much you're worth to the world, and then I do that to you."

"Forget about it," I say, smiling in a way I hope fools him into thinking I'm not bothered.

Jem reaches to touch my cheek and I shift so he doesn't. "Your face... If I ever see that fucker again..."

"Bit of a mess, but nothing permanent. At least he didn't break my nose."

Jem scowls. "The way you deal with this is wrong. Don't play this down."

"Jem, I've been to the police like I promised, but I'm too tired for any more lectures. I need to deal with this in my own way. Surely, you of all people understand that."

He nods slowly. "But we need to talk; we can't leave things as they are, you know that."

"I know. But not now. I need a smoke and a rest."

Jem drops his hand and I grip onto the illusion I've created around myself today, the strong girl coping with the pain and fear of the situation in a way that's had people commenting how brave I am. But I'm not fooling Jem; and if I stand here for a second longer, I'll break down in front of him, and if I do, I'm not sure what'll happen.

Aware heavy words hang between us and the anxiety growing with my nicotine craving, I offer Jem a reassuring smile I'm sure he doesn't believe and head toward his garden and the fresh air I'm about to pollute.

I take up my usual spot on Jem's patio, sitting on the edge of the wooden chair as I light up and stare at his neatly mown patch of green in the middle of the city. Of course, he has a gardener, to go with his cleaner; and God knows what other minions he has when he has a need. The garden is bordered with white and yellow roses, my favourite flower. The ones I have etched on my skin.

I stub the cigarette in the terracotta tray and sit back, focusing my mind away from anything Dan, Jem, or painful. The door bangs and Jem stands in the doorway, watching me silently.

"What?" I ask. "You're freaking me out staring like that."

"They both stopped me," Jem says.

I shake my head at his sudden comment. "Who did? What are you talking about?"

"The kiss." He rests against the doorframe.

"Jem. Forget it."

"I can't."

"You don't have to explain. It's cool."

Jem ignores me. "Liv." He shakes his head. "My Mum. I can't separate you; you're like both of them together. It's like being pulled back in time. The demons controlling you are the ones that torture me too."

I straighten, unsure what to think and why he's chosen to say something so strange out of the blue. "Do you speak to your counsellor about all this?"

He tips his head. "Do you mean shut up and talk to your counsellor?"

"No. It's just..."

"No stress, Ruby. You're right. I'll talk to my counsellor." Jem puts a hand on the door, ready to go back inside.

"No. Talk to me."

He smiles weakly and I realise I've killed his attempt to open up. "No. You don't want to hear."

"I'll tell you about Dan," I blurt. "About why. You asked once. Jax knows, doesn't matter if you do too."

Jem pulls on his bottom lip. "I don't know."

"You mean shut up and talk to your counsellor?" I mimic.

"No. If you want to talk to someone, I'll listen."

"That's not what I mean. Forget about it."

Jem walks over, sits in the chair next to me, and reaches out. That's exactly what he's doing - reaching out. But why? "I know that's not what you mean. I'm making excuses for myself. It's because if I know more about you, you're harder to keep away from."

When Jem takes my hand, I don't want to let go and squeeze his as I force back the tears in my eyes. "You mean if I let you know about Tuesday?"

"Such a weird name," says Jem.

"Such a weird girl."

"Weirder than Ruby?"

"She suits Jem more than Tuesday."

He frowns. "What?"

"Rubies – they're gems."

"Is she?" His mouth tips at the corner.

"Ha-ha." I pull my hand away, fighting the urge to light up another cigarette. "Dan was my brother's best friend."

"Was?"

"My brother died three years ago."

"Oh, shit. Sorry to hear that."

If I close my eyes, I don't need to be here. I could stay in the calm quiet, amongst the rose scent of the garden and not engage. But I have to. I want Jem to know me; and then at least, if he rejects me, he's rejecting who I really am.

"Quinn was more than a brother; he was the one good thing in my life, and some bastard drunk driver killed him." I rub my knees. Can I do this? Tell him who I really am? "He was only twenty-one, walking home from a night out and got hit. Instant. He was always there for me and I never got a chance to say goodbye."

"Fuck." Jem attempts to reach out again and I tuck my hands under my arms, tensing against any attempt by my body to breakdown.

"Quinn was older than me, things were shit at home, and he looked out for me when everything got bad." I catch Jem's eye. "My dad left when I was too young to remember him and my mum left when I was thirteen. She moved overseas to live with a guy who didn't want her baggage. Quinn and me moved in with my uncle and aunt. My aunt was great, but my uncle didn't want my mum's baggage either so things were tough. Me and Quinn helped each other, then Quinn left for uni and I was stuck there."

Jem shifts and stares at his bare feet. "Yeah, I get the shithouse parents thing."

This makes sense, another connection I suspected. "When Quinn left for uni, he asked Dan to keep an eye on me, a person to turn to when things got really bad at home. Dan did. He was a great guy, really, nice. Would do anything for me. Dan let me sleep on his sofa each time my uncle scared me enough to run away. I trusted him because my brother trusted him."

"Dan? A nice guy?"

I laugh softly at Jem's incredulity. "Yeah, but when Quinn died,

Dan changed. Slowly at first. He interfered in my relationships, my life choices, always throwing at me that my brother wouldn't approve. That was enough for me to listen; after all, my brother trusted Dan, so I should. When things got really screwed up at home, I moved in with Dan."

Jem looks up. "You moved in with him? He's my age. How old were you?"

I shake my head. "I was seventeen. We weren't together like a couple at first, but he was the only man apart from my brother who'd shown me attention. I craved Dan's love, and he said he loved me, wanted me, and took care of me. I believed him. Over the next three years, he took my control away."

Jem interrupts. "You stayed for three years? I never understand why they stay."

"They?"

"People hurt by others they live with."

"I had to leave my uncle's and had nowhere to go. I'd put up with abuse from my uncle since I went to live there; everything from him constantly telling me what a bad person I must be for my mum to leave me, to him slapping me around to prove the point. I believed him; my mum had screamed the same shit at me before she fucked off. Around the time I turned sixteen, he got weird." I inhale. "I'm not going into it all, but he wasn't looking at me or treating me like his niece anymore. He'd walk in when I was getting changed, that kind of crap."

"Shit, Ruby. Please don't tell me..."

I shake my head and a bloody annoying tear flies out. "No, no... that's why I got out. I didn't feel safe. Dan kept me safe. If I'd stayed with my uncle and aunt... I don't know, Jem."

Jem puts his elbows on his knees and drags his hands through his curls, swearing under his breath.

"I don't think anyone understands unless they've been there. Dan controlled my life. The psychological abuse came before the physical. He ground me down until I felt like he was doing me a favour even wanting me. That nobody else did or ever would. That I just had to look at how people had treated me, and that it was all my fault because I was a bad person. I tried to leave Dan a few times before but failed until last time. Now Dan's done what I always worried he would, what stopped me leaving before."

Jem stands and walks away from me. "This is the problem. This is why I can't get close to you."

"Because I'm a bad person?" I ask hoarsely.

"No! You're the opposite, Ruby. You're an amazing, strong person and my whole self screams to let you in."

My stomach lurches at his admission. "Let me in?"

He turns back to me. "They were the same as you. I grew up with a woman who was constantly abused and I fell into a relationship with a girl like you once before. That's why I stepped away when I kissed you. I realised I can't go there again. I can't fix broken people because I get cut on the sharp edges."

A girl like me? Realisation crashes down. I'm so fucking stupid, why didn't I see this before? "You think I'm Liv?"

"You are."

"How?"

"Similar then."

"Similar isn't the same, Jem."

He drags his hair away from his face. "Okay, similar, but I feel I need to rescue you."

No way. "Rescue me? What the hell are you? A super hero?"

"I mean fix you, make things better."

I stand. "You think I need fixing? Rescuing? That is so insulting! That's what you see when you look at me? A weak girl who needs protecting from the world?"

"No... Yes. Shit." Jem looks past me, chewing on his mouth.

"Is this why you hold back from me? You think I'm weak, like Dan thought I was weak? I'm stronger than you fucking think!"

His refusal to react after I laid myself bare to him does more than irritate me. All I've done is give him more ammunition to prove I'm like his ex.

I lean toward him, face close to his. "I'm not Liv! How can I be her? What was she doing with her life? Getting stoned with you. What else was she doing with her life, Jem? How was she changing?"

"She wasn't. She was stuck. I was helping..."

"Look at my face, Jem. If I needed rescuing, would I have been in the position to get this? Everything I've achieved in the last few months began before I met you. I started on a path away from Dan and you've helped me by helping the band. But you're not saving me. I don't want saving. I could've done all this whether you were here or not!"

Mind blown, I can't think straight. I need out. Away from him. "I think I should leave if that's how you feel. I doubt the police will bother you and the media will back off when they hear. Call Jax later about the band." I march to the door and yank it open.

"Ruby. Stop."

"I'll pack now. See you in the studio in a couple of days, once the swelling goes down."

"Wait. Please." Jem steps past, between me and the open door, and holds his hands up as he faces me. "I won't stop you physically; you know that. I'm asking you to stay."

"What? So you can look after me?"

"No!" He places a hand on my uninjured cheek. "Because I want you here; the house is weird since I got back from the States. Empty."

"Heard it before, Jem. This time you don't get the kiss." I twist my head so he's no longer touching my cheek. "You're screwing around with my feelings and I can't do it! I have enough shit to deal with; I haven't got time for yours."

He closes the door and rests against it, looking straight into my eyes, something he normally avoids. "I dream about Liv."

"That's supposed to endear me to you, is it?"

Jem continues to hold my gaze and I can't look away. This is the other Jem; the one I'm beginning to suspect only I see. "I have nightmares; the scene is on repeat in my head. Trying to wake Liv up and the gut-wrenching realisation, she was dead. It consumes me, Ruby. She's with me all the time. Everything reminds me of her, that's why you do too!"

"I'm not her!" I say through clenched teeth.

"Can you begin to understand what her dying did to me?" he shouts, and then lowers his voice as I stumble back. "Everyone thought Jem Jones didn't give a fuck, but I was terrified. Guilty.

They cleared my name, but I did it, Ruby. I hurt her and she took the drugs. It wasn't an accident."

"How could you know that? They said it was just a straightforward accidental overdose. Nothing else was found to indicate differently, I remember reading about it."

"She left a note blaming me. Nobody else knows about it. I took the letter and destroyed it before anyone else could see; but I'll never forget the words on the page."

"That doesn't make it your fault. She was on the edge before you met her."

Jem's paled; hands shaking and I take one. "Jem, why have you never told anyone?"

"How can I? I'm not being judged anymore!"

"Look at the mess you're in over it. The guilt is eating you. People who know you and care won't judge you. What the hell does it matter what strangers think?"

Like the rest of the world, I thought I knew Jem Jones. Then I met Jem and saw who he is, parts of him I doubt anybody else does. Yet, there's so much buried beneath the broken pieces nobody sees, not even me. His eyes are vacant and Jem's somewhere else, the space he shouldn't go to. I place a hand on his cheek and he blinks back to me.

"You're not responsible for another person's mental health; you weren't responsible for her death."

"If I'd got there sooner..."

"But you didn't. Okay, you had a fight, but that's not the only reason Liv chose to do what she did. It's a shit situation and it's hurt a lot of people, but it wasn't your fault."

"It fucking hurts." He grips my hand. "Everywhere hurts, and then I'm with you and the ache goes away. But that terrifies me because even though I'm happier when you're here, there's also need, jealousy and fear filling the space the hurt once did. How are they any better?"

"They're not."

"So that's why I want to be numb. Feeling nothing is better than feeling that shit."

"You're not thinking about..."

Jem drops my hand and shoves his hands into his pockets. "No! I'm done with drugs. I need to learn to control the thoughts myself. I can't give in to my emotions."

This is the core of who he is and who he needs to fight. This man was emotionally dead; how long for, I don't know. Then something triggered negative reactions, and by shutting down to avoid the hurt, he can't let himself feel the good too. My chest tightens because I know I'm the same and his words hit that home.

"You can't stop yourself feeling, Jem. Even if you shut the world out, there's another in your head and that place is harsher than the world you avoid."

He steps forward, back into my space, our space, the one between us we refuse to cross. "I don't want to replace one hurt with another, Ruby. I don't want to go down the same route. You overwhelm me because I'm a different person around you. You see the real me and understand, never judge. I'm happy with you. But if I let you in and you leave, it would fucking kill me..."

My heart pushes against my chest, as if wanting Jem to take hold of it the way I know he already has. His words reach my ears, but I can't take them in. Nobody has told me I mean something; that I make them happy. How can this mess of a girl in front of him be that?

Jem winds a hand into my hair and rests his forehead on mine. I flinch at his skin touching the graze on my forehead. "I want you. I want you so much. You're me. I thought you were the fucked up, broken me, but you're not. You're the talented, strong, and determined person I once was. So much about us is the same – not just the bad." He inhales a shaky breath. "You're not Liv. You just kicked that truth into my dumb head."

Hesitantly, Jem kisses the uninjured edge of my mouth, then presses his lips against my cheek, holding the back of my head gently as his mouth remains there, as close as he can get without causing pain. I want to cry because I want Jem to hold and kiss me, and I ignore the urge to push him away because he could hurt physically and emotionally if he closes me out again. Jem wraps his arms around me, carefully as if I might snap if he hugs too tight, and strokes my hair. Unable to hold back anymore, I rest against Jem's lean body, my face against his neck, my senses closed off from anything but the safety in his arms that he pulled me to last night.

"Stay with me," he says into my hair. "I know you don't want protecting, but until this shit is sorted with Dan, stay safe."

I place a hand on Jem's chest and his heart thumps against my palm. With Jem, we can be in a safe place together; we don't have to be alone in the world if we share the good in ourselves. Together, now, we're wrapped on the edge of this place we belong, the shattered pieces of our lives surrounding us. With the secrets we shared came the understanding that not everything is broken forever.

"I don't want to save you, Ruby. I want to mean something to you, because for the first time in forever, someone means something to me."

I listen to the steady beat of his heart, as I'm encompassed by the confusing, frustrating Jem who just laid himself open to me. For the first time too, I believe Ruby means something to someone else, and for the right reasons.

23

I wake confused by where I am and what the time is, my head pounding. There's light shining across the bed from the open curtains and my phone reads four p.m.

Jem's house.

The stress of the last day caught up and after our embrace, Jem hovered around uncomfortably until I told him I wouldn't get pissed off with him if he walked away again. Following my outpouring over Quinn and Dan, I wanted time alone to compose myself too. Our shared understanding that this isn't rejection; but dealing with our own headspace is another indication of how similar we are.

My body aches and I examine my face in a small pocket mirror. My lip isn't as swollen but the bruising around my eye and cheek has darkened. Add to that the grazes to my face and I'm a delight. I pull out the thick foundation and set about painting away Dan.

I haven't eaten since last night and the dizzying hunger forces me into the kitchen. My instant noodles I left behind last time I lived here are tucked in the back of the cupboard, so I pull them out and break them into a bowl.

Jem appears as I'm pouring boiling water onto the noodles. We eye each other warily; but I'm relieved to see a calmer Jem, one whose face has lost some of the strain from earlier. The loose white shirt he's wearing is unbuttoned far enough to see his ink underneath. One hug and my body and imagination firing to life at the sight of him isn't good.

"Please don't tell me you're eating that crap again," he says.

"I'm hungry and there's nothing else."

"What do you mean? There's a shitload of stuff in the fridge."

"Your food."

"So?"

"Don't you remember your housemate agreement? I'm not allowed to touch your stuff."

Jem flicks his tongue against his teeth and then realises what I mean. "Oh. That. You're a guest."

I turn back and rip open the packet of powder loosely described as flavouring. One embrace and suddenly the space between us feels smaller than it once did. Also, not good.

"Leave that. I'll order us some proper food. I'm hungry too." He crosses and rests against the counter next to me. "You put make-up on."

"Yeah. I'm sure nobody else likes looking at the mess; I know I don't."

He looks at me with concern. "Doesn't it hurt putting that crap over a cut?"

I shrug.

"I prefer you without make-up. I can see your eyes properly." Jem touches the skin under my uninjured eye, wiping at the kohl with his thumb. At his touch, I shiver and the softness in the way he studies my face grips me. People don't look at me like this. "You shouldn't hide."

I turn my face away. "Like I said, covering up."

Jem remains next to me and the physical desire I've fought against since he walked into the kitchen – since I met him - has intensified. He laces his fingers through mine and I look up in surprise.

"Are you staying? I know I upset you before."

I'm unaware of much, apart from how natural my hand in his feels. "Yes. If you want me to."

"Good." Jem takes his hand away and indicates the drawer I'm standing in front of. "Grab the menus from there. What do you want? Chinese? Thai?"

When he does his 'Jem thing' of breaking away the moment he's too close, my stomach knots. I shouldn't crave his attention let alone expect him to hold and kiss me.

Half an hour later and we sit in the lounge, boxes of noodles and rice spread across his low glass coffee table. I'm impressed by Jem's ability with chopsticks, instant noodles never called for such sophistication.

"I can show you, if you like?" suggests Jem, passing me a pair.

"It's okay. I'll use a fork. I'm too hungry to mess around with those."

We're on the floor and I rest against the sofa, holding a box in my hands as I eat. Jem sits in his favourite armchair opposite.

"What do you want to listen to?" he asks. "I can't sit in silence." He heads to his laptop that's hooked up to the sound system and the large plasma TV. "Pick a decade."

"Nineties?"

"Okay, who?"

"How about Smashing Pumpkins?"

Jem rubs his cheek. "Nah. Chili Peppers?"

I shrug. "Your house."

He scrolls through a list on his laptop. "Must be some classics we both like."

After more debate, we settle on a random mix of '90s indie rock. Back to Ruby and Jem whose strong wills won't bend, choosing a band we agree on isn't happening anytime soon. "Sounds awesome on your system," I say.

"One thing I'll always have the best of."

I twirl noodles around my fork, and side-glance him. "What colour is this song?"

Jem closes his eyes. "Red."

"Really? No, blue."

"No way, there's black in here too." He opens an eye.

"What colour is "Rising"?" I ask him.

"Orange."

"I always saw red. I guess you get to dictate the colour if it's your song."

"No, it's just what colour it looks. There's a lot of G in and that's red."

"No, G is green."

Jem pouts but his eyes show his amusement before he looks away and silently eats his meal, abruptly stopping the conversation. "I've never met anyone like you," he says eventually.

"A lot of people say that to me."

"Same. For the first time I feel comfortable around someone."

"You're comfortable around the band, surely?"

"Yeah, early days and as a kid we were all similar but never the same. Dylan's closest to me, understands the power of music like I do, but we lost each other."

"You lost yourself."

He frowns. "I guess. Dylan stopped the drugs, I didn't."

"If you were an addict, you wouldn't meet anyone you felt yourself around because you weren't yourself."

Jem sets his box on the table. "Have you known any addicts? Sometimes I get the impression you have."

"Some friends at school got into that shit. My brother steered me clear. I smoked weed a few times, but it wiped me out and interfered with the music too much. That's why I can't understand why you went that way."

"There's a lot we don't understand about each other." He tucks a loose strand of hair behind his ear.

A lot we don't want to share.

Again, conversation killed. Although Jem's different around me than a few days ago, loosened and a sense of humour poking through; he's still never far from the world of his memories. Jem finishes his meal and heads out of the room, leaving me and my disappointment behind. His habit of walking away without saying anything irritates me; does Jem realise what he's doing?

"Will you play for me again?" Jem's returned, holding the guitar I played in his hotel room.

"Why?"

"I like it." He looks at me as if I'm asking a stupid question.

If my playing means he stays in the room with me, forges us further, I will. "Sure, but you can play for me too."

Jem grins. "Cool by me."

Cross-legged on the floor, I take the pick he offers and strum a few notes, fine-tuning the strings. Playing the opening bars of "Stairway to Heaven," I grin at him as he rolls his eyes at the cliché.

"Don't worry, I won't play that."

I play the Ruby Riot track, "Beneath the Stars," lost in the world of colour. The rainbows of music illuminate the shadows of my mind, dragging me away from darkness and stars, until I forget where I am. I always do. Playing alone or performing, I'm on a different plane, body as tuned into the music as my mind. When I finish, I jerk back to reality and focus on the world again.

The expression on Jem's face tears the breath from my body. I've glimpsed the intense look before, on the days it sneaked through before he'd look away again. This time his eyes remain on mine. This is how people look at you when you mean something to them; he told me the truth in the garden earlier.

"Why did I ever think you were like her?"

I don't want Jem to elaborate, but I know who he means. I set the guitar down; I don't want to go back to old conversations. I make to stand and Jem sits forward.

"Don't go," he says. "Spend time with me before we go and hide in our dens."

I rub my forehead. "You're a confusing man, Jem Jones."

"Nah, I'm quite simple really.'

"That, I don't believe."

Jem shifts and takes the guitar. "Sit with me. Play again." I frown, unsure exactly what he wants. "Here. Lean against me." He indicates the space in front of him.

This man who doesn't like to be touched is asking me to sit

close? I hesitate; aware the intimacy of placing myself there is another step across our borders. I'm torn. I've craved nothing more than being held by Jem for weeks, but I'm vulnerable and hurting.

"I want to be close to you, Ruby Tuesday. I'm over the URST bullshit, I want you in my life, and that involves touching you." The abrupt words wipe out any doubt. He wants the same as I do; the same thing we've avoided for months. Not just a physical intimacy, but allowing in an emotional intimacy, too.

"Okay," I say quietly.

I move so Jem can put his legs on either side of me, my back against his chest as he rests against the armchair. He passes me the guitar. How will I play when all I'm aware of is being encompassed by Jem? He exudes calm and warmth, the thump of his heart against my back and his face close to my neck. His breath sets goose bumps along my skin, intensifying the situation. Is this how we can be close? If Jem can hold me, but I can't him. If I can't see his eyes.

Jem strokes my hair, the sensation tingling my scalp. "How is your hair so soft when you kill it with hair dye?"

I chuckle and he rests his chin on my shoulder. "What's funny?"

"Should we discuss hair care products? Which do you find gives you the best body and shine?"

"I don't use..." He pauses. "Ha-ha. Play."

I set the guitar down. "No." I want to twist around to look into his face, communicate without words.

He misreads my tension and closes his hand over mine. "Fine, I'll put the music back on but my choice since you're refusing my simple request."

I place a hand on the floor, preparing to shift away from him but Jem curls his arms around my waist.

"Sit with me. Relax. I'm not going to do anything you don't want me to."

I let go of the tension and allow myself to sink back against his chest and rest my head against his neck.

Jem Jones. Blue Phoenix bad boy, man-whore, and ex-addict is sitting on the floor with me and holding my hand. If there's one thing I would never have thought possible, this is it. But he's right; there's a little bit of us in each other. The music, our personalities, the past, and the understanding. Could this be more? We've formed a shaky friendship built on those foundations. But can either of us give more at the moment?

Jem nudges the hollow of my neck with his nose, shooting an unexpected warmth through me. Of course, I'm attracted to him; I have been since I was a teen Blue Phoenix fan, but the hormonal reaction annoyed me because I didn't like what I read about the man himself. Jem's lips touch my skin and I inhale at the gentleness. The times I imagined getting physical with Jem, gentle wasn't on the agenda.

When I allow him to trail small kisses along my collarbone, he slides a hand to my side, rubbing the edge of my waist with his fingers through the material of my shirt. I will him to touch my naked skin with the same softness, but when he slides his fingers beneath my shirt, placing his palm on my side, I can't help tensing.

"I'm not hurting you, am I?"

Not yet.

"No, but be careful. My ribs..." After all this time waiting for his touch, and I can't let Jem hold me without it causing the pain I want him to take away.

"I wish I could kiss you," he says in a low voice, pushing images of his mouth on mine back in where I've blocked them out.

"The same."

"I'll stick to kissing you other places." The first hints of a move from tender to sexual catches me by surprise. He misreads my breathy reaction. "But only if that's okay with you."

"Like my neck?"

"I was thinking other places, but neck is good." The sensation of his mouth and body surrounding me triggers a rush of heat, spreading arousal through. His heart beating against my back speeds up as I shift against his hips.

"Can I ask you a question?"

I tense. "I might not answer it."

"You don't have to."

"Fine." Jem entwines his fingers with mine. "Who named you Ruby? You?"

Now I know why we're sitting like this. Without eye contact, we can tell secrets. "My brother, when I was ten and some kids at school teased me about my stupid name. Quinn began calling me Ruby Tuesday, told me it was a cool name. When I was outside the house, that's who I was. I made everyone call me Ruby - friends, teachers, everyone. I refused to respond if they called me Tuesday. Quinn played me the song and I'd listen to it on repeat when he was away. My song. Since he died, I can't listen to it anymore."

"Sorry for playing it to you." His lips move against my skin as he speaks, not helping with the desire for his hands to move to other parts of my body.

"You didn't know."

"But it is you. So much you."

"I have a line from the song tattooed on my ribs, about how yesterday doesn't matter because it's gone. I wish I'd never done that."

"You tried to show me once," he whispers into my hair.

"What? When?"

Jem laughs. "You were drunk. I didn't see much, don't worry."

My cheeks heat and blushing isn't something I do. I grasp at a memory triggered by his words. The kitchen. Offering myself. Jem saying no. I'm surprised when tears spring to my eyes. Why? Because he said no? No, because he treated me with the respect I didn't have for myself.

I shift from his embrace and twist to look at him. "I've never met a man like you."

"A lot of people say that," he says with a smile.

Jem's face has lost the pallor he had when we first met, the lines softened. He looks at my mouth and then turns his darkened eyes to mine. Is he going to kiss me again? I want my mouth on his; but it would hurt, and my lip twinges in annoyance. I touch Jem's face, tracing the contours of his defined cheekbones, rubbing my fingertips along his scruff. Is he holding his breath?

"Are you okay?" I ask.

"You're looking at me in a way nobody has for a while."

"And how's that?"

"Like I matter."

"Jem..." I press my lips against his, briefly, gently, and then withdraw before he kisses me properly. Jem's lips move across my uninjured cheek before he buries his face in my hair.

"Every time I touch you, I hate that fucker more because I want to kiss you so much." He looks up. "When your mouth is better, I'm going to kiss you until you can't breathe."

He obviously misses my current struggle with breathing around him. "Suffocation doesn't sounds pleasant, Jem."

He laughs. "No, I mean the effect it'll have on you. I'm a fucking awesome kisser."

"I remember." He smirks. "Actually, no. It was crap."

Jem rests his head back on the chair. "Oh, really? I don't believe you."

"I'm sure your expertise in all things umm... physical is admirable, Jem, but there's a difference. You can kiss me like you mean it, or not at all."

Jem cups my chin in his long fingers. "I'll mean it, Ruby Tuesday."

His brown eyes tell me he already does and I ache with the frustration of wanting him to show me now. Instead, I shift around, curl into Jem and rest my head on his shoulder. He runs his fingers along my arm and strokes as we listen to the music in the peace we've created. I wait for him to be Jem Jones, to continue the path he started to something sexual but he doesn't. This is Jem, intuitive about the Hell I found myself in last night, and understanding how tender is the road to where he wants to go.

24

em

We bunker down in my house for a few days. I tell myself it's because I can't be bothered facing the media, but it's not. Even though Ruby pretends she's okay, the attack has shaken her badly. She doesn't want to leave the house, tells me it's because of her face but the larger part is she's traumatised. Ruby hates being weak, needing protection, and I don't want to be the one who craves to keep her safe. But I do, and I'm going to, whether or not she likes.

Opening up and sharing shit I've never told anyone scares me, but the pressure from keeping everything in built too much. I never knew saying the words to somebody else could help relieve some of that. Ruby is the person who pushed me to do this without realising, and all because she shared her own. She took the risk I never could.

She's under my skin, burrowing into my heart and soul, and I want her. The frustration is killing me. I catch Ruby watching me when she thinks I'm unaware; the confusion and desire reflected in her eyes. I hate people in my personal space; can't stand anyone touching anything that belongs to me. Hell, some days I don't want to share oxygen with people.

Ruby belongs here.

I have no explanation or experience of this, but I crave her. Not just the naked Ruby who's spent the last couple of months living in my fantasies, the one I'll get into my bed as soon as she's ready, but the comfort of her presence and understanding.

No longer hiding in bedrooms as we did last time she stayed, we spend hours together talking about music, life, everything but the past. We're in the world we were trapped in alone, but now we're there together. Secretly, I'll touch Ruby's hand, run my fingers along her arm, and we've even gone as far as cuddling up on the sofa watching TV like an old married couple.

Natural. Safe.

And fucking frustrating.

After the other night when I held her fragile figure to me, I've tried to touch her in the same way again but she stiffens. Ruby explains she won't do anything unless I kiss her, but she doesn't say why. I examine her lips twenty times a day, watching the split heal. When Ruby tells me she has a way to speed up the healing, pulling creams from her bag to apply, the anger seethes again. This has happened before, more than once, and Ruby deals with it as if she has a reoccurring medical condition.

Following a third restless night fighting against asking Ruby to get into my bed, I wander downstairs and find her sitting on a stool in the kitchen, long, naked legs crossed. She's dressed in a short black summer dress covered in a pink skull pattern. With no make-up to hide behind, the bruises visible on her face yellow. I watch as she slowly eats cereal, focused on her phone.

My heart is gripped by the inexplicable joy of seeing her in my space, relaxed as if it were her space too, although her brows are tugged together in consternation.

"Hey," I say.

She looks up. "Jax wants to know when we're back into studio time."

"Jeez, that guy. I've told him next week, about ten times."

"I think he's worried you're going to change your mind because of the... complications."

Unable to resist, I cross and kiss her soft hair. "You're not a complication."

"What am I then?" Her question is loaded and I step back, watching her warily. "What are we?"

"Whoa. Ruby. This is a bit left-field."

"Sorry."

She takes another mouthful of cereal.

"Friends?" I suggest.

She huffs. "Liar. You don't want to fuck your friends."

Actually, I have done. Often. "I don't want to fuck you."

"Liar," she repeats with a small laugh.

"Your mouth."

"Because I used the word fuck?"

"No." I move mine close to hers. "It's not sore anymore, is it?"

Ruby's breath rushes out, then she attempts to disguise the reaction. "Yeah, feeling better, thanks."

"You're funny. Don't you remember my promise to you?"

Ruby's nonchalant attempt to keep eating fires the situation further because she runs her tongue along her lip and licks the milk off, a gesture that edges me closer to her.

"Was that a promise? I thought we'd gone back to friends."

"Did you?" She's not wriggling out of this, and she's lying. The undertones have followed us; the looks, the touches, the teenage style glances. Either Ruby does this or I give up. I brush my lips against her cheek.

"Does anywhere hurt still?"

Her blue eyes meet mine. Of course, she hurts. I can see that but I can also clearly see her want matches mine. "No."

"About bloody time."

I want to kiss her gently. I really do, but I can't. The need for her that's built in the last two months explodes and I take Ruby's face in both hands and close my lips over hers, roughly pushing my tongue into her mouth. For a millisecond, I kick myself for my stupidity, waiting for her to shove me away, and yell at me Ruby-style.

Instead, she welcomes my tongue and holds my face in return. Devouring kisses follow, pulling us further into each other. The kiss less than a week ago was amazing; this is fucking stratospheric. I place my arms either side of Ruby, caging her. In response, she stands and shoves my arms down, so I pull her against my hips.

My desire for Ruby blinds common sense, and I slide a hand up her leg to run my hands across her skin, beneath her dress until I reach her ass.

Shit, shit, shit. Groaning, I attempt to back her toward the counter again and she stands her ground, placing a hand on my chest but not removing her lips from mine. I get it. I can't corner her. She needs to lead but it's bloody difficult. Ruby breaks the kiss, resting her forehead against mine as our mingling breaths come in short pants.

"Okay, I can't breathe; you're right," she says.

"Suffocated?"

"No, the effect you have on me."

"What's that?"

Ruby slides her hand along the front of my jeans and runs a finger along my obvious erection. "The same as I have on you."

We've reached the line. The one I swore I wouldn't cross with this woman; the one that I'm scared will resurrect the asshole who fucks around with women's feelings. Or worse, this might be the final fall into something I can't handle. Dylan's bullshit about love has circled my mind. I don't love, not in the consuming, selfless way he does. I was never loved, so how do I understand when it happens, if it ever does?

For fuck's sake, Jem. Stop thinking and be yourself.

"Did I kiss you like I mean it?" I whisper, running my tongue along her neck.

Ruby shivers at the sensation. "Yeah." She pushes her hands beneath my t-shirt, dragging her nails across my lower back. "Kiss me some more."

"So now I get to kiss you other places?"

"You're funny."

"How?"

"Jem Jones making requests." Her warm breath tickles my ear as she speaks.

I loosen my grip and slide my arms to her waist. "Because I'm not going to take from you what you don't want to give."

Ruby's eyes soften and her response is a soft, slow kiss. She tastes sweet, of Ruby and muesli; I'm going to love the taste of muesli for the rest of my life.

Pink-cheeked and mouth parted, Ruby touches my lips. "Can I make a request?"

"Anything," I say, hoping to Hell that it's not 'stop'.

Curling her fingers through the belt loop on my jeans, Ruby tugs me closer and whispers in my ear. "I want to go into your bedroom with you and not come out until this URST thing is dealt with."

"URST," I chuckle. "Fine, but don't think you're getting the kids and the house in the country."

Ruby

I'm in Jem Jones's bedroom. *Jem's bedroom.*

Jem disappears into his bathroom, leaving me a trembling mess of excitement and anxiety. What if I'm not good enough for him? I pull my dress over my head, dump it on the floor, and slide beneath his thick bedding. I tug the soft material to my nose, inhaling the spiced scent of the man who more than kissed me like he meant it, and keep myself in my Jem frame of mind.

Jem reappears with a box of condoms in his hand and halts, frowning. "What are you doing?"

I grip the duvet. "Um. Waiting for you?"

"Waiting for me?"

Why does he sound annoyed? "Yes. Why? Did you change your mind?"

"What the hell?" Jem crosses to kneel on the bed and cups my chin with his hand. He runs his tongue across my bottom lip, triggering the heat that had waned with my nerves. I part my mouth for his kiss and he pulls away. "I'm not doing this *to* you, Ruby. I'm doing it *with* you."

"Okay." I push his t-shirt up and he rests a hand on mine to stop me.

"You have no idea how long I've wanted this," he says hoarsely. "I'm not screwing this up. If I do fuck up and you never want sex with me again, it'd kill me."

He wraps an arm around my waist, I eagerly accept the way his mouth claims mine. Jem's kisses are unusual because I don't do this type of kissing. Dan couldn't care less whether we did or not, as long as I opened my legs for him. With Jem, I've learned there's an intimacy from a kiss that goes deeper, an inexplicable extra connection. With Jem's come an unspoken care and affection, his desire to be with me on my own terms reflected by the way Jem gauges my reaction to each stroke of his tongue or movement of his lips. And I can't get enough.

I push at Jem's t-shirt again and this time he drags it over his head. In return, Jem pulls away the duvet covering my chest. His eyes darken as his gaze soaks in the sight, and my skin tingles as he runs a finger along the quote beneath my breast.

"Worth the wait," he whispers and his mouth finds mine again.

I wrap my arms around Jem's neck, pressing against his naked chest. My nipples brush his taut skin, sending a frisson of sensation to my core as Jem holds me, one hand on the nape of my neck and the other in the small of my back.

I could spend all day kissing Jem, exploring the new sensations from the touch of tongues, the taste and heat of our mouths. An eternity pressed against his warm body beneath gentle hands wouldn't be enough.

But that won't be what he wants, and isn't what I've waited this long for.

I move to unbutton his jeans and Jem shifts, helping, then shuffles out of them and kicks them to the floor. I shift back and pull him close, lying against the pillows, then begin to wriggle out of my panties.

Jem puts his hand on mine to stop me. "Is this what you do?"

"What?"

"Do you just lie back and have this done to you?" He props himself up on his elbows. "I'm not going to let you lie down while I fuck you missionary style, Ruby. That's not enough."

Crap. I'm in a situation with Jem Jones who has more than likely tried every sexual position I can imagine and some I haven't. *I won't be enough for him.* I close my eyes in embarrassment and leave my panties on. "Sorry, what did you want me to do?"

Jem sits back. "Jeez, Ruby. Have you ever had sex with a man who cares about how it feels for you?"

I tug the duvet under my chin again. I can't answer. There's only been Dan, and a couple of five-minute sessions with guys from school, and I certainly wasn't the focus. I'm uncomfortable. Sex is something I do, I don't talk about it as well.

"I guess that's no, then," he says quietly and pushes my hair from my face. "I don't understand guys like that. Having a woman really enjoying herself is the biggest fucking turn on."

I chew a nail, increasingly out of my depth, and when he moves to kiss me again, I tense.

"Ruby... Come here." Jem drags me onto his lap and looks up at me with darkened eyes. "I have fantasied about this for months so this isn't going to be over quickly or without enthusiastic participation by you." When I turn away, he takes my cheek and moves my head so I have to look straight at him. "Otherwise, I'm not doing this, okay?"

"Okay, but I don't think I'm very good at... things," I whisper, desperate for him to stop talking and do what he's promising.

Jem traces the shape of the heart tattoo on my chest. "No problem, I'll make everything about you this time, and then I can show you how to be good at things." His eyes shine with the promise of his words as he looks up at me, a tug of a smile on his lips. "Okay?"

"Okay."

Holding my head, Jem kisses gently, tongue teasing my lips.

His attempt to cool the situation won't work; my awareness of Jem's muscled body against mine, of his arousal pressing against my thigh takes me further from my anxiety. He slides his hands along my back, heating my skin with his gentle stroke. I shift closer, wanting harder kisses, to lose myself in us away from the awkward I created. The whole time, Jem holds me as if scared I'll fall apart if he lets go, or he'll break me if he embraces too tightly.

The kisses intensify, his hands harder against my skin, exploring every inch with his fingers, until I'm shaking with the need for him. Jem shifts me from his lap and we tip onto the bed; I lie on my side, wrapping my legs around his, not wanting to lose contact for a moment.

"You're fucking beautiful, Ruby Tuesday." The hoarseness in his voice and truth in his eyes almost makes me believe him. He spots my doubt. "And I won't stop showing you until you believe me."

"I'm okay with that." I trace a finger along his firm abs, lower, and Jem inhales sharply as my hand moves to the band of his briefs.

He curls his fingers around mine. "Don't. I am so turned on right now; that's not a good idea."

My heated cheeks hide my reaction – not embarrassment but a pleasure in the fact I have this effect on him. I shift to face him. "Don't stop."

Jem grins. "Don't worry about that." He dips his head, leisurely moving his tongue across my collarbone to my breasts. I suppress a moan as he circles my nipple with his tongue before taking it in his mouth and sucking. Involuntarily, my body arches toward him and I grip his hair. His gentle touch changes, in response to my body's desire for him to take over, the gasp that escapes showing I'm more than ready to be enthusiastic.

As he continues his attention to my breasts, Jem slides a hand down my side and pulls my leg over his hips, pressing himself against me. The evidence how turned on he is pushes against my thin cotton panties and adds to the gathering heat between my legs, the longing for his touch taking control of my thoughts.

I push my fingers into the knotted sinew of his shoulders, as

Jem's focus remains on my breasts and intensifies this ache. Every place on my skin Jem touches jolts arousal and I move against him. Weeks of wanting this, of fantasising about Jem wanting me, and I'm here.

Jem's mouth finds mine again, as his large palm closes around my ass. Fiercely, I kiss him and pull Jem onto me, desperate to be as melded with Jem as our mouths are. He needs to know, though I may have been shy, this isn't doubt. Jem matches the ferocity of my kiss, as our tongues slide in desperate want; a greed for each other no longer held back. His hand moves down my belly, toward the edge of my panties and I moan into his mouth, and close my eyes.

He pauses and when I open my eyes, Jem looks back with eyes darkened by desire. He stopped though, is this not what he wants? Gaze remaining on me, Jem slides a finger between the fabric of my panties and my belly, across my skin, teasingly close, and I wriggle against his hand, needing him to move lower, find how much I want him.

Jem hesitates again watching for a reaction, chest rising and falling as rapidly as mine.

"Jem, please..." My heart thumps, skin alight and the blinding need to be touched consumes like never before.

My words are enough. Jem's kisses me again, a dizziness spreading through at the intensity, as he edges his fingers downward. Jem reaches my wet heat and skims a finger between my legs. I gasp, and buck against his hand as he strokes, but this isn't enough, why didn't he let me take off my panties before? I hold his shoulders and am suddenly aware he's trembling the same way I am, holding himself back.

"Fuck, you're wet for me. I guess I don't need to ask if you're enthusiastic."

"Jem, I want this."

Breathing hard, Jem kisses my face, my cheeks, my mouth, moving along my body kissing and licking. He moves downward, dipping his tongue into my bellybutton before he swirls his tongue to my hip.

He shifts, kneels on the floor and draws me to the edge of the bed, where he slowly kisses from my ankle and along my calf.

Jem's lips reach my inner thigh, venturing higher and part of me is screaming for him to keep going, over the building anxiety. I've no experience of this; it wasn't on Dan's list of things to do.

"Your legs kill me, Ruby. The first day I saw you I wanted them wrapped around me." The words are spoken against my skin and he hooks both thumbs into my panties and tugs.

I tense and look away, body tingling with anticipation of what he's going to do as he pulls them off until I'm completely naked in front of him. Jem runs both hands up my thighs, circling his thumbs at the edge of my flesh, eyes focused on his action. I feel exposed but before I have a chance to catch up with the thoughts, he runs his tongue along the seam of my sex. My mind splinters as he finds my clit, ripping any rational thought from my mind.

"Fuck!" I breathe out the word and arch against him. Jem laughs against me, the vibration intensifying the pleasure, setting my nerves alight.

Pulling my legs onto his shoulders, Jem holds my hips so I can't move, exploring me with his hot tongue. When he eases a finger inside too, I'm lost. Lost to Jem, to here, to never going back from this new world. Jem focuses on me, swirling his tongue, sliding his fingers, shifting his pattern as he pays attention to my reactions. I try to disguise the sounds, but these are the touches and kisses of a man tuned into me and inhibition won't work. As I edge further to a place that's blinding me with stars threatening to explode in sensation Jem stops. I groan at the loss of his mouth but his fingers remain where they are.

Kissing his way back up my body, Jem's lips meet mine again, and the taste of myself on his tongue shocks and arouses me.

"That was unfair," I push myself against his palm, not wanting the new sensation to end. Jem shifts and smiles at me; a lazy smile of a guy who knows what he's doing and knows that he's good at it.

"Didn't I sound interested enough?" I ask, genuinely concerned I'm not doing this right.

"You're enjoying yourself." His whisper is a statement, not a question and is matched with the slow slide of his fingers, teasing a place inside I never knew existed, a place hardwired to the rest of my body and flooding shocks to my nerves.

"I want you inside me before...," I say. "I mean, if you don't stop you're going to make me..." I can't say the words, wish my brain would let go that little bit further.

Jem moves his face to my ear, hair and breath tickling my skin. "Come?"

I squeeze my eyes closed. "Yes."

"Good." Jem plunges his fingers with a harder rhythm, rubbing my clit at the same time, whispering what he wants to do; what he's going to do as I spin away from the shyness I shouldn't have around this man who is already part of me. Every time I find myself reaching for the edge, he stills his hand and focuses somewhere else –taking my nipple in his mouth or leaving a trail of heat along my breasts and stomach with his tongue. My short breaths have become pants; the moans at each time he stops are met with a smug smile and heated desire in his eyes.

"Jem, please..." I say when he stops again.

"Now?"

"Inside," I pant out.

Jem shuffles back and I close my eyes. I hear the noise of the foil wrapper and jerk in surprise when he runs his tongue across my clit again as he rolls the condom on.

"Fucking amazing," he whispers, stroking me with his tongue. He pauses and I'm ready to scream at him. "I want to make you come first though."

"No, Jem!" I protest and he laughs, sitting back.

I prop myself up and stare at him kneeling on the floor in front of me, the sight of his muscled body, his hard length, tightens my stomach with anticipation.

Should I be doing more?

Jem moves up the bed, tautly muscled body covering mine as he presses me into the bed and settles himself between my legs.

"For now, we can do it this way." His eyes glint. "Later, other ways."

I'm shaking with the need for this, to have him finish what he's started. I inhale sharply as the tip of him touches my sensitive flesh, as Jem rubs with the same rhythm as his tongue once did and for the first time ever I'm giving, not accepting. I shuffle my hips closer as he slides down my wetness, holding himself at the edge of where I want him. I wrap a leg around his waist, attempting to pull him closer.

"I have waited too long for this and what makes it better is you're fucking loving it," growls Jem.

I dig my nails into his side and he rocks against me, slowly, teasingly pushing himself inside then edging back out. I lose the last control I'm holding onto. "Jem, just fucking do it!"

"Ah, your mouth... Jesus..." Jem lets go, plunging into me and I gasp as he fills me completely.

I grip him tightly, wrapping my legs around Jem's waist and dig my nails into his back. Jem has me consumed; body, heart, and soul whether I want him to, or not. We hold each other's gaze, an intimacy I've never had. The final connection, looking into each other's vulnerabilities, of seeing everything we're feeling in each other's expressions ramps up the physical sensations crashing through with each thrust.

Jem slides in and out of me, harder each time, and I match his rhythm with my hips, wanting all of him too. He moves a hand beneath my ass, pulling me upwards as he pushes deeper, bumping my sensitive clit with each thrust, sending me spiralling further to a new place. I hold Jem tightly; and he groans pushing his tongue into my mouth, joining the movement we create. I grasp his neck locked into my overloaded senses.

Unable to hold out any longer, the pressure built inside explodes. The tingle spreads, reaching from my scalp to my toes, deep inside. I'm aware of crying out; of gripping him tightly inside as the pleasure comes in waves and I open my eyes, vision blackened by the intensity.

Jem watches as I fall apart in his arms but keeps thrusting. "Holy fuck, Ruby..." He swears repeatedly and his face changes to pleasure that matches mine, lost in his own intense moment as he closes his eyes and slams into me one last time. He drops onto me, heart thudding against mine, gripping my hair, and covering my face with kisses.

I cling to Jem and he holds me close as we stay in a silent understanding, panting becoming sighs, kisses back to tender and our skin burning against each other. I bury my face into Jem's shoulder and he strokes my hair. We don't have words, although I burst to tell him what he did to me, how he showed me that I matter. The intense pleasure still coursing through my body is because this was for us, and not his own satisfaction and I'm fighting the tears that realisation is pushing into my eyes.

"Be right back," he whispers.

When Jem returns from the bathroom and climbs onto the bed, I rest my cheek on his damp chest and play my fingers along the defined muscles of the body that just connected with mine the way nobody's ever has. Sex takes on a new understanding, more than a one-sided act for gratification, not something that's done to me. But with that rushes the fear I shared more than my body at the point he looked into my eyes and saw my soul unhidden. Did Jem give me a glimpse of his too?

"I don't do all the post-sex loved-up bullshit, by the way," he says, winding a finger through my hair.

I smile; this is the Jem I expected. "I don't want you to lie to me. That's fine."

"Yeah, mind-melting orgasms I can do, sweet nothings, not so much."

"It's okay; you don't need to apologise."

"I'm not apologising. I'm stating a fact." He rubs his nose against mine. "Give me a few minutes and you can have something better than sweet nothings."

"A few minutes?" I say doubtfully.

"Oh, you bet. There is so much more I want to do with you."

Jem drags the duvet up so the soft cotton covers our bodies and our hearts slow together, to a shared rhythm. Sometimes words chosen contradict the reality. In this space, with this man, something is different. Whatever sparked between us, and was denied for weeks, has been kindled into something that burns stronger than I think either of us will be able to control.

25

Jem

Ruby's light shines through the broken glass of my world creating rainbows and filling my life with colour. What worries me is rainbows are illusions and when the darkness returns they disappear.

We're closer but the barriers are still there; me and Ruby don't talk about emotions or share ourselves outside of the physical intimacy. Not that we're hiding who we are in public, there's no way I can avoid touching Ruby's skin or stealing a kiss if I need a kick-start from the darkness.

A week passed since she gave herself to and trusted me, believed I had no expectations. We joke about the fact we've dealt with this and have moved on; but Ruby spends the next two days in and out of my bed. I tell myself it's the sex without drugs that makes the experience different with Ruby; the physical intensity of every sense operating at full capacity is the drug itself. Gradually, I realise I'm lying to myself. It's Ruby who makes it different.

I crave her more than anything in my life before, her presence a blinding light pouring into the shadows I'm surrounded by. I need her to stay, to never take her radiance away or leave me lost in the dark again.

But I can't fall in love with Ruby.

I don't love.

We return to everyday life, back to the studio and moving Ruby's life in the direction she spoke about: forward. The first time I slid an arm around Ruby's waist and kissed her cheek, the horror on Jax's face was unmistakable. I don't care what he says; Jax wants Ruby. They share a bond through the band and the music they create together. Ruby's adamant she's never seen Jax in a romantic way, but I know he does. Jax spoke to her about us the first day, throwing glances at me as he had a heated conversation with her in the sound booth.

From the look of her hand gestures, Ruby gave him a mouthful of unpleasant words.

The Ruby who lives in my house, who exists in my space, is a milder version of her public persona. I get that; I've done the same for years. As soon as you show people the slightest hint of vulnerability they poke until a hole opens up that lets out more than you want, and in turn lets in too much. Only because Ruby has vulnerabilities of her own can I let my guard down a little. Our unspoken agreement not to push each other into revealing any more of our hidden thoughts works. For now.

Inevitably, I fuck this up.

Since returning from the States, I lost myself in Ruby Riot and then Ruby. I forgot loose arrangements made. I missed a meeting with a pissed-off Liam and didn't notice today's date until it arrived. And until Kristie arrived.

I'm in bed and Ruby answers the front door. A few minutes later, Ruby comes into the room with pink cheeks. She's dressed in my t-shirt, always pulls one off the floor the morning after a night in my bed, and walks around in the shirt and her panties for half the day, which is bloody distracting.

"You have a visitor," she says coolly.

"Bryn?"

"Kristie."

I sit and pull back hair from my face. "Crap. Okay. I'd forgotten she was coming."

Ruby stares wide-eyed for a moment, then her face straightens into her neutral, closed-down expression. "I told her you would be down in a minute."

"'kay."

Shit.

Kristie Dawson is a friend from years back. She's older than me, widow of Sam Rayne, the front man of Easy Ride, who was as big as Phoenix in the '90s. Kristie has her own band, proving she had talent after accusations she only got a recording contract because she was riding the coat tails of her husband. When I was in LA last month, we hooked up as we always do. I completely forgot I arranged to meet Kristie when she came to London. She's over for a media tour promoting an art house movie she's in, playing someone who's basically herself. We share a drug-filled past and were fuck buddies before the phrase even existed.

Kristie is in the kitchen, sitting on the counter, when I get downstairs. Her platinum blonde hair is bobbed but styled to look like she just got out of bed. She favours the same style of make-up as Ruby and still wears the '90s bohemian mix of skirts and tatty jackets she always has. Although Kristie is ten years older than me (I suspect more) she's smoothed some of her drug-damage with plastic surgery.

"I'm sorry, Kristie," I say from the doorway. "I forgot we were meeting up."

"Hey, no problem!" She walks over and places a hand on my cheek, her strong perfume reminding me of sex with this woman. "I'm good for a few hours. We can go for lunch? Is that little cafe still open? Loved the fries there!"

"Yeah, I guess." I rub my tired eyes. "You should've called."

Kristie laughs and pokes my ribs. "Because of the chick? She'll know the score if she's screwing Jem Jones."

I cringe at Ruby being seen in that light. "She's cool." *I hope.*

"Shame, I was hoping you'd be alone," says Kristie and runs a finger along the skin above my open shirt. "We always catch up when we're in the same city, huh?"

As she moves to press herself against me, I turn to pull out coffee beans. "Make some coffee while I shower," I tell her.

"Me?"

"You do know how to make coffee?"

"Yeah, babe, but I don't normally make it for other people."

"Fine."

Kristie slides a hand in mine. "But, I guess you're not other people."

With a small smile, I tug my hand away and head back upstairs. Here's a new emotion I haven't had for a while. Guilt. But why guilt? I hooked up with Kristie last month but I hadn't kissed Ruby at that point, she was just a girl in my daydreams. But in my experience, chicks don't react well to other girls turning up at my house. Especially, when they've both been in my bed.

When I return to the bedroom, Ruby's cross-legged on my bed and engrossed in my iPad. She glances at me as I come into the room then returns to what she's doing.

"I know her," she says. "I should've guessed you guys would be friends."

"Yeah."

Why isn't she mad? I attempt to read her expression but we both know how good each other are at hiding.

"She said you'd arranged to meet up with her. You going out today then?" asks Ruby.

"If that's okay."

She arches and eyebrow. "Seriously, you're not asking for my permission, are you, Jem Jones?"

Now I'm a bit lost. Good, she's not being pissy and accusing me of sleeping with another woman and all the drama that entails, but not good if she doesn't give a shit whether I do or not. Plus, I've noticed she uses my full name if she's trying to distance herself by making me Jem Jones instead of her Jem.

Her Jem?

"I haven't seen Kristie since I came back from LA."

"You don't need to justify yourself." She scrolls through the iPad, not looking up. "I'm sure I'll be able to entertain myself."

"Just lunch."

Ruby shrugs, focused on the screen. Confused as hell, I head for the shower.

There is no reason for me to get upset about this. We never discussed exclusivity. I was dumb enough to think it was implied.

Tell that to the blotchy faced, teary girl in the mirror.

Did I honestly think Jem Jones would treat me any differently? That the guy who cares about nothing would care about me? Yes. Because he treats me as if I'm important. Hell, Jem even told me I was. Now I'm convinced I've spent the last week projecting the fantasy over the reality.

Well, then it's time I stepped back to that reality and away from the weird world I've ensconced myself in with Jem.

Jem returns early afternoon. I hear the heavy front door and his familiar footsteps as I'm packing up my things from the spare room I haven't slept in for days. One set of footsteps and no voices.

"Ruby?"

My hands shake as I pack a sweater into the rucksack, heart pushing into my mouth as Jem heads down the wooden hallway, approaching the room.

"What are you doing?" he asks.

Straightening, I take a deep breath, switch off, and turn to him. "I thought it was time I went home, back to the share house I mean."

Jem leans on the doorframe and crosses his arms, and all I picture is Kristie lying against him, his long fingers stroking her hair. I shift my look to his mouth, remembering his touch and kiss, and furious with myself for caring.

"I knew you were bothered," he says.

"Bothered? About what?" I pick more clothes from the bed.

"Seriously, Ruby? Don't give me that bullshit. About Kristie."

I straighten. "You went out for lunch with a friend. I presume she's some kind of fuck buddy, too. Why would I get annoyed about that? It's not as if..." *Shit*. I focus on packing.

His tone hardens. "As if what?"

"It's not as if we're a couple. I mean, a committed relationship, in love, type of couple. It's cool, Jem."

He continues to watch me silently, and the hidden, stupid teen Ruby Tuesday wills Jem to come over, hold her and declare his love. I refuse to look around and instead behave as if he left.

"No, I don't suppose we are," he says quietly and walks away.

Taking shaky breaths, I inhale and squeeze my eyes shut, head tightening with the attempt not to cry. I slipped into this. Jem didn't pull me. It's not his fault.

Bag packed, I head to the lounge to grab my keys and phone from the coffee table. Jem's watching TV, one arm across the back of the sofa as he flicks through the channels. He fills my life, and until this morning, it was as if nobody exists outside of us, but I know now he's not mine. This happening is good; I was falling back into something I wasn't ready for.

"I'll see you on Monday at the studio," I offer as I pick up my car keys.

Jem grunts. Oh, great, a male noise I recognise. An 'I'm not talking to you' grunt. What the hell did I do wrong here?

"Yes? Jem?"

"Yeah."

"Enjoy your weekend," I say brightly.

He turns to me, the expression on his face arresting. His eyes are darker, mouth pulled into a line I recognise from arguments we had early on. "Yeah, maybe I'll call my 'fuck buddy'."

I reel at his tone. "Whatever. Your life."

"Exactly." He returns to his clicking through TV channels.

"I'm not sure what I did wrong here, Jem."

"Nothing." He throws the controller onto the seat as a music channel appears.

"Okay, then. Bye."

My foot has barely left the bottom stair in the hallway before

Jem appears at the top of the stairs and calls my name. I turn back to him. "What?"

"I didn't screw her. I mean, I'm not going to. Not anymore."

"Please stop trying to justify yourself. I said it's cool."

"No, I want to tell you because if I did screw her, this would be over, right?"

I drop my bag. "Let me see. As an average person I think that my lover fucking another person may not be what I want."

Jem takes a step down. "So if I'm not, and you're my lover, what's the problem?"

"No problem."

"Then why are you leaving?" He walks down the rest of the steps. "I don't want you to go."

"It's probably time I left. Things are better now, Dan's under a restraining order and he hasn't tried to contact me. He's due in court soon, so I doubt he'll make things worse for himself. I don't need to hide here anymore."

"You're not hiding anymore, are you? You're here because you want to be. I want you around. No more surprise visitors, I promise."

I huff. "Jem, you are who you are. It's all good."

"No, it isn't if you're leaving. I said I don't want you to go."

"Why? Why do you want me around?"

Jem looks past me, the way he always does if I touch on things he doesn't want to talk about. *Fine.* I bend to pick up my bag and Jem snaps his attention back to me.

"Because everything's better with you here. I'm used to you being with me now." He closes his hand over mine. "In my space, in my bed. Everything."

"Used to me? That's not the most romantic..." *Oh, crap.*

Jem's eyes widen. "Romantic? You want romance?"

"No, I don't believe in romantic love. You know that."

"Hearts and flowers and teddy bears on cards are bullshit anyway. Stomach churning, breathlessness, and aching are closer to the truth," he says.

"Pain?"

"Yeah, love is painful."

"Then you're doing it wrong."

"I don't do it at all. I don't love."

"No, of course. And neither do I."

Touching on a subject we've never discussed is weird enough but the tension in the air between is stranger. In the small space, there's barely room for the two of us to stand and not touch, and I'm scared if I try to leave, he'll stop me. My legs wouldn't work anyway, my stupid self is still waiting for him to hold me in his arms and profess the love he's denying.

Jem takes my face in both hands and searches my eyes, the way he does when I'm sure he's trying to read my mind. "So why do I want you as much as I do?"

"I don't know."

"Is caring about you enough? Can we share enough of ourselves, but not so much we lose our grip on who we are?"

"Not all of ourselves?" I ask.

"Not everything."

"Jem, if we don't give all of ourselves, we can't commit. And if we can't commit, there's nothing to cement this. I think the problem is neither of us wants to have a relationship."

"Commit." He wrinkles his nose and drops his hands from my face. "I can commit to you that I won't touch another woman while you're in my life. Is that what you want?"

His definition of commitment is what I'd expect of him. Jem can give himself to me physically, but keep an important part hidden.

"What I want from you is something I'm not prepared to give you myself," I tell him.

"What do you want?"

"Your heart."

The expression that crosses Jem's face is wide-eyed shock, he turns away rubbing his neck. The link I felt to him snaps. "Shit, Ruby."

"That's the issue here."

Jem bumps his rear onto the bottom step. The light from the tiny window casts across the hallway, the dust in the sunbeams like stars in the sky. The silence tells me everything I need to know.

How could this ever work if we constantly push each other away? I can't have another relationship where I doubt my worth, where somebody takes but won't give. Realistically, I shouldn't get into a relationship at all.

"I didn't think I had a heart," he says, quietly. "But you found it and pushed life in. You already took my heart, Ruby."

My heart stutters at his unexpected words. "I didn't, Jem. I haven't tried to make you love me."

"I never said I love you. I said you've taken my heart." Jem's mumbling his admission to the floor, not me.

"Explain what you mean."

He shakes his head and looks up. "I'm a guy. I don't talk about this shit."

"Guess what? You're going to have to or I'm walking out of the door."

"I don't know what you want me to say!"

"I need you to explain what 'this' is. Then at least we both know and we can stop the second-guessing and confusion. Then we can decide what to do. *I* can decide what to do."

Jem taps the wooden step next to him, the sound echoing in the small space. He can't do this, refuses to do what we need to stop our merry-go-round of confusion. One tiny admission is all I'm getting, I guess.

I turn to the door.

"Ruby, I can't explain what I don't understand."

Turning back, I meet his hassled look. "I'll tell you what you make me feel and then if you recognise any of the symptoms, just let me know."

"Sure," he says with a small laugh. "Might help."

I've lain myself open to people before and ended up shredded to pieces, and the longer I leave it before I tell what's hidden, the harder I'll fall when I discover I'm alone in my feelings. This time I'll admit everything and if Jem can't tell me what I need to hear in return, I can end this before my need for love sees me making shit decisions again.

I cross my arms. "Well, there's the stomach churning,

breathlessness, and chest-aching I have right now which I'm sure isn't the flu."

"Yep. That's what I was talking about before, but that's not a good thing."

"There's the constant desire to be close to you I've had for weeks."

"Right."

I inhale. How much am I risking by doing this? "There's the calm of being in your arms and feeling as if the rest of the world doesn't exist and doesn't need to." *Oh, God, I sound like a bad romance novel.*

Jem stares at his feet. "Yeah. That too. Okay."

"Help me out here, Jem. I'm opening up to you."

"There's an emptiness when you're not here." Jem looks up warily and I raise an expectant eyebrow. "Shit. Okay, there's the way time stands still when I'm away from you and passes too quickly when I'm with you."

"Yes?"

He stands. "I can't do this."

"I didn't think you could; it's okay." I say and smile through the lie.

"No, it's not okay. Shit." Jem rubs his temples and closes his eyes. As he releases the breath, something else comes too and he closes the gap between us. Jem strokes my cheek with the back of his hand, the touch soothing the hollow ache that was beginning. "One smile, one look, and one touch from you blasts my world so full of colour it fucking blinds me."

Only Jem could use the word fuck in an explanation of his feelings... He circles an arm around my waist and grips my back, holding me to him so I can't move. This is safe. I can tell him. Tentatively I put my arms around his neck; if I touch him, I can say this.

"What hurts is, being with you is the most natural place in the world, and I'm frightened one day you'll push me out. Like today, her..."

Jem nudges my cheek, winding his fingers into my hair. "No, not her. She means nothing and never has. I'm not interested in anyone else because I have a gut wrenching fear of my own. If I lose you, I'll lose a part of myself I recently found."

I loosen his hands. "No, I'm not trying to take part of you."

"I mean you match me, a reflection of my past come back to show me who I can be again. I get you. You get me."

This. Why can't these words have been spoken before? "You make me feel it's okay to be me, not who you want me to be," I whisper.

"Never be anything but yourself, because that person means a hell of a lot to me." Jem cups my cheek in his hand and kisses me; his lips barely touch mine, but push away any remaining inclination I have to walk out of the door. "Don't leave. Please."

"So what is this?" I ask.

"I don't know what this is, but it's ours."

"I guess everything else about us is different to normal."

"Ruby, I'm crap with words and expressing myself, that's bloody obvious. But each time I touch you or kiss you, I'm telling you everything we just said." Jem runs his fingertips across my skin, tracing the heart-shaped tattoo on my chest. "I'm telling you, you have my heart."

"Jem, that's getting close to romantic. Next it will be flowers and teddy bears and texts with kisses."

"No way!" I laugh at his doubtful look. "But you're staying, right? I said enough?"

"Yes."

"Thank fuck for that!"

Jem seizes me around the waist and lifts me; I wrap my legs around Jem's waist, take his face in both hands, and kiss him. Kiss Jem as if it's the first time and only time, desperate and hungry. This isn't the first or last, but he's finally my Jem. He tastes of the man who's turned my body from something used or beaten to something filled with an intense desire I'd never dreamt of. I'm rewound to those times – from Jem holding me when I needed support, to the intensity of sex when I craved us. This desire burns through, intensified by the words exchanged and the pull into our safe place again.

"I don't deserve this," Jem says.

"What?"

"You. I do so much wrong to people; I'm scared I'll hurt someone else again."

I rest my forehead on his. "Jem Jones, shut up and just fucking kiss me."

He nips my bottom lip, and smiles against my mouth. "Ah, Ruby Tuesday, your mouth..."

No more words, enough have been exchanged today. If we carry on talking, I'll obsess about the words we can't use, at the place in our souls we can't allow anyone in. Jem's heart thumps against my chest at a speed to match mine, hearts marching in a new rhythm.

26

Ruby

Two weeks since our admission that our relationship is beyond friendship and sex, and life takes on a weird normality. Studio time finished, I return to my everyday job at the cafe and Jem fills his days too. I'm not a hundred percent sure what with. He mentions meeting people, checking in with counsellors, or catching up with Bryn or Liam occasionally; but even though he's going out more than he did, most of the time he stays in the house. I expected Jem to be more sociable, but after years of being overwhelmed by the outside world, I can understand why he prefers to hide for a while.

I'm living with Jem on a semi-permanent basis now; we've discussed this as a 'see how we go'. I'm wary, but a larger part of me knows this is where I should be right now.

For a few days, Jem insists on taking me to and from work until I assure him I feel safe. Since Dan was arrested, he hasn't contacted me. Maybe now someone outside of us knows, Dan realises he has to be careful; perhaps a lawyer has got through to him. I don't know. Jem's doubtful about letting me go alone, but knows my opinions on him trying to take care of me. After an argument about how he's trying to control me, Jem backs off. He doesn't always back off, and as we're both prone to moodiness, and because Jem is used to getting his own way in everything he does, we clash. Sometimes it's snide remarks; occasionally, it's arguments followed by sulking, but always ending up in bed working things out when words fail. This is how we'll always be together, because neither of us is likely to drop back on our personalities for another person.

Exhausted after a double shift, I go home to Jem's and flop on his sofa. Despite being in a busy suburb, I marvel at how quiet it can be here, even when the rush hour traffic passes outside. Jem's house is set back from the street, bordered by trees for privacy. Kicking my shoes off, I rest my feet on the coffee table and my head on the cushions, soaking up the peace.

Footsteps descend the stairs and I open an eye as Jem walks into the room. I tip my head back and he bends to kiss my lips as he stands behind the sofa.

"Hard day at work, darling?" he says.

"Terrible. Pass me my newspaper and slippers."

We both smirk at our daily joke and he moves around to sit next to me.

"Done much today, Jem Jones?"

"Yeah, I have actually," he replies and flicks my ear. "I've been listening to the Ruby Riot tracks and chatting to the sound guy about cleaning some of it up. I don't think they're quite there."

"Cool. Can we hear yet?" I twist around on the sofa and lay my head in Jem's lap, looking up at him. He strokes my cheek with his rough fingertips and I close my eyes. Something soothes whenever I'm with this man; and in a quiet moment, when we're both calm, the space we're in holds us together and happy.

"Patience, you will." Jem strokes my hair. "I reckon the tracks will be done by the time we get back."

"Back from where?"

"I want to go away. Take you somewhere for a weekend."

"I'm working this weekend and I can't take any more time off."

"Well, whenever you're not working for a couple of days. You can't work seven days a week."

"Where?"

"Dunno. Where do you want to go?"

My mind blanks. I've never left the UK. I longed to go to the States once-over and I know Jem has places over there; but what if there's a collection of Kristies ready to jump out of the closet?

"I think you have more idea of the world than I do."

"Do you like beaches? Cities? Countryside?"

"I wouldn't know. I don't go on holiday."

"No?"

"No." I chew my thumbnail. "I don't think I'd like the beach. And I don't want to go anywhere people will follow us around because they're starting to."

Jem huffs and twirls some of my hair around his hand. "Well, you are Jem Jones's girlfriend."

I can't help the little surge of butterflies in my stomach on the rare occasions he calls me that. "Yeah, I told you not to hold my hand in public, you old romantic."

"Shut up," he warns and pokes me in the side. "So that's a yes, you'll come somewhere?"

"Yeah. Somewhere quiet."

"All my places are in cities," he says half to himself.

"All? How many have you got. No, don't answer that question."

"They're mostly apartments anyway. I'm not big into entertaining so if it's small, no pressure to have parties. Dylan's is the party house." He pauses. "Was the party house."

"You know where I'd really like to go? Somewhere in the middle of nowhere with absolutely nobody, anywhere nearby."

"Okay. Do you know where I'd really like to go?"

"Where?"

"Wherever you are."

27

The sun sets in the Spanish sky, streaking a burning gold and red across the wide sky above the orange groves. I sit on the cushioned chair outside the old farmhouse; legs tucked under, as I drink freshly squeezed juice from the oranges I picked earlier. Jem appears from inside and perches next to me in a world away from the London we left yesterday.

"You're right about quiet. I can literally only hear crickets," he says.

"Not your thing?" I ask, hoping he's not going to hate every minute.

"Not what I said." Jem wraps an arm around my waist, our skin sticky in the evening warmth as we cuddle up. "This would never have been my choice in the past. I think I avoided places like this before because when it's quiet the thoughts sneak in."

"Really? I'm the opposite. When it's quiet my mind can be quiet too."

"I've spent a lot more time alone recently, so I'm getting used to it." He catches my look. "I mean away from the music world alone. You don't count."

"Sheesh. Thanks!"

"You know what I mean!" Jem hugs me to him and kisses the top of my head. "You count for more than you know."

When Jem told me he'd found a place to stay for a few days, he wouldn't tell me where. We flew to Barcelona and picked up a car before arriving a couple of hours later at the small estate in the Catalonia countryside. The huge building is expensively renovated with numerous bedrooms and luxuries I doubt the original owners had - swimming pool, terraced gardens, and even a tennis court.

Not the normal holiday destination of Jem Jones.

The house belongs to Steve and he brings his family here every summer. The rooms show evidence of children - shelves of books, kids' DVDs, and bikes in the converted barn adjacent to the house.

Jem and me take a downstairs bedroom with doors that open out onto a private terrace, overlooking the pool; and as I acclimatise to the surreal world I'm pushed into, and after weeks of stress and fear, the calm takes hold instead.

This is our second day lost in a place out of time. We've spent days together in Jem's London house, wrapped up away from the outside world, but this is a step further removed. The drive to the nearest village is twenty minutes but the small Spanish settlement only has a couple of shops and a bar. Real civilisation is several hours away.

"Here is so weird after London," I say.

"Life has taken on a lot of weird the last few months. There's you..."

"Weird?" I interrupt with a laugh. "The pot calling the kettle black much?"

"No! Everything. Being sober, no Blue Phoenix, meeting a crazy girl who stole my heart. Shit, I doubt life could be any more opposite than a year ago."

"Don't, Jem." I squeeze his hand.

"I hardly remember a year ago, but I do remember things were going downhill for everyone in the band; and in the middle of it all, I was lashing out in every direction, hurting people."

I softly place my lips on his. "Haven't you read my tattoo recently? Yesterday's gone. It doesn't matter anymore."

"Hmm... maybe I should take a look to remind myself?" Jem's eyes glint in the fading light as he slides a hand beneath my loose t-shirt.

I'm bra-less and he closes his hand over my breast, gently rubbing my nipple. I shift; whenever he touches me, it's as if Jem has a magic ability to trigger a hardwired need for more. As he slides his other hand teasingly across my skin, the spreading desire for him shifts downwards. The knowing smile he gives shows how aware he is of the effect he has with barely a touch.

"Plus, I don't think it's appropriate for you to wear t-shirts with other band names on them." He pushes the t-shirt upwards. "I feel as if you're cheating on me with Queens of the Stone Age."

I giggle at him as he pulls the black t-shirt over my head and dumps it on the floor next to us, then digs his fingers into the back of my hair, and pulls my face to his. I move my head back. "Go and grab me a Blue Phoenix shirt, then."

"If you want to be covered by something Blue Phoenix, I can do that job," he whispers.

Jem runs his tongue slowly along my bottom lip. My lips part in anticipation of one of Jem's kisses that empty my mind of anything but us. The communication of his kiss fills the gaps of what he refuses to say - what we both refuse to admit - that we belong together as much as any other couple, other couples who spend their days telling the world they're in love. We gradually piece together our shattered pieces; the kisses and touches, the times in bed melding our bodies is the glue that holds us together. We're still fragile and the mended parts could easily come apart again but every day the bond strengthens.

Sometimes the gentle isn't enough and Jem's awareness of my past means he holds back until I make it clear I don't want him to. I hold his head, our mouths moving together. He tastes of the sweetness of orange juice, and of Jem.

Jem pulls his t-shirt off too and lifts me onto his lap, his eyes level with the inked words. He runs a finger along the tattoo on my side, and up to the quote beneath my right breast. "Oh, you're right. I remember now." He circles my nipple with his tongue.

I grip his hair, and he runs his hand over my bare legs, squeezing my ass in both hands. "You drive me fucking mad the way you do that." He pulls away and looks up at me. "Always wearing just t-shirts and nothing but panties. I deserve a medal for the self-control I have every time you walk past me."

Holding his face, I kiss his cheeks across to his ear. "I know." I nip his earlobe.

He inhales sharply. "Why do you do it?"

"Because I feel comfortable around you, and it's comfy for me."

Jem holds my hips firmly and pushes against me, his arousal pressing between his jeans and my lace panties. "Quite often it's not very comfortable for me."

I smirk and wriggle against him a little more so he groans. "Sorry."

"Ruby..." he warns.

"Yes?"

"You know how you said this morning I didn't have to be so cautious about what I did to you?"

I run my fingers lightly up and down Jem's back, pushing myself closer so his mouth almost touches my breast. "I did."

"If you don't stop teasing me, I'm not going to be cautious." Jem presses his hot mouth to my skin.

I love the hoarseness of Jem's voice, the way he looks at me when I'm turning him on. The feel of his hard-on against me, his heat, touch, kiss... everything Jem. What we have is real, an intense physical need for each other that pushes colour into our world.

"Okay, I'll stop. Pass my t-shirt." I swing my leg to climb off Jem but he grips my hips and holds me in place.

"Um. No."

I giggle and fight to climb off him, but he wraps his arms around my waist in a vice-like grip, mouth on my breasts. As he sucks on my nipple, I gasp and dig my nails into his back.

"You're not going anywhere," he says as he pulls away again.

"Really?" I run my fingers into his hair, holding his curls so he can't put his mouth back on me.

"Really." Jem stands and I hook my arms and legs around him, expecting Jem to take me back to the bedroom. Instead, he backs me against the wall of the house and presses against me.

The bricks scrape my back and I wince. "Ow! Jem... That hurts; you're not doing this here."

Jem doesn't reply and glances around, his hold on me firm. The remnants of our meal rest on the smooth marble table nearby, plates and glasses, a half empty bowl of salad. Jem strides over, and one arm around my waist, he pushes everything to one side and sets me on the table.

"Here." Before I can respond, Jem covers my body with his, eager mouth and hands harsher than usual as he pushes me backward against the hard surface. I gasp as he nips at my neck, runs his hands across my breasts, and rolls my nipples beneath his fingers, hands not leaving me for a second.

I'd protest about being outside, and so exposed in the fading sunlight, but Jem switches everything off but the need for more. He pulls my legs to the edge of the table and opens them; pressing against me, his jeans and my panties barriers I don't want. I make an involuntary sound in my throat and wrap a leg around his waist pulling him closer. In response, Jem slides his hand up the inner thigh of my other leg, parting them further.

"Fucking gorgeous," he says and runs a finger along my panties. I suck air through my teeth, the barrier too much. Jem silently agrees, hooks his fingers around the edge, and pulls them down, the black lace rough against my thigh as he does.

As I kick them off, I sit and quickly unbutton his jeans, pulling out his cock. I run my fingers along the hard length, circling my hand around the base. Jem groans, fingers finding my wet centre, and I cry out as he pushes one into me, then shoves me back onto the table, so I'm forced to let go of him. Gazing down, Jem slides his finger out and rubs along the seam of my sex, thumbing my clit. I squirm, at the intensity of the touch and discomfort at Jem seeing me so clearly, so exposed.

"You look..." Jem swallows and reaches into the back pocket of his jeans, pulling out a condom.

As he opens the foil, I watch as he slides the condom on. Before I decide whether to help, he's done; the thick tip of his cock already against my sensitive flesh. Jem watches as he slides himself along me, breath ragged.

I sink back, head against the cool marble and look up at the emerging stars, the ones in the sky and my mind, my chest tightening as my breath shortens too.

"I want to go slow, but I fucking can't." Jem's voice is hoarser and he places a hand on the table next to me, leaning down to kiss my face.

"It's..." I barely get the words out and Jem plunges into me, hard and fast, stretching, and filling me. There's more friction than usual, I'm turned on; but without as much attention from Jem, I'm not as aroused as usual. "Fuck!"

"You okay?" He stills.

"Yes!" I push my hips against him. "Don't stop."

Jem moves back and places his hand on my stomach, then pulls out, sliding in again teasingly slow. "This looks so hot," he says, breathlessly, unable to look away from where we meet.

I shift and grip Jem with my legs, partly because I want him to stop staring at me, but also because the tighter they wrap around him, the more intense the sensation. Jem pulls my leg up, thrusting hard and pushing against the spot that guarantees me a place in the stars. I moan and Jem takes this as his green light, pounding into me hard and fast, propelling me to the magic place and tearing away any remaining shyness about being screwed in the open air by Jem. I can't hold back the groans I normally try to, and I get louder as the tingling spreads through me, pushing me closer to the building orgasm.

Jem stops.

"Don't do this again!" I complain, propping myself up on one elbow to give him a filthy look.

Jem grins then puts his thumb in his mouth, wetting the tip, not speaking. As soon as he touches my sensitive clit, I don't care that he's stopped. His thumb jolts the hardwiring that sparks into every nerve ending. He slowly thrusts into me again, smug smile on his face.

I gaze at Jem as he watches what he's doing, mouth parted. He responds to each sound I make, joining me with noises of appreciation as he carefully moves in and out. This is torture, I attempt to cling him to me again, but he pushes down against my thigh. "Come for me, Ruby," he says, hooded eyes on mine. He licks his thumb, making a noise of pleasure before rubbing me again.

The sensation blinds, taking me by surprise and I shout out his name. Immediately, Jem removes his hand and grips my ass, thrusting into me harder and faster as I climax around him, pleasure pulsing through as my tight grip on him intensifies with each push. Jem's fingers dig harder into my skin, breathing heavier as he swears repeatedly under his breath; eyes closed until he pushes himself to the hilt one last time and let's go a shout of his own.

Jem sinks onto me, kissing my mouth hard, before switching to soft kisses as he strokes damp hair from my face.

He bumps his nose against mine. "And that, Ruby Tuesday, is why you don't tease me."

The position is awkward but we lie together for a moment, caught in the afterglow as our sticky skin cools in the breeze. Never in my life have I trusted someone so completely with my body as I do Jem. Now all I need to do is trust him with my heart.

I busy myself cutting up fresh watermelon and strawberries and add to the bowl of breakfast fruit salad before setting it on the large wooden table. Jem watches me running a tongue along his teeth.

"Didn't you listen to me last night?" he asks.

"Which bit?"

"You're in a t-shirt and panties again."

"No, this is a bikini." I lift up my t-shirt to show him the plain black two-piece.

"Huh. I never thought I'd see you in a bikini."

"Never thought or don't want to? How else am I supposed to swim in the pool?" *Do I look that weird?*

"The sexy as fuck thing is still happening, don't worry about that." He runs an appreciative gaze along my almost naked body. "So, you can swim?"

I throw watermelon peel at his head. "Cheeky! Yeah, we had to learn at school in a bloody freezing pool."

"I couldn't swim until a few years ago."

"Really?" I sit opposite and pour the coffee.

"Nobody ever taught me." He focuses on the coffee pouring into his cup. "And I was umm... away from school for swimming lessons. Or too sick to swim."

Setting the pot down, I'm aware of the harder tone, the one Jem uses when he gets lost in his past. "Too sick or too many bruises?"

He looks up sharply. "How can you know that?"

"I'm guessing. You said something about shit parents when I told you about my past. Did your mum..."

"No!" He clears his throat. "Not her. The dickhead she lived with. The one she left with."

My throat tightens and I drink the coffee, attempting to moisten my mouth. Wasn't I the one saying yesterday doesn't matter? "Sorry. I shouldn't have brought this up."

Jem sits back in his chair and pulls his long curls away from his face. "Don't be. I always promised I'd tell you after you explained about Dan, but you've probably guessed most of it."

"Abusive childhood." I reach out and place a hand over Jem's, rubbing the back.

"Oh, yeah, temporarily from mum's procession of boyfriends who came and went. Not mum though, I guess people have to be around to abuse you and I was on my own a lot. Eventually my mum fucked off for good with her boyfriend and that was it. Just me on my own."

"How old were you when she left you?"

"The last time, I was twelve."

I refuse to hide my disgust. "Your mum left you to live on your own when you were twelve? What the hell? What happened to you?"

"I managed to keep it hidden for a few weeks; she left and came back all the time and I guess I was hoping that's what would happen. She didn't. They tried putting me in foster care, but I kept running away in case she came home and I wasn't there. When I was fourteen, I got pissed off with the constant merry-go-round and finally accepted Mum was gone for good. I agreed to stay with a family. They were okay, had a house full of foster kids nobody wanted, so I could blend in and avoid any attempt to fix me. I was never around much, spent most of my time at Dylan's or Liam's house. Then Blue Phoenix happened and I left St Davids."

I picture Jem as a little boy, hurting and alone. "She left you more than once?"

"All the time," he says, not looking at me. "I could never figure out what I did wrong, why she kept going."

"You didn't do anything wrong. She's the one in the wrong. You don't piss off and leave a little kid to look after himself."

Jem's disappearing, retreating into his mind as his shoulders stiffen. "As an eight year old, how else would I see it? I guess at least she used to come back to start off with."

"Fucking hell, Jem!" I half-shout. "Eight? Is that how old you were the first time she left you alone?"

And he's gone, staring at the table and mouth turned down by the memories he buries deep.

I push my chair back and cross to sit on his lap. Jem blinks in surprise and I pull his head against my chest, desperate to take away some of the pain surfacing. Somebody should have held him back then, told him this wasn't his fault, and loved him. No wonder Jem's so fucked up. He's spent years convincing himself he's unlovable. Shit, I went through those childlike rationalisations when my mum left, but my brother was there. Quinn held me through the tears, filling the emptiness with his love, and the gentle explanations that her behaviour wasn't my fault.

Jem had nobody.

Any words I have right now would never express the intense anger and despair adequately. If only I could go back to the twelve-year-old Jem and tell him it's not his fault. Jem wraps his arms around my waist and crushes me, resting his cheek against my side. I hold him, rubbing his back.

"If my own mother didn't think I was worth her time, who else would?" he says. "I lived with that thought until one day everybody wanted me. The whole fucking world loved me, but I was still empty. The past hung over me so I kept people at a distance by behaving like a selfish dickhead. It worked."

"You let me in," I whisper, the awareness what a massive thing this was for him hitting me fully for the first time.

"Mostly," he says. "Even though you have my heart, there's a part locked away that I can't give you, Ruby."

"I know." I brush my lips against his forehead. "You have all of mine though."

Jem releases my waist. "I don't think that's a good idea. I'll trash it; it's inevitable."

"No, it's not inevitable. Nothing in life is. I believe we're more than that; you know we are."

Jem sighs and looks up at me, face pale. I brush his curls from his eyes, willing him to see the truth. "I can never replace the love you lost as a kid, Jem, but I can love you now."

My heart thumps into my ears, at the fact I told him the one thing I swore not to. Jem's face remains inscrutable and our new world drifts away with each second of silence.

"Don't. I can't say the words you want to hear."

Tears prick at my eyes at Jem's admission and I climb from his knee. Jem watches me warily as I return to my seat and pick up a slice of melon. The reason my tears don't fall is because Jem didn't deny he loves me; he just has the truth locked away. How much time before I can unlock this? Will I ever be able to?

"Sorry," he says quietly, "you do know how important you are though? How much you mean to me?"

"I just dredged your mind of painful memories, a world where love didn't have a place. It's all good."

Subject closed, we finish eating. I can switch off too. I have as much practice. I'm not spoiling my peace and happiness of this place with Jem, or the calmness that surrounds us by obsessing on unspoken words.

We have a long path ahead. Time will tell if we can navigate it together or get pulled away by the control of the past.

28

*em*

Six weeks with Ruby.

Forty-two days of somebody living in my life and head, consuming my every day.

How do I feel about this?

Torn.

I live and breathe her; and I'm terrified this air supply to my emotions will be cut off, and I'll be suffocated by the vacuum again. Each day this worry lessens, but it's there.

Tonight, I watch Ruby on stage and she thrills me as ever. Jem Jones is lucky to have what he doesn't deserve - the love of this amazing, talented, sexy chick that the world is sitting up and taking notice of. Ruby Riot has done a couple of press interviews recently where Ruby refused to dress in anything suggested by PR for the photo shoot. She wore her striped leggings and baggy sleeveless top, and I smiled when I saw this was a Blue Phoenix t-shirt, faded grey with the sleeves roughly cut off. I hung around, let her vent the frustration over being told what to do for the shoot; but in her eyes, I saw the anxiety. My beautiful girl is out of her comfort zone, moving into a world that I'm going to guide her through.

The venues get bigger as word about Ruby Riot grows. They're not touring but gigging regularly, playing new tracks from our recording session. Steve agreed to sign them based on those tracks; a full album is scheduled for April after the tour with Blue Phoenix in January. I'm proud – and vindicated. This isn't because of my fantasies about the lead singer.

Ruby arrives offstage half an hour later, hair damp, and heat radiating from her skin. She's on the high she always is after performing, the one that twinges jealousy because I want to be up there again. I've nagged Dylan about starting rehearsals for the tour, but he's still on his own world tour with Sky. Liam and Bryn have agreed to start in November. Nearly two months.

"You okay?" she asks, sliding her arms around my waist.

I smooth a tendril from her forehead as we head to the Green Room. "Yeah. Some nights I'm jealous of you getting to do this."

"I bet you won't be saying that a month into a tour," she says. "Anyway, you're always welcome to play onstage with us."

I push through the door to the Green Room. "Sure, Jax would love me taking his place."

"Just a couple of tracks would be cool." Ruby kicks off her shoes then roots around in her bag and pulls out a fresh t-shirt. "He'd be okay with that."

I can't respond because Ruby unzips and steps out of her red dress. Does she still do this in front of the other guys?

"What?" She pushes her arms through the t-shirt.

I soak in the sight of her lace-covered tits and the tiny panties before the material of her t-shirt covers them. "I wish you wouldn't do that. It switches my brain off."

Happy memories of this morning skip into my mind and I go from wanting to chat about Ruby Riot to wanting to pin her to the wall and screw her hard. Ruby gives me a warning look.

"Come here." I beckon with my finger.

"No." She deliberately bites her lip coyly.

"Right. I'll come over there then." I take the couple of steps across the space between us and back her to the wall. Her breath rushes out but not from the force, but the reaction to my hand sliding around to that perfect ass. I play my fingers at the edge of her panties. "You know not to be alone in a room with Jem Jones, especially if you're stripping for him."

Ruby laughs and winds her fingers into my hair, holding her forehead against mine. "I like being alone in rooms with Jem Jones."

"Yeah, but you never know what he might do to you." She inhales sharply as my finger slips beneath the lace, toward the wet heat that'll be there for me. I taste the perspiration on her skin as I lick from her neck to her ear.

"He never wastes any time, does he?" She shifts and presses into my hand.

"Makes a change that I'm the groupie," I whisper.

Ruby thumps my chest with her palm. "Do you mind not mentioning groupies when you're about to screw me?"

"Am I?"

"Ruby, Ruby, Ruby!" calls a voice to the tune of the Kaiser Chief's song, followed by a knock. *Jax.*

"For fuck's sake..." I mutter and let go of her.

"Yeah?" she calls.

Jax continues to sing the song as he opens the door, then stops dead as he sees me. "Oh. Hey, Jem."

That bloody song. Jax sings it around Ruby a lot and I've yet to figure out whether he's attempting to communicate something. I'm aware that he's torn between not accepting her involvement with me and needing to hide this because of the role I have in his life.

Jax is shirtless, hair as damp as Ruby's, every bit the rock star he's morphing himself into. Ruby's t-shirt barely reaches her thighs and if he doesn't stop staring at her legs... Jax has his own chicks now; he can keep his eyes and mind off mine.

"Were you wanting the room?" I ask. "Got someone with you?"

"Nah. Not tonight, too tired. Besides, we're doing some celebrating with Ruby, aren't we?"

"No, we're not," warns Ruby.

"Why? What happened?" I ask.

Ruby shoves her discarded dress in her bag and pulls her jeans on. "I'm tired too. Let's go home, Jem."

Jax crosses his arms and pulls his brows together. "It's your birthday!"

"And we went through this last year; I don't do birthdays!"

Jax looks at me and waves hand at Ruby. "Tell her!"

Ruby focuses on the wall over my head.

"Tell her what? You can't make her celebrate her birthday."

"So you knew too?" he asks.

"No. But I don't like celebrating mine, so I understand."

"But it's your twenty-first!" protests Jax, ignoring me. "At least have a drink with the guys."

I recognise Ruby's stance, the tension beginning in her stiffening shoulders, and spreading toward her hardening mouth. I get the brunt of this enough to know when to calm things down. But it's her trembling hands as she puts her shoes on that worry me because I'm not entirely sure this is anger.

"Ruby doesn't want to do anything," I say. "Leave it."

"Jesus, Ruby!" snaps Jax.

"If you hadn't nagged me or mentioned my birthday I might've stayed, but you're stressing me. I'm going home." Ruby grabs her bag then pushes past him and he swivels his head to watch her go.

"But, Ruby..." Jax is rewarded with a one-finger salute given to him over her shoulder.

"How long have you known her?" I ask. "Long enough to understand Ruby doesn't operate on the same level as you. This is a situation connected to her past and you pushed it!"

"What, so she's like you? You understand each other?" he asks, voice laden with sarcasm.

"I understand the world is different shades and not black and white. Maybe when you grow up a bit, you will too." I pause. "And yeah, we understand each other."

Jax chews hard on his bottom lip, his silence telling.

"Spit it out," I say.

"Don't hurt Ruby."

"We're none of your business."

"She's my friend and I watched her moving from a bad place.

Then you came along. You helped, but now I think you're going to make things worse."

"I don't abuse her! Don't you fucking accuse me of being bad for Ruby."

Finally alone with me, he has the balls to say what he thinks. "I'm not going to fight with you, but think about where she came from. Don't fuck with Ruby's self-esteem by screwing her over and kicking her to one side."

"Watch who you're talking to, little boy," I growl.

"Hit a nerve, have I?"

"I suggest you stop now before this gets nasty."

Jax drops his aggression, eyes taking on a look of concern. "Ruby deserves to be loved. If you can't give her that, do you deserve hers?"

Before I can respond, he turns and walks away. For all his bravado and swagger, this guy has an intuition I wouldn't expect. He's naïve, his sheltered background protecting him from the bad in the world, but he understands chicks in the same way Bryn does. How do guys do that? Maybe he grew up in a house full of sisters like Bryn and got conditioned the same way. Yeah, I get Jax's worried about Ruby; but he has no place to interfere, and if he says anything again, I doubt I'll react as calmly.

The topic isn't mentioned on the way back to the house. Instead, Ruby chats about the gig, over analysing every track the band performed as she usually does.

"You guys rocked, as always," I tell her as we head into the kitchen.

And as always, my approval of her musically makes Ruby smile. She rewards me with a slow, soft kiss, wrapping her arms around my back, and gripping me close. I lift Ruby onto the kitchen counter and put a hand either side of her, shifting so her legs circle my waist.

"So, it's your birthday, Ruby Tuesday?"

"I don't like celebrating my birthday," she mutters. "All it does is remind me of loneliness. I rarely had friends to share birthdays with; and after mum left, my uncle and aunt forgot half the time anyway."

"Twenty-first, though."

"So?"

"I don't remember my twenty-first," I tell her. "I know it involved a shit load of alcohol and drugs, and more than a couple of girls."

Ruby scowls and drags both hands through my curls, and tugs my hair to shut me up. "The birthday subject is closed, Jem."

"I know why you don't celebrate, and I have to tell you the reason isn't true."

The grip on my hair tightens. "Really?"

"Yeah. Because if people want to celebrate your birthday, it's because you mean something to them. They want to make you feel special, and you don't believe you are."

"Thanks, Dr Freud." She shifts away from me and attempts to climb off the counter, but I grip her legs.

"I understand. I'm the same about my birthday for the exact same reason."

"Cool, well if you understand, drop it. Get me something to drink." She pokes me with her foot.

"But I'm going to buy you a cake tomorrow."

She drops her mouth open. "Piss off."

"And a present."

Her face darkens. "Don't you dare!"

"Tough. You're my girl; you're unbelievably important to me, and I want to let you know how special you are. Is that a problem?" Ruby won't meet my eyes so I twist her face to mine. "You tell me I avoid how I feel, so don't shoot down my attempts to show you."

Ruby's eyes soften as she recognises the truth in my words; how her attempt at hiding something has failed because of my choice not to disguise my own thoughts. I do understand. I'm telling the truth and I'd be furious if she said the same to me.

"When's your birthday?" she asks.

"November 13th"

Ruby pulls her phone out of her back pocket and swipes the screen. "I'll make a note."

Closing my fingers around Ruby's hand holding the phone, I place my mouth on hers and press myself closer. Ruby turns her head away and pulls her hand from my grip. "Nice try, Jem." Ruby nudges my chest with her knees, so I have to step back. She hops off the counter, focusing on the phone as she types, before tucking it back into her pocket.

"Done. Now you can kiss me," she says, a smile playing around the edge of her mouth.

"Kiss you? After you stripped in front of me earlier, I want to do more than kiss you!"

"Uh huh? Stripped?" Ruby slowly pulls her t-shirt over her head and curves her warm body against mine. I run my fingers across her velvet skin and grab her ass. When she wriggles out of her jeans and sits back on the bench, any thoughts about birthdays vanish as my head switches to the things I like to do most with Ruby.

29

"I am not going to one of your bullshit awards ceremonies," I inform Jem as I pull my boots on.

He laughs at me as I search around for my leather jacket. "Ruby Riot will be going to them one day, best get used to them."

"Screw that. I'm already over all the 'Jem Jones's girlfriend' crap and the insinuation I'm screwing you to get a recording contract."

The man who completes me sits on the bottom stair in his house, watching with increasing amusement. "Now, now, everyone in the industry knows that's bullshit; don't get all high and mighty."

"Plus, they don't like the foul-mouthed rock chick who throws things at them."

"I'll keep anything away from you that could be used as a projectile missile. I'm not paying off another photographer for minor head injuries from flying phones."

I switch tactics and pull an exaggerated pout. "Jem, please..."

"Nope. You're coming."

Sulkily, I stomp out of the house with Jem in tow, as we head to our favourite coffee haunt. The autumn sun hovers behind clouds and the chill of the air heralds winter. Winter. That means it's only a few months until the tour.

"Naw, c'mon, stop it." Jem slides a hand around my shoulder and kisses me fiercely on the head, his hair brushing my cheek. "I want the world to see us, to see the changed Jem Jones and the foul-mouthed rock chick who kicked his backside into line."

I humph but smile as he traces a heart shape across the back of my hand. We still won't say the words, as if what we have is greater than everyone else's lesser description. Ours is honest and open, scary but getting easier. Jem slides his hand into mine and squeezes, the simple gesture flooding calm over my growing anxiety. Two months ago, we took our lives, shook them up, and watched as the pieces settled into a crazy, mixed-up Jem and Ruby world. What other place could we live in?

"Fine, I'll go, but I don't think I fit in with the other Blue Phoenix girlfriends."

"Talk to Bryn's then."

"He doesn't have one, does he?"

"Exactly. So you won't be able to piss her off."

I smack his arm. "Ha fucking ha."

Jem neglected to tell me the awards ceremony is in Germany, which doubly pisses me off. Bad enough when English-speaking paparazzi mob me, now I don't understand what they're saying. They seem to understand the English swear words I throw at them though.

My sulking intensifies when a Blue Phoenix PR girl suggests I dress up, indicating I could get paid for kitting myself out in some up-and-coming designer's creation. I pretend to comply by accepting a dress, and then deliberately leave the expensive item on the bed in Jem's house. Hence, I'm sitting around a table, in the star-studded venue amongst the overdressed in my black dress covered in skulls and unicorns. Jem comments that at least I match his black shirt even if I do fail at looking like a normal person. I stomp on his foot with the heel of my matching green and black shoes.

"No, look, I put a sparkly clip in my hair," I say as he pours me a glass of water.

"Right. A sparkly skull shaped clip."

Jem in a suit amuses me, the PR girl's magic works better on him. I'm not into men in suits, but I can look forward to removing his designer clothes later. He's already dispensed with the jacket and hung it over the back of the dining chair. Yes, I'm definitely unbuttoning his shirt and getting my hands on the taut muscles barely hidden by the cut of his shirt as soon as I can. Jem spots my scrutiny and arches an eyebrow. When I smile, he bends closer and kisses my cheek. I run a hand along his arm, hoping his stressed aura over the last few days is about coming to the ceremonies he dislikes, and nothing to do with us.

A woman – an actress I vaguely recognise - sashays past our table. Perfectly primped in a sparkling silver designer dress I can only describe as unique, her disdain for me is obvious. I lift my glass in a toast and she looks away.

Liam and his fiancée, Cerys, sit across the white-clothed table. I haven't seen them since they came to a Ruby Riot gig a few months back, and they're a nausea-inducing, lovey-dovey, holding hands under the table couple. Cerys has also foregone the designer clothes trap, opting for a simple black dress and an inexpensive-looking necklace with a heart-shaped pendant. Liam's arm is across Cerys's shoulders, as he rubs her neck with his thumb. She's what I'd call down-to-earth; and not the kind of girl I'd imagine falling in love with a longhaired rocker. But what do I know? Nothing about these people, Jem barely discusses them.

Despite the fact Jem forced me to come to this, his stiffened shoulders and fingers tapping on the table reinforces he doesn't want to be here either. Why make us come?

"You okay?" I ask.

"Yeah. You having a drink?"

I shake my head. "How many times? I don't drink around

you, Jem."

"Everyone else is, it doesn't bother me," he says tersely.

"Water's fine." I pick up my glass and drink to reinforce the point.

Dylan appears with Sky who looks as happy about being here as I am. The venue is filled to the brim with star power; musicians from all genres rub shoulders, and in some cases, clash egos. Jem always has an energy humming around that sets him apart from others, and Dylan shares that. More eyes follow Dylan than anyone else I've seen arrive today. Perhaps his natural comfort in his own skin, an assured poise, is what eclipses Jem slightly. Not to me, but to those around.

Sky grips his hand, dressed in a short blue dress that matches her eyes, hair loose and curling to her shoulders. She wears little make-up, doesn't need to. Dylan rubs a hand along her arm and whispers something that breaks her look of concern into a smile. They sit and he takes her hand.

I've not met either Sky or Dylan before, and he scrutinises me before glancing at Jem.

Jem shifts in his seat. "This is Ruby," he says with a half-hearted hand gesture. His under-enthusiasm prickles.

"I know," says Dylan. "Hey, Ruby."

"Hello."

"Did you want a drink?" Dylan asks, taking the champagne from the ice bucket.

"No. Thanks."

"Sky?" Dylan hovers the bottle over her glass

Sky places her hand over the top of the flute glass. "No, I'm not feeling well."

"Still?" Dylan's face creases with concern.

"I'll be okay, feeling sick, just gastro I think, but coming here doesn't help," she mutters and picks up the water jug to pour herself a glass.

"Yeah, I'm with you on that one," I say.

"I can imagine. Nice to finally meet you." Sky gives me a small smile before turning to Cerys. My stomach sinks, my reputation obviously precedes me because, despite her words, something in her expression is distrust. Of course, any chick with Jem is going to be far too obnoxious to join their gang. *Like I give a shit.*

I jump as Jem squeezes my knee under the table. "You okay?" he whispers and when he closes his warm hand around mine, I place the other on top. Who cares what they think?

Liam and Dylan chat, too. Are they deliberately ignoring us? I know Jem's usually pretty closed off from people, but they could involve him. Perspiration begins along my back. Is it me? Do they not approve of Jem being with me?

Fortunately, Bryn appears and distracts everyone. He looks as pissed off as I feel. A girl is with him and the rest of the group switches their attention to her. She's as skinny as me, and taller with dark brown hair shining in the light like she's stepped out of a shampoo commercial. Maybe she has, she looks model material. This girl is perfectly made-up; and I don't know much about dresses, but what she's wearing looks like the kind you see reported in magazines when awards night chicks have their clothing rated out of ten. I'm fairly sure I can guess my score; the looks I was given as we paused for the inevitable pictures when we arrived said it all. As the girl approaches, I try to gauge her age. Teenage? Older? Her layers of make-up make my thick kohl and bright red lips look minimal.

Bryn sits, ignoring her.

"Who's your new friend?" asks Jem.

Bryn gestures at the girl who perches on the seat next to him. "Mia. Mia this is... well, the guys."

Mia smiles broadly. "Hey, everyone! How awesome is this?"

Young...

Mia's oblivious to the surprised looks the other table occupants are giving Bryn and her. Bryn pours himself a drink and slumps back. Interesting date if they're not talking.

"Can I take pictures?" she asks Bryn.

Bryn snaps his head around. "Pictures of what?"

"You guys. Everyone." She leans in. "Kelly Holland is at the table behind. If I take a selfie, then she'll be in the picture too." Mia giggles.

I don't know Bryn well, but I thought I knew him well enough never to pin him as a guy interested in someone like Mia. Her fingers and neck are covered in expensive jewellery and the red dress is one I'd label 'barely decent'. I hazard a guess at spoilt, rich girl.

"Do what you like, but don't piss anyone off," mutters Bryn.

Mia kisses his cheek. "You're so awesome!"

As Bryn shakes his hair from his face and rubs his cheek. Jem laughs. "Don't worry, Ruby will have the pissing people off part covered.

"Yeah, I'm just awesome too," I say snidely.

Mia purses her lips for a moment then tips her head at Jem. "Bryn told me about you guys, so cute that Jem Jones finally fell in love."

Jem chokes on his water before turning a sour face to Bryn's companion. "I don't fall in love, sweetheart."

"Oh, okay, well, you guys are so cute together. Ruby and Jem. Precious. Gems? Rubies? Get it?" She smiles at her obvious joke.

So cute. Awesome. How old is she? But all I can hear is Jem's words about not falling in love. I thought we were over this; that we had what he termed our own version of love. We have mismatched ideas still it appears. This doesn't help the insecurity caused by his recent whispered phone calls, which he claims are from the guys we're sitting with now.

"Sorry," says Bryn, "she has no internal filter. She's a bit of a pain in the ass."

"You love me really," says Mia and pinches his cheek.

By this point, Liam and Dylan have joined in the stunned, silent staring at Bryn and Mia. If the Phoenix guys have no idea who she is then the media will get a story that happily pushes me off the radar.

"Quit it, Mia," says Bryn.

Pulling her hair over a shoulder, Mia picks up a glass of champagne and surreptitiously looks around at the other guests as she drinks, mouth open goldfish-style between sips.

"Where do you know Bryn from?" asks Sky. "I didn't know he'd started dating." Dylan digs her in the ribs. "What? I'm only asking what everyone else is thinking."

Mia sips her champagne. "Oh, we're not dating. Not yet anyway." Bryn crosses his arms. "He's keeping an eye on me."

"Ah, Bryn, the Babysitter!" says Jem.

"Piss off," he replies. "Do you seriously think an eighteen year old princess is my type?"

"Princess?" says Dylan.

"Eighteen?" splutters Jem.

"Not a real princess, jeez. You know what I mean, look at her!"

I cringe for Mia who appears to think the insult is hilarious. Is she stupid?

"He's always so rude to me," she says, "but I know he loves me really, otherwise why would I be here?"

"You just said why! I'm keeping an eye on you," snaps Bryn.

"Keep telling yourself that," she says with a smirk then catches the looks from Jem and Liam. "Oh, I'm winding him up! He's used to it."

"Weird," mutters Jem too loudly, echoing what I'm sure are the thoughts of those around.

Following an excruciating evening of back-slapping amongst the music industry darlings and the fact only the obvious people win awards, including Blue Phoenix, and Jem decides we should go to the after party. I protest again; but Jem says there's people he wants to chat to.

In the semi-darkened function room filled with the A Listers, I sit with the band on a plush sofa and stare at the contents of the low metal table in front of me. I give up on the water and start on the champagne. I don't normally drink wine; but it's closest and flowing the most. Jem disappears and I sit awkwardly with Liam and Cerys. Sky and Dylan have the right idea; they don't hang around and leave straight after the ceremony. Skulking in the darkened corner, I'm not interesting to anyone around so I wait for Jem to return. This is a side of Jem's life I've not seen before and hope it's not one he indulges in too often. I wish the Ruby Riot boys had been invited too.

"Jem hates these too, but he wanted the press to see him

sober," Liam remarks as if reading my mind. "And calm; he's calm when you're around which is why he wanted you here."

Calm? They haven't heard us when we disagree over something. Hell, sometimes one wrong word, and we don't talk for half a day. Jem's been edgier over the last week too and my fear that our three months of Jem and Ruby's happy place is on the wane increases.

"He said that?"

"In not so many words."

Cerys reappears from the Ladies and tugs Liam's arm. "I'm tired, can we go yet?"

"Having as much fun as me?" I ask, twisting my glass in my hand.

"It's overwhelming," replies Cerys. "But I guess you'll get used to it once you're up there getting the awards."

I smile at her taking time to talk to me. "Yeah. Maybe."

"Oh, you will," says Liam, "otherwise Jem's going to kick some ass until you get recognised."

If Jem doesn't come back soon, he's going to be the one getting his ass kicked.

Once Liam and Cerys go, I decide it's time me and Jem left, too. If this was a normal party, I'd keep going but this fakery... no thanks.

Unable to find Jem in this room, I head to the hallway outside, past the bouncers. I hope they take a good look and allow me back in because they already stare as if I crashed the place.

Kristie heads down the hotel hallway toward me, her assets spilling out of her tight white dress, unsteady on her sky-high heels. She pauses when she reaches me, attempting to focus on my face.

"You looking for Jem?" she asks.

"Hi, Kristie. How are you?"

"Pretty good." She rubs the pink lipstick at the corner of her mouth with a finger. "He's back there. I just finished with him."

However hard I try, I know my reaction to her words isn't hidden on my face. "Right. Okay."

"Interesting that he's chosen you," she continues "But then he's always trying to put back together the broken little girls."

"Rather than fucking ageing rock widows?"

"How do you know he's not doing both?" For emphasis, Kristie adjusts the front of her dress.

Bitch. "Right. Sure."

Kristie cocks a brow. "You know what me and Jem have in common?"

"I'm too polite to say," I snap, my distrust of Jem morphing into anger. He said he wouldn't screw anyone else. He promised.

"More than he does with you."

"Mm hmm." I look past her, hoping Jem appears from the nearby bathrooms, but praying he doesn't at the same time.

Kristie bends toward me. "Silly girl. Why would a man who cares about nothing care about you?"

"Then you don't know Jem," I retort.

"And you do?"

"Yes."

"Ask yourself that question again."

Jem appears from a doorway down the hall and stops dead as he sees me talking to Kristie. She's saying something else, but I'm not listening. Kristie practically said he'd just fucked her and now here he is appearing from a room in the direction she came from. Catching site of someone behind me, Kristie air kisses a false goodbye and teeters away. I step to one side and rest against the wall waiting for Jem to reach me.

"You okay?" he asks warily as he approaches.

I check out his clothes for disarray and step closer. Jem's clothes are intact but he smells the same as the woman who stood in the same spot a minute ago.

"You fucking, asshole!" I yell and shove him hard in the chest before he tries to touch me.

"What the hell? What the hell have I done now?"

"You mean who have you done!" I shout.

Jem grabs my arm and steers me to a quieter part of the hallway. "What the fuck are you talking about?"

"How dumb do you think I am?" I hiss, trembling. "You disappear for ages and then her!"

"What?" Realisation dawns in his eyes. "No! Jesus, Ruby."

"You smell of her! You bastard! Why bring me here at all if you were going to spend the evening with your fuck buddy!"

Before he can answer, I stomp off to the elevators. "And don't follow me!"

Jem makes the wise choice, and I'm alone in the elevator when I head up to our suite.

30

Ruby

I wake the next morning with a dry mouth and headache, the extra champagne I drank when I got back to the suite last night seemed like a good idea at the time. Stumbling out of bed, I head to the kitchen area, passing Jem on the sofa, who's sleeping under a white hotel blanket. The tears threaten again; but I cried enough of those last night, my aching chest a reminder of how much.

How could he? Jem promised we were exclusive, I didn't think things had changed. If anything, I thought we were stronger.

This is the real Jem Jones and he's a still a fucked up mess if this is how he's going to behave.

"You calmed down yet?" he asks as I reappear with a glass.

He's naked apart from his briefs, tight abs tensing as he bends down to pick up his jeans. He pulls them on and pushes his hair from his face. My shocked silence hides my level of pissed off.

"Calmed down?" I say with a short laugh.

"Yeah. What the hell was that about? Do you really think I'm going to hook up with another chick when you're nearby?"

I grip the glass. "When I'm nearby? Oh, so when I'm not nearby, you do?"

"Don't twist my words, Ruby! Seriously, you think I screwed her?"

"Yes."

Jem's brow tugs down and so does his mouth. "Is that what you think of me? Three months and I've not been near anyone else. I don't want to."

"Right. She lent you her perfume, did she?"

Jem opens his mouth to respond then changes his mind, blowing air into his cheeks instead. I expect anger but he looks tired, like he can't be bothered.

"You know what? I'm not going to have this discussion with you. If you're going to behave like a jealous teen the first time someone hits on me, then this won't work."

I step back. "What?"

"I'm Jem Jones, it happens. If you can't deal with it, then that's your problem."

If I had anything in my mouth, I'd choke at his arrogance. Ensconced in our life of every day work and home life, away from his public persona, I'd shaped him in my mind as my Jem. Does he exist?

"What's going on with you?" I ask. "You've been odd for the last week. Have you had enough of us?"

"I'm stressed and you're not helping. This isn't helping."

"Stressed about what?"

"Nothing. I'll deal with it."

"Why not talk to me about it?"

"I don't want to." He grabs his t-shirt. "Just because we're in a relationship doesn't mean I have to tell you everything."

His words are a blow to the chest. Why is the Jem who hides back again?

"So you didn't screw Kristie?"

"No! So stop behaving like a high school kid and trust me."

"If you can't confide in me, we're not as close as I thought!" I shout.

"You're as close as I want you." He stands. "I'm going to order breakfast. Do you want anything?"

Conversation over as far as he's concerned, he pulls the hotel menu from the low table nearby. That's it? He thinks this is dealt with?

"I'm not hungry," I retort and head to the shower.

We cross paths as I come out of the bathroom and he goes in, not speaking. I'm genuinely not hungry; the rough edges of our relationship apparent all of a sudden. Why can't he trust me enough to confide what's bothering him?

The last few weeks he's been cagey, not only the phone calls; but Jem's hiding something and now he's admitted he is. I pushed down my insecurities, but the way he looks at me has changed. The guard is back up in his eyes. Are we getting too close? Is that what's bothering him?

Is Kristie who the whispered phone calls have been to? I don't want to be one of 'those girls,' especially considering the way Dan stalked my life, but my urge is too strong. When the water starts trickling in the shower, I grab Jem's phone. He doesn't lock the screen, which is a pretty stupid move because if he lost his mobile his life would be accessible to anyone.

He doesn't have a lot of people he messages. Bryn, Dylan, Steve, Liam, and occasionally Tina, the PR girl.

And Marie. Not Kristie.

A desperate need to know the truth overriding my guilt, I scroll through the messages. They're similar in tone.

<Are you coming to see me when you get back?> is her last one and Jem hasn't replied.

I look through the others.

<I need to see you> is another from Marie.

Jem's are typical Jem. Two or three words indicating he'll call when he can. Nothing intimating his feelings. One in particular kicks me in the stomach.

<I'll try to visit but it's complicated>

Jem

The steaming water runs over my skin, washing away the aching of a night sleeping on a too short sofa, and I want to stand under here forever. Life gets better, and then it gets hard again. People are so fucking complicated, Ruby has everything I can give her. Why isn't she happy with that? I'm okay with what she gives me.

Accusing me of sex with someone else. Not trusting me. And she wonders why I don't share what else is going on. Why the hell would I want to screw Kristie? Yeah, Kristie came on to me, couldn't understand why I'd be faithful to Ruby, but I didn't do anything, for fuck's sake. After a few minutes of Kristie pressing herself against me while I explained I didn't want her, she got the message, shoved me to one side, and walked away.

Have I backed off from Ruby recently? Yeah, probably a little; but that's because my head is messed up, and I'm trying to contain everything. If this pours out, and Ruby can't cope with the fucked up Jem Jones returning, things will get worse, so I keep him contained. If I let Ruby in and she rejects me when I need her most, my life will go full circle. Best solution? Don't need her. Don't need anyone. I haven't spoken to Bryn or Dylan about this, and I'm running out of excuses not to go and see Marie.

What sort of a person doesn't visit his dying mother?

31

em

A tense morning with Ruby isn't the best start to a day that's going to be a test of the new life I'm trying to hang onto. Another night unable to sleep hasn't helped either. Ruby's interfering, asking me what's wrong. Since when did we go back to the 'talking about how we feel' crap? Everything has been discussed and dealt with, why rehash? Ruby's not coming into my safe place. This has pissed her off because breakfast again involved slamming around of cups and bowls, and silence. I left without saying goodbye and hope she's in a better mood tonight.

The hospice is in Reading, a short drive from London; but I intend to make it there and back in one day. If I do, I can pretend to myself it never happened.

Sure, Jem.

Since Marie contacted me a couple of weeks ago, the walls between my childhood memories and reality have crumbled. She left when I was twelve, and I haven't seen my mum since. I vowed to myself I would never see her again or allow myself to be hurt on that level by anyone else.

Is there any bigger hurt in the world than not being good enough for your own mother? A part of me yells Ruby would understand, her mum left too; but I can't talk to her about this. I just can't.

Each rehab stay, a counsellor has attempted to get me to open up and acknowledge the power this has over me still. I'm not fucking stupid, I know I'm screwed up by my childhood; but ripping open that wound isn't helpful when my stability is shaky in recovery. So, I refuse. The past should be buried. Forgotten. Over.

So why the hell has the past become my present?

As I sit in the car, outside the single-storey building, I stare at the gardens full of yellow and white rose bushes that I bizarrely notice match the ones in my garden. I'm dragged back to memories of helplessness, and confusion, of wounds piercing so deeply the damage severed my nerves and left me unable to feel again. Recently this has changed because Ruby crosses my mind; the irritation over this morning's argument includes a small part of wishing I was with her instead. I shake the thought away. See? I'm allowing in emotion and here's a reminder of why I shouldn't.

I don't have any pictures of my mother, only the suppressed memories of her long, curly brown hair and a vague recollection of her face. Besides that, nothing. She wasn't a hugging mum, but at least she didn't hit me around like the guy she walked away with.

The middle-aged nurse in the hospice recognises me straightaway, of course, but doesn't make a deal out of it and leads me along a carpeted hallway. The yellow furnishings and watercolour pictures dominating the building don't hide the institutional smell of the place. Not as bad as a hospital, but uncomfortably reminiscent of rehab centres.

The nurse knocks on the door of a room at the end of a bright hallway and informs the woman inside that I'm here, before smiling encouragingly and leaving.

Fourteen years.

I step inside. This woman doesn't have curly brown hair; hers is short. Cancer patient short. Her sallow skin and frail frame shock me. The woman from my memories doesn't match the person sitting in the high backed armchair by the bed. She could be anybody. This isn't my mum.

But she is. Her eyes are my mum's; they must be because they look like mine, eyes brimming with tears she doesn't deserve to shed. For a couple of minutes we stare at each other saying nothing. I stand in the open doorway, debating whether to turn and leave. Why the fuck didn't I talk to someone about this rather than doing this alone? Bryn, Dylan... even Ruby.

I close the door behind and rest against it. "Hello."

"Thank you for coming to see me," she says and her voice tears at me. There's a weakness that drags me back to the bad times; the days she was weakened by the men; the days, they injured her.

I close my eyes and inhale. When I open them, she's still there. My mum, broken as she always was but this time by something killing her, rather than by someone.

"How have you been?" she asks.

"Don't you read the papers?" I reply a little too harshly.

"I don't believe everything I read, Jeremy."

"Don't call me that. I'm not Jeremy."

Mum looks at her hands. They age her, the skin drawn across pronounced veins like an old woman's would be. Mum's mid-forties and the illness has pushed her looks into old age. "I know. Sorry."

To her, yes. I'm her Jeremy who had to become Jem to forget him. I pull up the plastic and metal chair near the drawers containing a vase of white and pink flowers, and sit. Shit, I should've bought flowers.

"I'd ask how you are, but it would be a stupid question," I say.

"I've been better."

"You've looked better."

She rubs her head, pale fingers touching her short hair. "I have."

We have nothing to talk about. Reminiscing about the past is out, and I've no interest in knowing what she's been doing with her life.

Life. Mum told me she had weeks left, the cancer breaking her body more readily than anybody broke her in the past. As I look at her, Jeremy hurts for his mum the way he used to; but Jem has to stay strong against the threatening tide. Since she contacted me out of the blue and ripped me back in time, the bottle, drugs, and void have called more loudly than in a long time. If Ruby wasn't in my life and house, I reckon I'd have slipped by now.

"I haven't heard from you for years," I say pointedly.

"You made it clear you didn't want to see me about six years ago. I wasn't going to be one of those relatives of famous people demanding money."

"You needed money?"

"Everybody needs more money, Jem. After Paul left, things got harder."

"Didn't you find someone else? You always did."

"No. I left him for a shelter; he hurt me badly. They helped me, and then I helped them. Others."

The woman who refused to help herself? "Oh."

"I knew it was too late for us."

"Was it? You didn't try that hard to fix things."

Mum rests back in her seat, her breathing laboured. "Would you have let me? Look how long it took you to arrange to see me. It's almost a month since I asked you to visit."

"Probably not," I say quietly.

Mum reaches out to her bedside table and takes the plastic tumbler, hands shaking. She sips; swallowing as if it hurts her and my resolve wavers.

"But you're here now." She gives a weak smile. "I'm glad you came to see me before... well, before."

Before she dies. Before time runs out and she can't assuage her guilt. So she can fuck me up one last time.

But as I look at her, I know that's not her motive. I believe she thinks she's doing this for me. For both of us.

"How long?" I ask.

"I don't know. Weeks."

My throat thickens, why am I feeling? Where's the wall gone? "Oh. Right. I'm not sure I can come again."

"I understand. But you'll stay and talk to me this afternoon?"

"Yeah."

Mum tells me about the work she's done, with domestic violence victims like herself. Helping families stay together. Did this help her? She abandoned her own family; how many others did she need to save before she felt she'd atoned her behaviour? I tell her things about Blue Phoenix, about the boys, but she never knew them. My mother was locked in her own world and her own pain; pain I had no comprehension of as a kid.

The conversation tires her, Mum's breathing becomes shallower and speech slower. As usual, she doesn't have the energy for me.

"I'm proud of you," she tells me.

"Proud of me?" I ask hoarsely.

"Look at what you've achieved. Things could've ended so badly for you."

I slump back in my seat. "And look at my screwed up life. This man you're proud of, that you've watched over the last few years, is he happy?"

"You've come through that though. You're sober now."

"I'm still fucked up." *Because of you.*

"I'm so sorry. I wish I could change what happened, but I can't. Don't let the past stop you being happy now. I've seen you with a new girl...did you say her name was Ruby?"

"Do you follow my life?" I interrupt. "You seem to know a lot."

"Of course I do, and you looked happier recently. Are you happier?"

"I don't want to talk about my life."

"You're right. It's not my business." She inhales a shaky breath, and I see her energy fading in front of me. "I wish you'd brought your guitar though."

"What?"

"I listen to some of your music, not all of it; but you wrote some beautiful songs. My talented son."

This is too much. "Your son? By blood, yeah but not by love."

"Don't, please."

"I didn't come here to tell you I forgive everything because I don't. I live with the scars."

"I'm not expecting you to. I wanted to see you; that's all. I missed you."

Fuck. I stand. Am I shaking too? "Don't. You don't have the right. You made your choices."

"And now you make yours, Jem. Make the right ones."

The sun shines through the open curtains. A bright autumn day fills the room with a humid warmth that isn't helping my dizzying pain. "I think I need to go now."

Mum sits forward and grips the chair arm with pale hands. She wants to stand and can't. "Okay."

The unrelenting ache grips and the words spill. "Mum, you left me. Not just once but again and again."

"I'm sorry."

"So am I."

I hesitate. She'll leave me one final time, and I'll never see her again. Every other time Mum left, I couldn't understand why she didn't say goodbye. Often it was when I was at school, and I'd come home to find a note and some money.

When people leave, they should hug you with the promise they'll see you again.

This is what she wants to do now, but there's no promise of a next time.

"Bye, Mum."

The decision is made in the moment, without thought, without rationalisation. How can I leave and not hug her goodbye? I pull the chair over, sit, and hesitantly place my arms around my mum. She's all bones and I'm frightened of hurting her. Mum hugs me back, hard; but not as hard as I think she'd like. Her back shakes, face buried into my t-shirt; and I fight, fight, fight against the tsunami of pain engulfing.

People say they love you. Then they leave you. Or they die. Sometimes both.

When I walk back to the car through the afternoon sun, away from the smell of the hospice cloying my senses, I clutch the emotions and drag them back inside. I'd forgotten how severe the suffering other people cause can be, how the need to obliterate this is what pushed me into a life of addiction.

This can't happen again. I won't fall into loving another person who'll leave.

I can't get any further into whatever is happening with Ruby because when she leaves, the fallout will send me back to my old life and this time it will kill me.

32

Ruby

I sit in the lounge of Jem's quiet house watching TV in a failed attempt to distract myself from the growing unease that something's going wrong between us.

Germany was three days ago and the tension between me and Jem intensifies daily. The last three months evaporate, content replaced by tension. I haven't questioned Jem about the texts and today he's home late; I'm scared about what's coming.

Something is wrong; this Jem is the guy I first met. The one who doesn't sleep; who once let me sleep in his arms, now pulls away and turns his back as soon as he thinks I'm asleep. He's withdrawing and I'm being edged out.

Jem arrives a little after eight p.m., the dark rings around his eyes from lack of sleep more pronounced. He gives me a gruff greeting and disappears; returning five minutes later, then hovers in the corner of the room, near the TV.

"Can I talk to you?" he says.

"Sure." I pick up the remote and click off the TV. "Are you okay? Has something happened?"

The nail chewing is odd for Jem and he stops, pushes his curls from his face, and looks at me. "I'm just going to come straight out with this."

"Okay."

"You need to move out."

He may as well have slapped me in the face, the shock and watering eyes come so readily. "Oh. Okay. Sure."

"And I don't think we should continue this…" He pauses. "This."

Another slap. "Right."

"Okay." He tucks his hands beneath his arms. "Sorry."

I'm not one of those girls, the ones who collapse in tears and beg to stay. Definitely not the sort to ask the guy to change his mind. They all realise eventually: I'm not worth it. "It's a bit late to go now. Can I stay until tomorrow?"

Jem rubs his cheek. He looks confused. I guess he expected a stronger reaction. Right, like I'm about to show him how I really feel.

"I'm not going to kick you onto the street!"

"No, but you are going to kick me in the heart."

Emotion shows through at last, the hidden distress in his eyes I want to ask about. What's happening here?

"I thought I could do this, Ruby, but I can't. I can't give myself to you the way you want. This isn't working."

"Have you been rehearsing these lines? How about 'it's not you, it's me'? I've heard that's a fucking good one."

Here she comes, if he's rejected one Ruby, he'll get the other. I knew something threatened our relationship; but for Jem to take what we have and smash it to pieces without any discussion is beyond what I imagined was coming.

"What's happened, Jem? Talk to me."

"I tried, but I can't do this," he continues.

"Define 'this'. Monogamy?"

"What?"

"You're fucking someone else."

"For fuck's sake, Ruby, is this about Kristie again?"

"No. Marie," I blurt.

Jem's stance changes, shoulders stiffening. "What?"

"Marie. I saw the messages."

"Shit!" He walks out of the room to the kitchen, slamming the door. My rapid-fire heart thumps in my ears as I scramble to catch up. I thought things were going wrong, but why this?

Jem returns, his face dark. "You read my phone messages?"

"I'm sorry. I don't know why I did. I shouldn't have."

"Correct. If I let you into my life, it's on my terms and they don't include spying on me."

"Wow, so you did me a favour giving me some of your precious time?"

Jem's tone softens, but the cold remains. What happened today that tripped the switch and re-erected his force field? "I don't want to fight with you."

"No, you wouldn't, because you have to feel something to fight. How long have you lied to me about how you feel?"

"I *feel* pissed off that you invaded my privacy, Ruby."

"I feel like an idiot." I grab my coat and phone. "I'll leave you alone."

"It's late. You can't go," says Jem in alarm.

"What the fuck, Jem?"

"Wait until tomorrow. I don't want to worry about you."

"You bloody hypocrite! You don't have to. If this is over, leave me the hell alone!"

Jem shook up our world again and scattered the pieces. Do I grab at them and try to push everything back together? As I stand, trembling, Jem closes his eyes, blocking me out.

"I don't understand, Jem," I say hoarsely.

"No, neither do I."

"Talk to me."

Jem turns away. "I'm sorry."

I wait. I don't know what for, but he doesn't speak again. I could touch Jem, try to get through to the truth, but I'm scared. No explanation from Jem is better than one from him containing words I can use against myself to rip apart my new self-belief. I know Jem lashes out when we fight, can say hurtful things, and I'll use the words as weapons against myself if this happens. With calm from years of practice, from hiding the distress and keeping control, I walk away to pack a bag.

I play over and over in my mind what I might've done wrong. I backed off on being needy, or I thought I did. He has to be screwing someone else; otherwise, why would he drop what we had so easily?

Jem has gone when I leave the bedroom with my bag and I stand in the lounge of the place I began to call home, overwhelmed by the grief twisting around my insides, strangling the life from me. How can he do this?

I climb into the car as anger joins the hurt, at being treated by him in such a dismissive way. Jem knows my self-worth is practically non-existent in personal relationships so I challenge myself to accept this is nothing to do with me. This is Jem, the fucked up guy who can't admit he feels.

Perhaps I should be thankful that, although he shattered my fragile heart into a multitude of pieces I won't find again in a hurry, he gave me the strength to leave Dan and push Ruby Riot's need for success. I can be who I want and achieve the dreams I never thought possible. In the future, I can take what I've learnt from this.

One day I'll have a relationship with a normal man.

Jem

I'm doing the right thing.

Exhausted, I go to bed, wrap myself up in the sheets, and fight away memories of seeing Mum today. I wake in the night and put a hand out for Ruby, but she's not there. Of course, because I screwed up. I pull across the pillow she slept on and bury my head into the cotton, inhaling the scent of her shampoo.

I'm doing the right thing.

Sleep eludes me and I pull myself out of bed, the process automatic. Get up. Get dressed. Treadmill. My guitar is propped against the drawers; the guitar Ruby likes to use on the days I persuade her to play to me. I should give her it, when she comes back to pick up the rest of her gear.

A spike of regret shocks me; an ache filling the void, reminding me it's not only my bed that's empty. I blank any thoughts of Ruby, retreat to the numb world where I'm on my own and I'm safe.

I'm doing the right thing.

Keep telling yourself that, Jem.

33

A couple of days later, I'm settling into my new place, the boys' sofa. I gave up my share house when I gave in to my feelings about Jem and moved in with him. Again, living and breathing Ruby Riot isn't as fun as it should be and I set about looking for somewhere else to live. November isn't the best time of year for doing this; most are already taken by students. Moving in with Jem and giving up my share house five minutes into a relationship with him wasn't the smartest move.

Jax hasn't said anything yet, but I knew what his first thought was when I arrived on his doorstep and told him about me and Jem. We're booked to tour with Blue Phoenix in late January onwards; Steve gave us the green light. Will that still happen if Jem Jones's ex-fuck is part of the package? Two months until we leave, I can be over him and we can behave like adults about this surely?

A few days after Jem ended us, Bryn calls out of the blue.

"Did something happen?" he asks abruptly. "I asked you to call me if you thought Jem needed help."

I'm put out I should be expected to care about the man who

fucked with my heart. "He finished our relationship and asked me to leave. I didn't think I needed to tell you everything."

"Why did he end things?"

"I don't know. Ask him. I think he's screwing around and is too scared of a real relationship."

Bryn goes quiet. "Oh. Okay. Maybe that's why I can't get in touch with him."

My stomach flips at Bryn's easy acceptance that this is probably the reason. "Check up on him."

"I'm overseas. I'll see if Dylan or Liam is around. Someone needs to see if he's okay if you think it's needed."

"He was behaving oddly, shutting down. I don't know; it's not as if I was around him long, but to me he seemed... wrong."

"But this is why I'm surprised. He was different around you. I don't get why he'd screw up something good for him."

"Because he's Jem Jones?" I suggest.

"Yeah, there is that." Bryn swears under his breath. "I'm worried because he won't answer my calls. I told him a relationship was a mistake... He'd better not have done something stupid..."

I should've called Bryn as soon as we split; but I wanted to blank Jem from my mind, so I didn't have to deal with the tears. Not that the attempt worked, fragments of Jem's splintered life pierced mine and I'm left with painful shards trapped beneath my skin.

"I don't think he would"

"You definitely don't know him then. Thanks for the info." Bryn hangs up and I stare at my phone.

Should I check on Jem? I can't switch off my feelings the way he did to me, and Bryn's woken the worry I have that Jem could relapse. I drag my fingers through my hair. I'm pulled in two directions. If I go to him and he refuses to see me or talk to me, the glass beneath my skin will cut deeper. If I leave this alone, and the man who was the world to me for those short months disappears back into addiction, I'll hate myself.

No, he has others who can help. I make things worse.

Jem

Dylan.

Wow, I'm honoured.

He shoves his way into the house and stands in my lounge, casting his gaze around the room. The place is covered in all kinds of crap; fast food boxes, empty cups, and glasses but not what I know he's looking for.

"Wanna sweep the house too? Should've just brought a sniffer dog," I snarl.

Dylan crosses his arms. "You look like shit, Jem."

"Nice."

"Where's Ruby?"

"Gone and if you're here you know that." I flop onto the sofa and rest my head on the cool leather. "I'm tired, man. Could've called before you landed on my doorstep."

"What happened with her?"

I shrug. "Got too hard."

"Bullshit, Jem. I saw you guys together and you were good."

I regard him with tired eyes. He's tanned, curls returning as his hair reaches past his ears again. Yeah, he's looking more like the old Dylan; but his new life with Sky means he never will be.

"How's things in your love life?" I put my bare feet on the low coffee table.

"Why the snide tone, Jem?"

"The love-struck thing you have going on. Doesn't suit you."

"Why? Because you want me to be unhappy like you? Throw away the right girl because of my past fuck-ups?"

"Just saying."

Dylan pushes a pizza box out of the way and sits on the armchair. Resting his elbows on his knees, he fixes me with a look

I recognise. "Tell me what's happening. You just threw away something good. I thought you'd dropped the self-destruct act."

"I'm not on self-destruct! See any drugs? Booze? No. I'm good."

He sinks back and makes an exasperated sound. "Give me your phone."

"No!"

"Just fucking do it. I want to show you something."

"What?"

Dylan holds his hand out and beckons with his fingers. Huffing, I slam it into his hand. "Don't read my messages."

"Not gonna." He swipes a finger across the screen. "Looking at your photos."

"They're not that interesting. Been a while since I had pictures of naked chicks on there."

Dylan laughs. "I'm only interested in one naked chick these days. So are you." He turns the phone to show a picture of me and Ruby on the screen, my arm around her shoulders close-up on our faces. Relaxed. Happy.

"Yeah? There's a picture of us."

"A few pictures, Jem." He keeps scrolling. "Look at yourself in these pictures and see how the outside world saw you and Ruby; how good you were for each other. You were happy, Jem. I hadn't seen you so alive for years." He tosses the phone and it lands on my lap. "So, I'm asking again, what the hell happened?"

I scroll through my phone absent-mindedly looking through the pictures I couldn't bring myself to delete because that'd be the final removal of Ruby from my life. Dylan's here, I should've called him weeks ago. I had a chance to talk to him about this in Germany, but I'm unsure he understands anymore. I lost him like I lost everybody else; pushing and pushing until I became such a pain in the ass that he gave up on me. I swallow hard and look to the concern in his eyes. If there's one person in the world I can share this shit with, it's Dylan.

"This happened." I click over to my messages and throw the phone back. Dylan's brows tug together as he reads.

"Marie? What the hell, Jem. Why screw around?"

"You too? People have such a high opinion of my morals," I say sarcastically.

"So who's this?" I cross my arms and wait for the penny to drop. His eyes widen. "Is this... Jem, is this your mum?"

I clap my hands slowly as Dylan carefully puts the phone on the coffee table. "Good guess."

"You seen her?" he says in a low voice.

"Yeah, but won't be seeing her again anytime soon."

Dylan rubs his forehead, the concern softening the frustrated anger he had a few minutes ago. "Whoa. No wonder your head's fucked. Does Ruby know?"

"No. Why would she?"

"Because when you're in a relationship you kinda discuss this shit!"

"We're not in a relationship anymore."

"Because of this?"

"No. Leave it. You have your answer." I stand. I can't discuss Ruby as well as my mum; this is too much.

"A clusterfuck like this, Jem? Why the hell didn't you call me before?"

"Dealing in my own way."

Dylan stands too. "I'm here, Jem. I understand this. You know that."

Dylan was the first person who ever found out what was going on in my screwed up childhood. He was in a bad place too, his dad had left, and he shared my anger. Everything came out - where my mum was, her boyfriends' treatment of me and her. The next time Mum went away, Dylan told his mum he was staying over at mine. And the next time, until Dylan was always there when she wasn't. We'd go back to my place and get drunk; we were twelve years old.

One night Dylan picked up my guitar and I started to teach him with the aid of one of my 'how to play guitar' books. Our shared bond over the hurt surrounding us found its way into another outlet, the one that bonded our lives forever after. Music. We were shit when we first started playing covers of classics, three years later we began writing our own stuff.

Not long after, we discovered Liam, Bryn, and Blue Phoenix.

Then we found drugs and fame; until eventually, me and Dylan frequently lost each other. He's the only person I've ever let in and that's only through a lot of shoving on his part.

"She's dying."

Worried he might hug me, I step back.

Dylan chews on the corner of his lip. "Shit, Jem," he says softly.

"Pretty much."

"And you've seen her?" Dylan sits again, watching me with the old concern.

"Yeah. First time since she left me."

When it happened all those years ago, I never knew Mum had left for good, not for a while. The days following my realisation she was never coming back were numb; a week later, I fell apart, and so began the pattern for my life. Switch off and if I can't numb myself, I use something to help me. I think I was drunk for two weeks straight. Right now, I'm close to stepping back there.

Dylan was there all those years ago, supporting, channelling my destructive needs into writing new songs and pushing me into music as my salvation. One person in the world knows who I am behind the Jem Jones mask, and I've also pushed him away when he's got too close.

Two people, Jem. I shake the thought away.

Other shit has happened between me and Dylan, complicated crap from drug-induced mistakes; but we always come back together.

Now he has Sky.

"How long until...?" he asks.

"She dies? Not long. She's really sick. Cancer." My staccato answers to the questions coming will have to do. I don't have it in me to delve back to that day at the hospice.

"When was this, Jem?"

"Four days ago."

"When did you end things with Ruby?"

"Four days ago."

Dylan throws his hands up. "So, rather than turn to her for support, you pushed away the person who loves you. What the fuck for?"

"She doesn't love me! We don't do love, Dylan. I'm not you."

Slowly, Dylan shakes his head. "How do you feel right now?"

"We gonna talk about our feelings?" I say with a snort. "Maybe we should hold hands."

"Fine. Shut me out too. What happened to living your life after rehab, Jem?"

"This is a hiccup. I'll move on."

"You don't see your mum for fourteen years, and then you do and she's dying? That isn't a hiccup. You need support." He sighs. "Come and stay with me and Sky."

"No bloody way!"

Dylan runs a hand across his mouth. "Okay, I'm staying here. I'll call Sky and tell her I'll be away a few days."

"I don't want anyone here!"

"Have you thought about using again?" he says in a low voice.

"No!" My face betrays me; Dylan knows me too well. "It's harder to control, yeah. Bryn was right, getting into a relationship was too much."

"You're a bloody idiot. Please explain to me why you pushed her away. I don't give a shit what you say, that girl loves you, and you love her."

Does she? How would I know? The concept is weird. I have no comparison. Spending a week waking and aching for her isn't love; that's not good. Ruby consuming my thoughts - how is she? What's she doing? Unhealthy. I miss her with a despair that's too familiar.

"She'd only hurt me," I say eventually.

"So you decided to pre-empt it by hurting both of you? Smart move."

"I'll get over it."

"Will you? 'Cause I don't think there's any other Rubys out there. It's like rewinding and watching a female version of you, Jem. That's how close she is. And you saw that too; I know it."

Dylan's right. Of course, he's fucking right. I pushed her away because I worried she'd push me away, that the fall-out would send me spiralling back into addiction. I didn't bargain on being unable to switch off how I feel about Ruby, unaware of how deep in my heart she'd settled. Guilt over somebody else's feelings is new – over my stubborn stupidity that blew apart the one thing holding me together. Us. We opened up, cared, saw each other's truths and the broken pieces fell into place. I threw the fragile relationship as hard as I could away from me and shattered everything – me, Ruby, the new place of peace we'd created.

I don't know what to do. I've never wanted to fix anything before. However hard I try, Ruby is someone I can never obliterate; but if she has any sense, she'll already have blanked out Jem Jones.

34

Life takes on a routine that I follow, a monotonous constancy to keep my head in check: work, home, sleep. There's a deep hole I keep tripping into when I'm not paying attention, but apart from that, I push on. The biggest thing that's pissed me off is I can't play right now. I'm so frustrated by life that even trying to hide myself in the colours of my music world won't work. So when I get a midnight text from Jem asking to see me, after three weeks of silence, I'm angry and respond with a colourful version of that fury.

Jem doesn't reply.

The one text is enough to tap into my brain, a searing pain forcing Jem back in. The nausea and twisted stomach, the unrelenting ache of being turned inside out at the loss of him, grips again.

This isn't fair. Two weeks of dazed acceptance and a week of tentatively re-joining the world, my head finally disconnected from the idea I can have what nobody can, Jem Jones's love. I won't let him rip off the skin I've grown over the raw wound he caused.

A second text wakes me at two a.m. and when I squint at the phone, I see Jem's name. A pang of worry over his not sleeping and what that indicates about his mental state pushes in momentarily, but I firmly shove it back out. Not my problem.

But as I close my eyes to go back to sleep, I can't let the worry go. Images of Jem surrounded by broken glass, the first day I realised how shattered he was, won't leave my head.

Swearing at my decision, I drag myself out of bed, dress, and head to my car.

November isn't the best weather for hanging around the streets in the early hours. Luckily, I still have my key; I don't know why I kept it. False hope? Deluded thoughts things would mend? Cautiously, I climb the stairs.

"Jem?"

For a horrible moment I think he's been robbed, the lounge room is trashed. Sure, there's half-empty pizza boxes and food wrappers strewn around, but more than that. A table lamp lies on the floor, bulb smashed and the glass table it once stood on is upside down. The large white cushions from the sofa are halfway across the room and glass picture frames are shattered. No, if he'd been robbed, the expensive sound system and TV wouldn't be here, and neither would the rare guitar that's survived amidst the chaos.

A noise alerts me from upstairs. The crash of something heavy as if thrown, loud enough I'm convinced whatever it is will fall through the ceiling. My heart sounds in my ears. What if this isn't Jem? No, the front door was locked and I needed the key code for the secured gate. I creep up the polished wooden stairs and listen. Jem's bedroom door is open. Hoping whoever it is, will be too distracted to see me, I peer around the door.

Jem's room is as big as mess as the rest of the house, drawers knocked over, clothes scattered around, even his mattress is upended. The house is unrecognizable beneath the chaos.

A figure stands in the darkened room. Jem. He faces the window, staring at the closed curtains.

"What's happening?" I ask him quietly.

He turns. In the shadows of the room, Jem's face is hard to

make out; but he looks confused, chest rising and falling rapidly. His hand shakes as he pushes it through his hair.

"Jem?"

"Why are you here?" he asks hoarsely.

"You asked me to come."

"Did I? Oh."

"I can go."

"No!" He tempers his tone as I step back. "No. Don't."

I rest against the doorframe, the space between us a gulf filled with the unspoken. "What happened?"

"I think I broke something." He gives a small laugh.

"This is a bit more than a broken glass in the kitchen, Jem."

"Yeah. And I'm a bit more fucked."

With those words, the crack in his voice, and the tired defeat, every fibre of me wants to cross the room to Jem, hold him, tell him I'm here. I've known Jem long enough to recognise the despair.

But he rejected me, doesn't want me.

"Do you want me to call Bryn for you?"

Jem sits on the low windowsill. "No."

"Then what? What did you want me for, before you forgot you asked me to come over?"

"In the kitchen."

"What?"

"Go in the kitchen and do something."

I rub my head; this man makes no sense as usual. "What? Make you a drink?"

"Shit!" Jem doubles over and wraps his arms around his head.

I freeze. He hasn't, surely... Heading downstairs, I halt in the kitchen doorway. Glass from a broken bottle covers the floor and a strong smell of whisky accompanies the brown liquid seeping across the tiles.

Jem, you fucking idiot.

Glass crunches under my feet as I walk into the room. An empty tumbler rests on the counter and I smell the inside. Nothing. Maybe he didn't. My first instinct is to clear this up. If Jem's slipping, then the smell of alcohol won't help. I pick up the largest parts of the broken glass and set them on the counter. I can't do this. I don't know how to help him right now. Stepping back out of the kitchen, I pull my phone from my pocket and search for Bryn's number. Jem needs his friends, not me.

"Don't call anyone." Jem's low voice comes from the doorway behind.

"Have you been drinking?" I demand.

"No!"

"So where'd the bottle come from?"

"I didn't drink anything, but I was fucking close!"

Hesitantly, I move closer but there's no alcohol smell on his breath. The curls hang into his reddened eyes; and in them, I see a suffering my heart can't handle; something has really hurt Jem. I reach out and touch his hand, attempting to take Jem's fingers in mine. When he snatches his hand away and tucks both beneath his arms, backing away, the rejection hurts as much as the day he told me to leave.

"So you want me here to babysit?" I say harshly. "Wasn't Bryn available?"

"I didn't try Bryn. I wanted to see you," he says in a flat voice.

"Why?"

"Because you won't judge. You won't push. You'll just be."

"I'm not staying if you don't tell me what's going on. You can't randomly contact me three weeks after breaking my heart, and then expect me to be okay with it."

Jem rubs his temples. "Breaking your heart?"

"Of course, you fucking did!" His eyes widen. "Jem, just tell me what's going on."

He mumbles something in the direction of his feet and I huff and step closer. "What?"

"I saw my mum," he tells his feet.

His simple words smack understanding into the situation around us. "When? What did she do?"

He ignores my response. "And she died yesterday."

Jem's despair washes over me, sweeping away the wall, and dragging my heart back to him on the tide. I'm on the verge of breaking down with Jem because this is something that would kill me too. Jem faces a resurrection of the past, heart ripped open for one last time by the person who failed him. My mum left once and forever. Jem's did it multiple times, mending the wound then tearing it further open each time she did it again. I had Quinn. Jem was alone.

Jem's alone now, struggling to swim against the tide of the memories he'd fought to keep away. In front of me, the devastation drowns him, he's fighting his pull to relapsing; but he reached out – for me.

I have no words. I grab Jem's stiff figure and bury my face into his chest, holding as tightly as I can. I want to give Jem some of my strength, help him cope.

Jem remains stiff. "Yeah. So that."

"I didn't know she'd been in touch with you."

"No. Only Dylan knows." He disentangles himself and rests against the wall, arms tightly crossed as if he never wants to let anybody in again. A bolt of realisation hits.

"Is she Marie? Was that who I was accusing you of cheating on me with?"

"Yeah."

"Jem. Why didn't you tell me?"

"Couldn't."

"Why? I'd have helped, been there for you. I care about you more than you realise. I can't stand to think you were going through that alone."

He peers up at me from beneath his fringe. "It hurt. I didn't want to go back there."

"Back where?"

"To the guy who let someone in, and then got screwed over again."

Every word he says adds more sense to the last few weeks but this isn't the time to dig into there. "If you've finished destroying your house, will you sit and talk to me?" I ask gently.

For a moment, I think he's going to tell me to leave again; that he's closed down. "Jem, you asked me to come. There must be a reason."

He nods and heads to the sofa, picking up the leather cushion and pushing it back onto the seat so he can sit. I turn the coffee table the right way up and perch on the edge.

In stilted terms, Jem gives me a bare minimum explanation about his mum's illness, his decision to see her. Anxiety joins the words, his breath short, as he continues. I place a hand on his. "Don't say more if you don't want to talk. I understand now."

"Do you? I don't."

"I understand that you're stronger than you think. The broken bottle in the kitchen tells me that."

His eyes darken. "Yeah. That was you."

"It was broken when I got here, Jem."

In a shift in mood that takes me by surprise, Jem grabs the side of my face, digging his fingers into my hair. "You stopped me. I had a choice - lose myself in that shit or lose myself to you. That's why I called. I remember now."

His grip hurts and I extricate his fingers. "That was a big ask after how you treated me."

"But you came. I hurt you and you came. Why?"

"I honestly don't know. Because I pictured this - you needing help and reaching out."

Jem stares ahead. "I fuck everything up."

"No, you don't, only the things you choose to."

"I fucked us up. I didn't want the pain." He grips my hand. "That didn't work because the pain came anyway; and now when I need the good to deal with the bad, it's not here. You're not here."

I shouldn't be here. This goes against everything I promised myself; but the distress on this man's face, the destroyed look I see in his eyes, is why. "I am."

"Why?" he repeats.

"Because I can't switch off how I feel about you. I can't stop caring about the man who's a mirror of me. If I can help you, then I know I can survive shit too when it's my turn."

"I fucked up."

Jem's not in a place to talk, like a child he's seeking reassurance; but I doubt anything I can say will help. He needs what he always did; quiet understanding from somebody who cares. Jem can't be alone with options that would set him careering into the past again.

"I'll stay if you promise you'll talk to someone tomorrow. Your counsellor or one of your friends, somebody you trust to help you through this. If I stay tonight, you don't get to push this into the 'not dealing' part of your mind because it'll never stay there." I climb onto the sofa next to him.

"You, I can talk to you," he says quietly.

"No, I can't help with this. I'm in the middle of that screwed-up mess of hurt in your head. I'll be a friend to you until you decide if you want more."

Who am I kidding? I love this man. Why else would I be here? I'm risking so much and possibly for so little.

I take Jem's hand; and for a few minutes, we sit side by side, but the waves of suffering coming from him are palpable. Giving in, I wrap my arms around Jem, and pull him close. Jem responds by gripping my hair, mouth crashing onto mine. He told the truth; he doesn't taste of alcohol, but of a kiss that wraps around my soul and drags mine into his.

I recognise this urgency of Jem's mouth, the sheer force of the desire rolling from him. With the kiss, comes Jem's frantic need to fill the empty spaces inside, as if I'm the only one who can. But this is the man who emptied me and pushed me aside, and I don't have the ability to give him what he's crying out for now. One day, I will if that's what he wants, and when he's dealt with whatever is happening here. For now, I'll lose myself too, in the illusion that the man with me now is my Jem.

35

Jem doesn't sleep. He calmed after we kissed, pulled away, and held me tightly as if I'd change my mind and leave. How could I? Jem can't be alone right now. I doze on the sofa as Jem repeatedly gets up and wanders around. When the sun filters through the curtains, I wake to find him attempting to straighten out some of the mess in the lounge.

"Do you have work today?" he asks, holding a broken lamp in his hand. The wild confusion held in his eyes last night has softened but the stress hasn't left his face.

"Yeah. This afternoon." I rub my bleary eyes. "I'll go home when somebody else gets here. Have you called anyone yet?"

Jem says nothing, walking to the kitchen instead. *Great...* I follow. "Jem?"

The room still smells of alcohol but the glass has gone. "Not yet. It's early."

"It's an excuse." I drag my phone from my pocket. "Who do you want me to call? Bryn? Dylan?"

"Dylan." He sinks against the bench. "I need coffee. You want some?"

"I'll get it. Sit down."

Jem nods and leaves. He's compliant, definitely not back with us yet. I chat to Dylan briefly as I make coffee, tell him the minimum about last night, and ask him to come. He sounds surprised to hear from me. Yeah, I'm not entirely sure why I'm here either. I return to the lounge where Jem sits, chewing a nail, the way he does when he wants the nicotine his body misses. For the first time in months, I crave a smoke too. We worked on kicking our nicotine habit soon after we got together, which worked more easily than expected. Someone told me it was the endorphins from being in love that helped us break the addiction. You can imagine mine and Jem's reaction to that.

Five months ago, I saw Jem Jones in a bar and I fought between the desire for his attention and the excitement he'd come to see the band. I was in a bad place; a fucked-up place that he gently eased me out of. Our lives entwined because of Ruby Riot and then because of the place inside we live. There's a piece of Jem in his music that he shares with the world when the rest of the time he hides. I'm unsure if everybody sees this or whether he realises how much this pulls people to him. When Blue Phoenix's music spoke to me as a teen, Jem was speaking to me too.

Did fate bring us together when we needed? Two broken people recognising each other's demons and understanding how to begin to exorcise them? The man on the sofa, lost in the place he'd begun to drag himself out of, still has his demons. Jem can't shake his as easily as I'm able. His have lived with him longer and he feeds them. Jem needs to sever them and live his own life again, not one full of pain from being strangled by a past that needs putting back where it should be.

"Dylan's on his way. I'll need to leave when he gets here."

Jem looks up and his eyes tell me so much. Jem knows I'm here for him too; the suspicion I saw in his face the first time I tried to help him that night amongst the broken glass in the kitchen has gone. Nobody has looked at me in this way before. He sees through everything I have built around, looking straight into my heart.

The one he shattered.

36

em

I hang outside the Chapel of Rest, watching people I don't know talking to other strangers; I'm on the fringes as always. The sombrely dressed men and women climb into cars, negotiating who travels in each. A few tried to talk when they noticed me at the back of the chapel, but I deliberately arrived late in order to avoid them. There isn't a single person here I recognise. When the service finished, I ducked out of the place before anyone else could speak to me and hid around the corner of the building with Dylan and my grief. Do they know who I am? Did she ever tell people about me? Or was I something Mum tried to forget until she couldn't anymore?

The early December weather freezes the afternoon and the coastal wind smarts my face. The physical numbness helps dull the pain gnawing my insides too. I don't think I hurt; I don't know. I've hurt so much in the last month I don't know what feels normal and what feels wrong anymore. I'm terrified because I'm slipping into the lost place in my mind, where a path leads to the old methods of oblivion.

As I watched the coffin leave the Chapel of Rest for cremation today, the pain of the battle to stop the tears split my head; and as the room spun, I realised I was holding my breath against the final goodbye. Dylan's quiet support helped, he understood my need to be left alone and didn't touch or attempt to speak to me in the service. Heaving in the breath I'd neglected, I pictured my suffering and memories burning with her. If Mum doesn't exist anymore, how can they?

But if Mum takes away all that with her death, what am I left with? An emptiness I need to take and fill with something, but what with is my decision.

Dylan steps forward hands in the pockets of his dark suit. "Are we going with them to the wake?" He inclines his head to the funeral goers.

"Nah. Don't know any of them. I'm done now."

Dylan places a hand on my arm and I brace myself. I don't want his comfort. He hugged me fiercely the day I told him Mum had died, rewinding us to who we are and always have been. The twelve year old Jem and Dylan— the boys who forged a bond that loosened, but never broke— are here. Brothers. "You okay, man?"

"No. But come on."

I wish Ruby was with me, but I couldn't ask her to come. We haven't spoken properly since the night she appeared like a scarlet-haired angel and pulled me out of the Hell I was falling back into. Ruby left the day after she helped me. I called a couple of times and we chatted, but Ruby says she's not ready to see me. I'm proud of my beautiful girl who found the strength finally to believe in herself, to know she deserves love and happiness instead of walking back into my mess. I will fight for her when I've finished fighting for myself. Until I'm in the right space, there can't be anything more.

Will I ever be in the right space?

Today I'm laying to rest my past and I'm not including Ruby as part of today for a bigger reason. I don't want to lay us to rest.

"What do you want to do?" asks Dylan as we climb into his black Audi.

"Dunno. Go home."

We return to my house empty of life, tidied and fixed, back to my barren life in just one or two rooms. Dylan stayed with me the last week, refusing to leave because I have nobody else. I once had somebody else. The woman who I reach for in the night and she's not there; the one who would sit half-naked on my bed with her guitar and play when she knew I needed her to, but never asked why. There was a beautiful, loving girl who held my face, looked me in the eyes, and told me she cared and just as easily told me when I was being an asshole. And I fucking threw her away.

Ruby Riot has a gig tonight and on the drive home through the greying skies, I suggest to Dylan I go there. He launches into a lecture about being around alcohol when I'm in a mess, considering my almost relapse when I heard Mum had died. I explain that's why I need to be around music, the good that can drown out the thoughts looping in my mind.

No, I can't wait until I'm in the right space because until I have Ruby, I never will be. A year ago, in this state of mind, all I would've wanted was drugs. The only thing I want at this moment in time is Ruby.

I'm late to the gig, Ruby Riot's familiar sound blasts through the open doors as I arrive. There's a strange irony in Ruby Riot being here tonight; the venue I first saw her in months ago. The last time Ruby Riot played here the crowd was half the size, the band relatively unknown. The few tables are empty as most people are standing and under Ruby's spell. I slide onto a seat so I can stay in the shadows.

Watching the band achieve what I hoped, the shit of today is wiped from my mind and filled with colour and sound. Dylan offered to come with me and when I got snarly with his undertone that he wanted to keep an eye on me, he backed off. Dylan knows I need to be alone; this is me locking myself into a different space and not slipping. The band gets tighter as they gig more often. As Blue Phoenix's support act for the next tour; the whole world will get to share them. Accusations they only got the gig because of Jem Jones's involvement with the lead singer fall away as the music world recognises what I did that first night at this same venue. Talent.

The power Ruby had over me the first night never wanes. The woman on stage, hair tumbling across her face as her powerful voice competes with Jax's heavy guitar for supremacy and inevitably wins, is a fucking goddess. This goes beyond her looks: her strength, her passion, the new self-belief all make up this phenomenal person who reached into herself, grasped the vines of the past strangling her, and tore them out. I saw Ruby grow in front of my eyes and this allowed her to turn away from me when I started to break her apart.

She's the Ruby she deserves to be, free from assholes who can't tell her when they love her.

I imagine the colours we talked about swimming around her head; the ones I see too if I close my eyes. Regret coils around my heart the longer I look at Ruby. She's me, or the me I would like to be.

If I were in the movies, I'd walk on stage and kiss the girl beneath the strobing lights. I'd confess my undying love with a song dedicated to Ruby. But life isn't like the movies, and we're certainly not typical when it comes to that shit. Probably, she'd tell me to piss off. Instead, I watch and wait. When the set finishes, I don't move. The crowds thin as the evening ends with only a couple of double-take glances thrown my way, most don't notice me.

Half an hour later, the band re-appears to get drinks and dismantle their gear. Ruby sits on the edge of the stage, long legs crossed and barefoot. Her skin shines, hair damp, my post-gig Ruby soaked in happiness. Jax approaches with a bottle of water and she smiles as he passes it to her.

Then he kisses her forehead, running a finger across her face as he steps back.

My world of colour darkens as I watch them, the old insecurity niggling. Are they together? Is this the real reason she's keeping me at a distance? Jax wanders over to where Will and Nate dismantle the drum kit, and I'm on the verge of leaving as the turmoil of my day is joined by more. This is exhausting. A few minutes later, Ruby disappears and my inner debate rages. Do I follow or stay?

She's better off with Jax.

But I can't let her slip away, not without a fight.

The door to the Green Room is open and Ruby sits on the edge of the dilapidated sofa, gripping her water. The dampness on her face isn't only perspiration. Tears travel slowly down her cheeks and she stares at her boots, mouth turned down. But she looked happy?

"Ruby?"

Looking up sharply, she scrubs away the tears with the back of her hand, but new ones shine in her eyes.

"Can I talk to you?" She nods but doesn't speak, and her distress radiates across the room. Quietly, I close the door. "Are you okay?"

"I'm surprised to see you, Jem," she replies, turning concerned eyes to mine. "It was the funeral today, wasn't it?"

Now it's my turn to nod.

"You were good tonight," I say after a few moments of silence that shouldn't be as awkward as we make it.

"Thanks." She pauses. "How are you?"

"Pretty crap. You?"

She gives a small smile. "About the same."

"What's wrong?"

Ruby's hair hangs in her eyes and she blows it away. "Jax is still worried about the tour in January."

"Why?"

"In case we... this between us means Blue Phoenix don't want Ruby Riot to support anymore."

"Huh. I'm not that unprofessional. I put a crap load of time and money into you guys."

"Okay." She's still fighting tears. This isn't her; this isn't about the band.

"Stop avoiding my question. What happened? Is Dan back on the scene?"

"No! He's gone, moved somewhere else with another girl. I don't know where, a bloody long way I hope."

"But I haven't seen you like this before, not for a long time. Is this because of me?"

Ruby fixes me with a curious look. "Don't flatter yourself, Jem Jones." I smile and she half-smiles back. "What did you want?"

"You."

The words echo our first meeting and she recognises my lame attempt to reach out. "This time do you mean Ruby Riot or me?"

I tuck my hands into my pockets, playing over the rehearsed words. They all sound wrong but so right at the same time. "You. I miss you."

"Well, you'll get to spend plenty of time with me on tour in a couple of months." She stands. "The guys are in the bar if you want to chat to them. I'm sure they'd love to know you came to see us."

"I came to see *you*."

Her hands tremble and the fought-back tears are ripping me apart. Something's wrong. She could be lying about Dan. I scan her naked skin for signs of bruises, nothing.

"Why? So you can screw around with my feelings again?" Ruby would've snapped this, but she's Ruby Tuesday and speaks with a defeated hurt.

"I didn't mean to. I just fucked it up like everything else."

Ruby rubs her head as she considers what to say. "You probably did the right thing; we'd have hurt each other more than we did."

"You think?"

"We can't give the whole of ourselves, so how could we avoid this happening eventually?"

No, she's so wrong.

This is it, I have one chance. If opening the final part of my heart to Ruby doesn't work, I'll know there's no future. If there's no chance for us, I can shovel away all the crap in my life in one day, and start again. "I already gave you the whole of myself, Ruby, that's why I got scared."

"Stop it, Jem."

I take a ragged breath and the words fall out, because if I stop they'll never find their way to the ears of the girl who needs to hear. "You have a part of me; you always had a part of me, Ruby." I resist the urge to stare at my feet, willing her to look at me too. "I came here because I have to tell you the truth that I've lied to us both about."

"Stop talking riddles."

I push on. "I was scared to admit what was happening; terrified of the emptiness I'd be left with if I gave you too much and if you took everything away."

Ruby makes a derisive sound. "So you told me to leave? How am I supposed to believe what you're saying, Jem?"

"I threw us away because the reality scared the hell out of me."

She turns her reddened eyes to me. "No, you threw us away because you can't love."

Shit. I rub my temples. Why the hell am I putting myself through this?

"So you've come here to tell me what?" she continues when I don't respond. "That you care and want to try again? I don't have anything for you, Jem, not right now because you left me empty too."

"What do I have to say to make you understand what you mean to me?"

"Just tell the truth."

I snatch the glimmer of forgiveness and move closer; there's a chance she'll let me in? Hesitantly, I touch her damp hair. "I'm lost without you. Hell, I've spent most of my life lost, but this time it's worse. All the colour in my life has gone because you're not there." I pause and whisper. "Every song I hear makes me think of you."

She gives a small smile to my admission. "What? Even the boy bands?"

"Even the fucking boy bands. Do you know how embarrassing that is for rock god, Jem Jones?"

Ruby's smile grows and she shakes her head at me. "So you're saying you miss me?"

"I ache for you. When you left, you took the part of me who could be a decent person, and the only way I can get him back is be with you."

"You kicked me out! I didn't leave!"

I rub my temples. "Yeah, I know. Shit, I'm no good at this, Ruby. I don't know what else to say to you because this obviously isn't working."

She crosses her arms. "I'm not helping you out this time."

My heart hammers against my chest, skipping out of its normal rhythm for a split second, the way the drugs used to cause. I take another shaky breath and push against Ruby's barrier some more. "I belong with you."

The tears remain in Ruby's eyes, the crossed arms indicate I'm no closer to being let back in. "Ruby, there's so many things I can't put into words; I should just leave."

When Ruby's expression changes to alarm, I know leaving would be the end. The real end. I swear my perspiration matches hers right now. Why is this so fucking hard?

Ruby touches my face, the surprise like an electric shock across my skin. "You could save yourself the explanations if you just used one word, Jem," she says softly and runs her thumb along my lip.

She knows. I know. We've both known for months. The girl in front of me who blew my mind the first night I saw her, who stepped across the broken glass and dragged the hidden Jem into her light deserves to hear the truth from him. "I love you, Ruby Tuesday."

Ruby's expression changes, but I can't read it and she doesn't speak. Shock? More tears... *Shit, she doesn't feel the same.*

"That was easier, wasn't it?" she whispers eventually, cupping my cheek in her hand.

"No, so you'd better fucking kiss me. I need mouth to mouth after that; it almost killed me."

Ruby laughs, the sound letting in light over my shadows. She winds her arms around my neck and plants a sudden, surprise kiss on my mouth. "How could I refuse such an eloquent request?"

Then Ruby *really* kisses me. She actually bloody kisses me with the mouth I was terrified would never touch mine again, the warmth and taste flooding a new energy into my life. Ruby wants me and is prepared to forgive my shitty, asshole behaviour. In this embrace is the pull back to our place, the one we escaped together, the new path we started on and I sabotaged.

Ruby stops and grips the hands that are wrapped around her slim frame; but I won't let her go, her long legs wrapped between mine, my face buried in her neck.

"Look at me, Jem. I love you, too, and it frightens me. Look at what happened, at what you can do to me when you're hurting. I can't cope with that unpredictability."

My heart stutters for a second time, is she saying no? "I will always tell you everything. There isn't anything I want to hide from you ever again. You're in here now." I place her hand on my heart. "You always were, just this stupid fucker had to catch up." I touch my head. "Can we try again?"

Ruby's smile cracks through the concern. "Can you accept you're worth loving?"

"If I'm worth you reaching out that night I fell apart, I must be worth something. Come home with me. I promise that from now on it's me and you; we're the only people who matter."

Ruby's smile leaves and she pushes both hands into her hair. "I'm worried about something that'll screw this up before we've even tried again," she says hoarsely.

I frown. "Like what? Nothing you could say would change my mind." *Unless.* Jax? "Or is there someone else?"

"No, no. Not that" Ruby continues to shake her head and pushes my hands away. She sits on the sofa again. "I don't want you to think... If this is a big deal to you, I'll sort it."

"If what is a big deal? Now you're the one talking in riddles. Something that keeps us apart?"

I sit next to Ruby and touch her bare leg. She laces her hands in mine. "I'm scared."

"Why?"

"Shit!" She slams her head against the back of the sofa. "You said I took a part of you when I left."

"When I made you leave."

"Well, I literally did." Ruby looks at me warily.

"Oh. What did you take? I'm sure it wasn't important if I haven't noticed. The guitar? I said you could have that."

"Jem, I'm pregnant."

The world shifts into slow motion, the words exploding through my mind as I grab at the scattering thoughts; make attempts at sentences, a reaction. Ruby launches into a burbling breakdown of what she'll do, how she'll fix it. I grip her hand. "Ruby, stop talking. Are you sure?"

"Yeah. Not very pregnant, I mean, it's early days and that makes it easier to decide." The breathless words are accompanied by her staring at the wall.

Finally, my brain processes the world-shattering information. "Holy fucking fuck."

"I thought something along the same lines. I didn't do this on purpose, Jem; it's not something on my life plan for the next few years."

"Or mine."

Ruby chews her mouth. "Yeah."

"No, I don't mean..." I tip her chin to me. She's scared and I hate Ruby scared. "Falling in love wasn't in my plans either."

Ruby tries to move, but I hold tight. "I need time to process this. I just came from my mum's funeral and that was a big enough headfuck."

"I didn't plan on telling you right now; but I thought before I went home with you, I had to, in case it changed your mind." The realisation she might not have told me at all hits. Surely, she would? "I couldn't stand to go back, spend a night with you, and be kicked aside."

She's rambling again, and I wipe the worry from Ruby's face with both my hands, kissing her cheeks, lips, forehead, anything to show her that words don't matter even though the ones I heard blew my world so far off its axis there's no way I'll ever get back into the same orbit again.

"I can say with complete honesty and certainty that whatever happens, this will not change my mind."

I squeeze Ruby to me, in case she changes *her* mind and wants to run or doesn't believe my words. I came to speak to her tonight because I put my past to rest and had to know if Ruby belonged there, or in my future. Now Ruby is where she should be: in my arms and my heart.

Ruby's body trembles against mine and I hold her tighter. I will never, ever, let this girl go. Whatever she needs, she gets; and if that's my love, then I have that covered.

"I love you," I whisper against her hot cheek. "I have never loved anybody before, never knew how until you. You found your way to the deepest part of my heart where that love hides and claimed it."

"Only because you were ready to love someone," she says against my neck.

"No, only because I love you. I was always waiting for Ruby Tuesday to come into my life and show me who I really am. Hers."

I find out I'm going to be a dad on the day I say goodbye to my mum and the crap of my childhood. Can I do any better? This is fate's ultimate demonstration I belong with Ruby. For the first time, the future exists and life is no longer the past or the day-to-day survival against relapsing. I have a place to go and somebody to take with me.

Sure, this isn't tied up in a neat little bow or a verse in a Hallmark card, but we can do this. I will always give Ruby what she needs because I'm not giving; I'm sharing a part of myself that has always belonged to her.

More than that, somebody somewhere decided we should share ourselves in another person, and that's fucking fine by me.

37

Ruby

I head out of the Ladies and back to the sound check. Morning sickness? All bloody day sickness. This accompanying lack of energy and exhaustion isn't helping. Shouldn't this have stopped by now? The tour will be over before I'm whale-sized pregnant so I thought everything would be okay. I'm past the twelve weeks and I read things are supposed to be easier now. The fact my body hates being pregnant worries me, as if telling me something. What the hell have I decided to go through with?

Jem hovers outside and comes straight over. "You okay? You been sick again?" He puts a hand on my clammy forehead. "You have!"

"Jesus, Jem. What are you going to be like when I go into labour?" I hiss.

"I worry about you."

"I'm coping with the tour, aren't I?"

We're four dates into a two-month tour, trawling around Europe. The Ruby Riot boys are doing the tour bus experience; I'm flying with Jem as much as possible. I received some teasing about being too good for them now I'm rock royalty, and I retorted about how unpleasant their house is so why would I want to share their equally confined space on a bus?

Jem wipes my face with the sleeve of his shirt then kisses my forehead softly. "But if you need to..."

I shove him in the chest. "Don't start getting all 'you're a fragile flower' with me. I'm fine."

"I want to take care of you, okay?"

"On my terms, remember?"

He laughs. "Oh, how could I forget, Ruby Tuesday?"

Circling my arms around his waist, I press my mouth to his. "Don't fuss. People will notice."

"I think they might notice soon, you're more than three months and in the book it said..."

"I don't want yet another update on how big it is. You're obsessed by that book!"

"Baby. Not it. And I want to know everything I need to!"

God, if only Jem's band mates knew how he spends his spare time these days, I think he knows more about pregnancy than I do.

We head back to the stage where an impatient Dylan fixes Jem with a sour look. "C'mon, I don't want to spend all afternoon doing this. Sky's over from England today."

Jax sits with the sound engineer watching proceedings. Ruby Riot finished the sound check an hour ago, Will and Nate disappeared to try out the local bars but Jax is eager to learn everything. He helped the roadies and is now annoying the sound engineer with questions.

"I'm heading back to the hotel," I tell Jem.

"Rest." Jem holds my head in both hands, kisses the top of my hair, then walks back to the stage.

The rest of the day disappears into sleep and I wake about three p.m. How can I sleep so much and still be exhausted? I head to the hotel restaurant and buy a salad; the smell of anything else nauseates me. As I look for a table in the cafe area, I spot Cerys with her daughter, and she waves. I haven't seen Cerys since the wedding at Christmas and although she's more approachable than Sky, I'm awkward around her. Walking away would be rude; I don't have any choice here.

Cerys smiles warmly as I approach. "Hi, Ruby, how are you?"

"Yeah. Good. You?" I sit and put my salad and bottle of water on the table.

The kid sits next to her mum picking lettuce out of a sandwich and putting it on one side. She's wearing a costume, including ribbons in her long brown hair and oversized jewellery and stares at me.

"Are you a princess?" I ask, feeling awkward under her scrutiny.

"I'm Elsa."

"I thought you were called Ella?"

"I am; but when I'm wearing this, I'm Elsa."

I don't have a bloody clue what she's talking about.

"Ella, eat your sandwich," says Cerys.

"I don't like it! The bread tastes funny!"

"Eat that up or no treats for you later," her mum says firmly.

I watch the exchange and the nausea returns. I could be Cerys soon. Am I ready to do this?

"How old are you?" I ask Cerys.

"Twenty-two."

"You had her young then."

"Too young. Not that I'd change that now," she adds hastily. "The timing wasn't great and yeah, Liam's not her real dad so that should tell you how not great it was."

"Liam is my dad!" protests Ella. "I have two dads."

"You did the single mum thing, huh? Must've been tough."

Cerys shifts in her seat and twists the cup on the table. "It was, but better that than staying in a relationship that was hurting me."

"Yeah." I continue to watch Ella and picture my own child. Will she be like me, or a little boy with Jem's curls? Crap, I don't think I've ever held a baby, let alone looked after a little kid.

My biggest worry surfaces. What if I end up a single mum? When I decided to go ahead with the pregnancy, I knew I was taking a risk. Jem's transformed his attitude toward our relationship, but what if he has another emotional freak out like he did over his mum's death? I'll love this kid whether I'm with Jem or not, care for him or her better than the job my parents did with me. I psych myself up for the possibility I may end up doing this alone though; and if I want to be brutal in my honesty, if Jem kicks us to one side, he'll need to pay. I'll have enough love for my child to cover Jem's if this does happen.

Deep inside, I know he won't. I'm surprised Jem hasn't blabbed to everyone. Once the shock wore off, he was more into the idea than I was at the time, which stunned me. He's adamant this happened for a reason; that we came into each other's lives when we needed. I would never have pinned Jem as a believer in fate; personally, I believe in cold hard facts and being responsible for everything that happens. We changed to a more reliable form of contraception once things got serious and the chances of this failing were supposedly low. Yeah, maybe fate did have a hand in this.

Jem has grand ideas about buying a place in the English countryside and living a new life with me and the baby. The holiday to Spain inspired the 'country Jem' and I have an amusing image of Jem growing vegetables and collecting eggs from his chickens. I also have an equal image of a little boy holding his hand as he does. I've told him I need to keep going with Ruby Riot and the kid can't stop me, so Jem immediately set about planning Ruby Riot's year around ours. No tours for a few months after this one, and plenty of studio time.

For the first time in his life, Jem is planning the future.

"Are you okay?" Cerys's brown eyes are full of concern. "You're miles away."

"Sorry, thinking about something."

"You look sick; Liam said you've not been well since the tour started. Are you okay?"

"Yeah, I'm going to the doctor if it doesn't get any better. You staying with the band for long?" A subject change is needed. I'm not discussing my health with her.

"A couple of days between gigs, we're doing the Paris thing."

"Romantic."

"In January? Cold." She laughs then whispers, "Especially since missy here found out about Disneyland."

"Right."

I eat my salad, fighting the anxiety, and don't remember a word of the rest of the conversation with Cerys. My decision and the reality of how my life is about to change for the second time in a year hits harder than ever after this one conversation.

38

*uby*

Playing to Blue Phoenix stadium venues is a different experience to small clubs. The intimacy between the crowd and band is missing, especially as most are here to see the Blue Phoenix boys and not us. People hang out at the bar for drinks before Phoenix perform, leaving the floor of the venue half-empty when we do. Jax is put out by this the first time, but the other perks of touring with the guys soon make up for it. With three out of four of the band in a relationship, it doesn't take much charm from Jax or the brothers to hook up after each gig if they want to.

Some nights I loiter offstage and watch Blue Phoenix play close up, caught in my old passion for their music, which is now replaced with the passion I have for the lead guitarist. Jem never notices, he's like I am when on stage; lost in his place of sound and colour, occasionally interacting with Dylan or playing the crowd. I cast a look over the screaming girls at the front; it's weird witnessing the adulation of the guys by others at such close quarter. Fans swarm outside every hotel and airport; most often, we duck out the back but Jax "somehow" tends to get lost and find himself mid-fans and media.

Blue Phoenix encore done, I head back to the Green Room; one where the backstage offerings from the venue are more than a single six pack and the bags of crisps supplied to Ruby Riot on their UK club circuit.

"You swearing off alcohol again?" asks Jax when I refuse a post-gig beer.

"Yeah." I glance over at Jem who's chatting to Dylan. Jem and Dylan appear closer, the strong friendship he mentioned clearer; but it worries me he hasn't confided in Dylan about the baby yet. I passed Bryn, outside the room, talking intently to somebody on the phone. Liam ducks his head around the door to tell us he's leaving to see Cerys.

"So much for the famous Blue Phoenix party animals," complains Jax and takes a beer from the counter.

"I think they're too old for that shit now," I say.

"Twenty-six? Fuck, I hope I'm not old and boring then."

Jem sits next to me, places his feet on the table and drapes an arm across my shoulder. "Who's too old?"

"You guys. Behaving like old men," says Jax. "Yeah, I get you don't drink, but we could at least party a bit more!"

"Kinda burnt out, Jax," says Jem. "You're welcome to have your own parties; but make sure you don't get into a life where a doctor tells you to stop or you'll be dead before you're thirty."

I grip Jem's hand. Was he told that? "Thanks, Dad," says Jax with a laugh.

Jem tips his head at me. "Did you tell..."

Eyes widening, I shake my head vigorously. "He means you're behaving like a dad."

Jax doesn't miss a beat. "What did you say?"

"Nothing."

Bryn wanders into the room, humming and grabs the unopened beer from Jax's hand. "Cheers, mate."

Jax doesn't respond. I can practically see his brain whirring as he looks between us.

"How're you feeling now, Ruby?" Bryn asks. "Still sick?"

Nice timing.

"Getting better," I mumble.

"Better in the evenings, huh?" He sits in the armchair next to Jem and leans forward to poke him. "Something you want to tell us?"

"No," Jem retorts.

I stand and tuck my trembling hands under my arms. "I'm tired, Jem. Let's go."

Bryn sinks back and watches as Jem stands too. "I always know when you're hiding a secret, Jeremy."

"Shut up," he warns.

Jem's doing it again, the protective arm around my shoulder, fingers rubbing my neck. We're a tactile couple since we allowed ourselves; but this kind of touch is more proprietary, and it annoys me. I duck from under his arm.

"Ruby," says Jax, standing too. "Please don't tell me you're..."

"I'm not feeling well, okay! Just leave it!" Since performing earlier, I'm light-headed, the lack of food not helpful. I slump back onto the sofa and Jem immediately joins me.

"You are! You're fucking pregnant!" Jax waits for my denial, the shock on his face growing with each second I don't respond. "For fuck's sake!"

Jax grabs a new beer from the table, pushes past Bryn, who steps to one side in surprise, and storms out of the room.

"Are you?" asks Bryn. "Is she?"

The yellow-stained ceiling spins in a change of reality. If the words are spoken to someone outside of Jem and me, somehow the reality is clearer.

"It's okay," I murmur to Jem.

"Yeah. Ruby's pregnant."

I focus on the ceiling so I don't have to see Bryn and Dylan's expressions. "Umm. Congratulations? You're happy about this, I guess?" asks Bryn cautiously.

I twist my head against the cushioned sofa. I need to see Jem's reaction around his friends. Whatever he tells me about how happy he is this will speak more.

Jem's grinning. "The best fucking thing."

I look to Bryn whose shared smile doesn't match Dylan's stunned expression. *Please let Dylan say something positive.*

"Aww! A baby Phoenix. The world is gonna love this! Especially as it's you," says Bryn.

"Why?" asks Jem

"HELLO! magazine: 'At home with Jem Jones, ex-bad boy and now doting father.'" He gestures in the air, creating the headlines with his hands. "'Jem and Ruby at home in the nursery'." He snorts. "Man, this is hilarious!"

Jem's hand closes on my knee. "Why?" he repeats. "Can't you just be happy for us?"

"I am! Jesus, man, this is the best bloody thing that could happen to you." Bryn looks at me. "Apart from the lovely Ruby, of course."

I told myself everyone else's approval didn't matter, but Bryn's counts. I don't know why, maybe because whatever Jem says about Dylan being the guy he's closest to, Bryn understands Jem. Bryn was there for him at the dark times when Dylan couldn't manage because his own demons were eating away at him.

"I need to talk to Jax," I say and stand.

"The baby. When?" asks Dylan, breaking his silence.

"July," I say. "Jem, I need to talk to Jax."

"Tell him to piss off if he says anything that upsets you."

I arch an eyebrow. "Do you think you need to tell me that?"

"Good point." He rubs my leg and looks up at me. "Are you okay?"

"Not the reaction I was expecting." I smile weakly.

Before I can leave the room, Bryn seizes me in one of his signature bear hugs and when I make an 'oof' sound, Jem springs to his feet. "Careful, man!"

"I'm not that delicate!" I snap at Jem.

Bryn releases me and laughs at us. "Shit, this is going to be funny. You two are hilarious!"

"And these hormones suck because my eyes are starting to water," I mumble and head out of the room.

Jem can deal with his fallout. I need to deal with mine.

I find Jax sitting in the plastic seated stalls of the stadium, beer in hand, as he watches the roadies packing up. The large venue is clear, cleaners wandering the rows of seats; and the crash of the equipment being moved echoes across the empty space of the stadium. I sit next to him silently for a few minutes.

"All this." He waves his bottle. "This is what we wanted. I thought you wanted it too."

"I did...do."

"Then why get pregnant?" He turns his ice blue eyes to mine, I expect anger; but worse, it's pity. "Why ruin what you have?"

"I'm having a baby, not dumping the band."

"Oh, right, so you can do both?" he snorts.

"What the hell? Are you in Victorian times? Is my life over if I have a baby? News flash: people have kids all the time and go back to work."

"Seriously? You think you can do both?"

"Now you're pissing me off. People do harder jobs than this and go back to work! This won't interfere with the tour. I'm not having it... the baby until later in the year."

He pouts and swigs his beer.

"That's not the issue is it?"

Jax pushes his blonde fringe from his eyes but doesn't look at me. "You jumped from a controlling relationship into this. You never got a chance to find who you are, and now you're tied to him."

I swallow down the fact he's voicing a concern that follows me but there's a bigger truth. "Have you ever thought that I found who I am in Jem?"

"Sure. The man who says he doesn't give a shit about anyone else and you got pregnant by him. Smart move..."

"What's this about, Jaxon? Me or the band?"

"Both. When he fucked you over a few months back, you were a mess. Worse than you ever were with Dan."

"With Dan, I was numb; with Jem, I'm alive. We've worked through shit."

Jax shakes his head slowly, staring at the floor. "You deserve more from your life, Ruby. You're young."

"Why are you so against Jem? Is this because of me and you?"

Jax's gaze remains on the floor as he picks at the label on his bottle. "Probably. Sometimes I think if it wasn't for him...yeah, anyway."

I link my arm through his. "Come on, Jax. We'd never have worked. I never really felt anything with you; you know that. Besides, your endless stream of chicks seems to keep you happy."

"Yeah, for now, until I find someone I really want. Maybe a bit like you, but a bit less complicated." He smiles. "And a bit less pregnant."

"I love Jem," I say quietly. "I can't imagine anybody else."

"Yeah, you two match. I always saw that, but at least you match in a good way now."

"So, I have your blessing?" I poke him in the ribs.

Jax shrugs. "I guess. I'll always look out for you though and if he messes you around..."

"You know what, Jax? Even if he does, I'm sure I'll cope. I'm not putting up with crap from men anymore. Look at us; we're fucking awesome with or without other people in our life."

Jax puts an arm around my shoulders. "Okay, I'm happy that you're happy. It makes you easier to be around; you're less of a bitch."

"Huh!" I shove him. "Cheeky bastard."

"Admit it."

"Yeah, okay..."

We lapse back into silence, the tension gone. I leave Jax alone with his thoughts and text Jem to ask him to meet me outside the Green Room. I'm too tired to face the questions; they're Jem's guys and not mine. Jem has people to tell who'll be pleased for him. He has a family who replaced his old one and he's finally begun to realise that. The sadness that I don't have anybody to share my news with is tempered by Bryn, Dylan, and Liam accepting me as one of their own. For now, I want to go back to the hotel with Jem and the peace and safety of being alone with him.

39

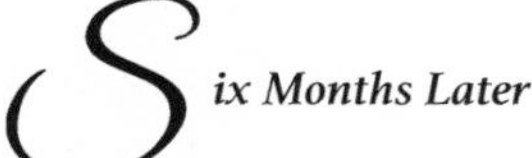

Six Months Later

Jem

Swaddled and held against Ruby's chest, a white blanket shielding her from the cameras, sleeps my beautiful, baby girl. The commotion around us as we step from the hospital, and the tears that spring to Ruby's eyes, surges my anger as I push through the bottom feeders trying to get their scoop. I grip Ruby's shoulders, this shouldn't be happening. The car is parked somewhere close, but private. Obviously not private enough. Who bloody leaked this?

"What the fuck? Why are they all here?" I ask.

"Let them have a picture," says Pippa.

When the latest member of Blue Phoenix's PR entourage arrived at the hospital and informed us there was some media interest, she wasn't joking. "No fucking way," I growl. "She doesn't belong to them; they're not having her."

"They might back off if you do."

"Yeah, right," says Ruby, adjusting the blanket to ensure our daughter is hidden.

"My car's parked out the back of the hospital," I say. "We should've just driven instead of Pippa sending someone to pick us up!"

"I don't care. I just want to go home," says Ruby, turning back to the building. Her pale face and wide eyes annoy me more. Ruby's exhausted and doesn't need this shit.

"You okay? Want me to take her?" I ask.

"We're fine, Jem." She ducks her head, allowing her hair to obscure her face as we head back inside.

"Deal with them!" I snap at Pippa and follow Ruby.

A couple of young nurses glance over as we head inside, and then turn back to their conversation. I guess they're used to famous babies at the exclusive London hospital.

We expected media interest, but not getting mobbed the day after she was born. This proves again how Ruby and me should stay in our world and do things our way. Why the hell did I allow Blue Phoenix PR in to try to arrange things? The three of us should've snuck out in the first place.

Ruby hovers by the car in the July sunshine, red hair spilling across her short black summer dress, and I kiss her forehead before opening the door.

"I'll put her in the seat." I hold my arms out and Ruby gives a small shake of her head, gently placing my daughter into my arms. She makes a strange baby sound, lips moving as if dreaming and I kiss her head, rubbing my nose across the blonde wisps of hair.

"Stop sniffing your daughter and strap her into the car seat. I want to go home," says Ruby softly.

Awkwardly, I attempt to push tiny arms through straps and figure out how to clip her safely inside. I catch myself against swearing and Ruby places a hand on mine. "I'll do it."

I rub my tired eyes, studying how Ruby fixes the seat, then

stands back. Now her arms are free, I encompass Ruby in mine and hope I take some of her stress away. "How are you?"

"Not pregnant anymore, thank God. How are you?"

"Apart from the bruises on my arm and the abuse you yelled at me yesterday, I'm great."

Ruby smiles her magic smile that lights my world. "Yeah, sorry, but I can assure you it hurt me a lot more than I hurt you."

I twist Ruby's hair from her shoulders and kiss her head, remembering how frightened I was for her yesterday. No way, I'd go through that and not break someone's face. I think I'm lucky I got away with bruises. "I love you," I whisper. "Both of you, forever. Our forever."

"Careful, Jem, you're getting close to romantic bullshit there."

"Not bullshit, Ruby Tuesday."

She hugs me tightly and the tension leaves her shoulders. "Just take us home."

Ruby

I wake from dreams of babies and Jem, immediately on alert for her cry, exhausted after the third night of parenthood. I'm surprised to see the sun shining through the window and the large bedroom missing Jem and our daughter; how did I sleep so late? I head out of the bedroom in my t-shirt and pants, and downstairs as I search for them.

The tiled floors of the old farmhouse are cool against my feet as I check the large kitchen, and the silence worries me; this hasn't been a feature of our house recently.

Then I see them.

Stretched out on the long sofa in the lounge lies Jem, shirtless with his daughter resting on his chest. His tattooed arms look odd surrounding her pink suit, the girl tiny against his broad chest.

She's facing me, her cheek pressed against her dad's skin and lips parted, sleeping as peacefully as him.

An overwhelming surge of love for both of them pushes through my heart and soul. The calm of the scene and the peace on Jem's face removes any doubt that when the baby arrived, he wouldn't cope with the reality. His constant attention to us both, the pure love in Jem's eyes when he looks at her, at both of us, is more than any child could ever want. Jem can give his daughter everything; but the most precious thing he can give her is in front of me, all-encompassing, selfless love that holds us together.

Jem shifts and tightens his grip on her, a curl falling across his face as he moves. I cross and kiss his forehead and he opens his eyes, looking at me in sleepy surprise. "She wouldn't settle and I didn't want to wake you," he whispers. "She likes to sleep like this apart from when she's hungry and I don't have the equipment."

His mouth tips a smile at one corner and I kiss him. "Thank you."

Jem cups his large hand around her head, stroking her face with his thumb. "Can we sort this name thing out, please? Bryn's started calling her Diamond which is bloody stupid."

I sit on the chair arm. "But we can't agree and that never ends well."

"Yeah, but this is one situation where we can't give up; we have to agree. I don't think she'll appreciate the name when she's twenty."

"I know, but after my mother's fail at my name, I'm cautious."

"I had a thought, but I'm not sure what you'll think."

"A name?"

Jem nods and closes his other hand around mine. "I thought... Quinn."

His words strike my heart. I haven't heard anybody say his name for a long time. "Quinn?" I whisper.

"It's a girl's name too, and it's pretty cool. He sounds like he was a cool guy."

My eyes fill with tears. Stupid hormonal tears come so quickly these days; but despite the ache in my chest Jem's suggestion causes, the name makes perfect sense.

"Ruby?" Jem's tone is cautious.

"I guess..."

The little girl shifts and murmurs, rubbing her face against him.

"See!" he says triumphantly. "She likes it!"

"You're funny. And yes. Quinn. You win."

"Wow, I'll add that to the short list of times I have." He sits, carefully holding his daughter in place against his chest. "Come on, Quinn, let's take a walk outside before your mum changes her mind, and wants to call you something boring." He pauses. "What about her other name?"

"One thing at a time, Jem."

The topic of marriage came up once and very briefly because I shot the conversation down before he got more than one sentence out. Not a proposal but one of Jem's 'we need to plan the future' sessions. Jem bought me a ring and gave me it the day Quinn was born, insisting it wasn't a proposal but a commitment that he'll be here forever. I wish I could believe that in every corner of my soul, but I think it will take time before I do. Marrying Jem won't take that doubt away; but I suspect my heart will win over soon enough. I twist the diamond and ruby ring around my right ring finger as we edge around the topic.

"She can have both surnames," I say.

Jem smirks. "Quinn Butler-Jones. Makes us sound like landed gentry."

"Says the man who bought a country estate!" I indicate the world outside the glass doors leading to the huge gardens. No longer city Jem, he's moved us onto a property surrounded by fields, into a converted farmhouse and away from prying eyes.

Quinn begins to grumble and I recognise the signs, and what's coming next. She's calm for a baby according to Cerys, which amuses the hell out of our friends considering how they perceive us. But they don't see how, most of the time, me and Jem operate on a calm and intuitive level; that our desire for stability in our new world sees conflict dealt with quickly, although occasionally, loudly. Quinn's snuffling turns to whimpering and my hormones kick in. I hold my arms out to Jem and he reluctantly hands her over.

Jem bends his head and plants a kiss on her head. "You saved my life," he whispers then looks to me. "Both of you."

"No, we killed your old one," I reply and sit down to feed Quinn.

"Yeah, I guess. Yesterday doesn't matter." He indicates my tattoo under my breasts, revealed as I position her.

"It's gone." I no longer regret choosing to etch the words from 'my song' onto my body. They are the truth and a connection to my brother, the part of yesterday who'll never leave.

Jem curls up next to me as Quinn feeds, as if he wants to be part of our bonded closeness and by touching my skin, he can be. I rest my head on his shoulder.

"I love you, Ruby Tuesday." Jem says this every day, a reminder I don't need because even when he refused to say the words, I knew this was true. Jem says the words simply and with undisguised love in his eyes, not with a desperate need for me to reciprocate with the same words. But I always do.

"I love you, Jem Jones," I whisper.

He touches Quinn's head as she feeds. "My life is fucking perfect." Then winces as I jab my finger into his side. "What?"

"We don't swear anymore, remember?"

Jem bites his lip in amusement. "Sure, let's see you try with that."

I poke my tongue out and Jem laughs, capturing my mouth with his, leaving a soft kiss on my lips to reinforce his words. I shift, snuggle into him and he wraps his arms around my shoulder.

Jem spent a lifetime hiding how he felt and attempting to contain the depth of the emotions he holds inside. Although he refused to believe it, Jem Jones has always been filled with love he wanted to give, but had no idea how to. If Jem didn't feel so deeply about others, he wouldn't have needed to cut away such an important part of who he is in order to protect himself. If he honestly didn't give a crap about anything, why would Jem need to obliterate his world? Jem took the love he tried to give, which was rejected as a child, and turned this back against himself into hate and inadequacy. Finally, Jem's lost the self-hatred and shared the love he deserves to get back.

Jem gave me the one thing he could never trust anybody with: access to the deepest parts of his heart where that love lives. He once told me the darkness could never hide me because I shine so brightly; that stars can never be lost in the night. In the same way, Jem needed to break apart; because how else would the light shine through the cracks into his shadow world.

Look what came from our pain and confusion, from our coming together. Not only a new world together, but also a new life, a new person. I could never doubt the goodness in a man who has poured himself into changing and becoming who he needs to be, for himself, for me, and for Quinn.

We're still locked in our own world, but we're no longer trapped. This is the place we've chosen to be together, and here is where we belong. Ruby Tuesday, Jem Jones, and Quinn live here in a new reality; one nobody gets to take away from us.

The End

The Blue Phoenix books

Summer Sky (Blue Phoenix #1)
Falling Sky (Blue Phoenix #2)
Forever Sky (Blue Phoenix #3)
Unplugged (Blue Phoenix #4)
Rising (Blue Phoenix #5)
Reverb (Blue Phoenix #6)

Other Books by Lisa Swallow

The Ruby Riot Series

The Ruby Riot series is a spin-off from Blue Phoenix. **Cadence (Ruby Riot #1)**

Shuffle (Ruby Riot #2)

Reprise (Ruby Riot #3)

The Unscripted Duet

Hollywood Romance

Unscripted

Spotlight

Butterfly Days Series

New Adult Contemporary Series

Because of Lucy

Finding Evan

The Same Deep Water

New Adult standalone

Snow Kissed

Holiday themed sweet novella

ACKNOWLEDGMENTS

My biggest thanks go to my Rising beta readers: Anne, Kaylene, Leeann, Lou, Teresa, Tarsh and Victoria who helped me through the ups and downs of Ruby and Jem's story. You're amazing and I'm honoured you gave me so much of your time.

Thanks go to my wonderful editors Peggy and Becky at Hot Tree Editing, and Najla at Najla Qamber Designs for making Rising beautiful inside and out.

I'm writing these acknowledgements at the end of 2014 which has been my first full year as an indie author, one I spent almost exclusively with the Blue Phoenix boys (although a paranormal romance snuck in mid-year). This has been a crazy roller-coaster journey where I went from selling only a handful of my previously published books to suddenly selling enough to hit Amazon bestseller lists and reach new readers. My journey is just beginning and although it's hard work, I love that I can call this my 'job' now. Thank you to every single person who has supported me in the smallest way over the last year. I try and thank everybody but if I miss something you've done and don't, I'm sorry.

Thank you especially to the bloggers who have supported my indie publishing journey - so many of you to mention. I tried to write a list but was scared I'd offend by leaving someone out so decided not to.

And thanks to every single reader who has left a review, signed up to my mailing list, spoken to me on Facebook or emailed me. You make my dreams a reality. I'm overwhelmed by the support for the Blue Phoenix series and can't wait to share more with you!

About the Author

Lisa is a USA Today bestselling author of contemporary romance and writes paranormal romance under the name of LJ Swallow. She is originally from the UK but moved to Australia in 2001. She now lives in Perth, Western Australia.

Lisa's first publication was a moving poem about the rain, followed by a suspenseful story about shoes. Following these successes at nine years old there was a long gap in her writing career, until she published her first book in 2013.

Fore more information:

lisaswallow.net
lisa@lisaswallow.net

60877592R00184

Made in the USA
Middletown, DE
05 January 2018